THE FREE LUNCH

BOOKS BY SPIDER ROBINSON

Telempath
*Callahan's Crosstime Saloon
Stardance (with Jeanne Robinson)
Antinomy
The Best of All Possible Worlds
*Time Travelers Strictly Cash
Mindkiller
Melancholy Elephants
Night of Power
Callahan's Secret
Callahan and Company (omnibus)
Time Pressure
Callahan's Lady
Copyright Violation
True Minds
Starseed (with Jeanne Robinson)
Kill the Editor
Lady Slings the Booze
The Callahan Touch
Starmind (with Jeanne Robinson)
*Off the Wall at Callahan's
*Callahan's Legacy
Deathkiller (omnibus)
Lifehouse
*The Callahan Chronicals (omnibus)
The Star Dancers (with Jeanne Robinson)
User Friendly
*The Free Lunch
Callahan's Key
By Any Other Name

*A Tor Book

THE FREE LUNCH

SPIDER ROBINSON

A TOM DOHERTY ASSOCIATES BOOK TOR® NEW YORK

THE FREE LUNCH

Edited by James Frenkel

Design by Jane Adele Regina

A Tor Book
Published by Tom Doherty Associates, LLC
175 Fifth Avenue
New York, NY 10010

www.tor.com

Tor® is a registered trademark of Tom Doherty Associates, LLC.

Library of Congress Cataloging-in-Publication Data

Robinson, Spider.
    The free lunch / Spider Robinson.—1st ed.
        p. cm.
    ISBN 0-312-86524-4
    1. Runaway teenagers—Fiction. 2. Amusement parks—Fiction. I. Title.
PS3568.O3156 F74 2001
813'.54—dc21

                                                              2001027196

First Edition: August 2001

Printed in the United States of America

0   9   8   7   6   5   4   3   2   1

FOR HERB VARLEY

AND ALSO FOR
DAVID GERROLD AND SUSAN ALLISON,
UNINDICTED CO-CONSPIRATORS

ACKNOWLEDGMENTS

This book began in 1984 as a conversation at a certain California theme park with my friend John Varley, and quickly swelled into a full-fledged literary collaboration. By the end of the day, with some help from bystander David Gerrold, we had our premise, lead characters, and title. Susan Allison of Ace Books then graciously suggested an excellent plot no one was using at the moment, which helped considerably. The next thing I knew, I was flying from Halifax, Nova Scotia, to Eugene, Oregon, to spend a week hunkered down in the bunker with Herb—as I call John Varley for no particular reason—working on the book. (And wearing the same clothes all week: the airline lost my luggage, and Herb, unlike me, is built like a Viking chieftain.) We refined our characters, fleshed out our plot, defined our themes, and settled on a classic working method: we would alternate chapters, then each do a final rewrite of the total manuscript. I drew the first straw, typed out a first chapter, passed the ball to Herb, and flew home.

Fifteen years later I broke down and inquired as to his progress, and there wasn't any.

Furthermore, Herb said, he had gone stale on the idea. Somehow. "It was your idea to start with—why don't you write it yourself?" he suggested. "Oh, by the way, your luggage finally showed up. By now some of the stuff is almost in style."

And then—*in the very next breath*—he suggested another collaboration.

You see why I love this man? So I won't kill him.

Well, the last one had turned out so well, what could I say? And so I'm pleased to report that Herb and I have begun another book together, tentatively titled *The Little Spaceship That Could.* (His original idea, this time.) We spent months of e-mail time plotting it and creating characters together, I completed the first chapter and sent it to him in May 1997 . . . and I'm sure chapter 2 will arrive any day now. I'm holding my breath, in fact.

Wish us luck. . . .

—Spider Robinson
June 1998

TANSTAAFL:
there ain't no such thing as a free lunch.
—Robert Anson Heinlein

It is often the fifth ace that makes all the difference
between success and failure.
—J. B. Morton

THE FREE LUNCH

CHAPTER 1

GOING UNDER

The fourth time was the charm.

At around sunset on a Monday, a well-dressed man in his late forties with a beard and old-fashioned eyeglasses surrendered his bracelet to the attendant and left Dreamworld, unaccompanied by children or other adults. He seemed to float through the exit turnstile, a dreamy smile pasted on his face. He looked, for the moment, much younger than his age. As he reached the edge of the parking lot, near the roped-off area where the evening crowd were lining up for admission, his visual-focus distance dropped back from infinity to things as near as the solar system, and he noticed the pastel sunset. It was more than he could bear. He stopped in his tracks, drew in a great bellyful of air, threw back his head, and bellowed to the emerging stars, "Thomas Immega, you brilliant benevolent old son of a good woman, *I love you!*"

There were giggles from some of the children who waited for admission, and warm smiles from some of the adults leaving along with him, but only one of the admitting attendants looked up from his work. He was new at the job.

"I'm going to find out where they've got you planted," the bearded man raved on, "and dig you up and kiss you right on the moldy lips. You did it *right*, Cousin!"

The ticket taker could see how it must have been. The fellow had come to Dreamworld for the first time *old*. Jaded and cynical, he had been told what to expect but had not believed it. He had arrived expecting to sneer. Now, only hours later, he was stunned by his own monstrous arrogance, and terribly grateful to have been forgiven for it.

The attendant felt nostalgia and kinship. He hoped the bearded man didn't live too far away. If his home was outside practical commuting distance to Dreamworld, the bearded man was going to have to move. The way the attendant had.

He yanked his attention back to his work; his own line was starting to build, and his supervisor would be offering him help in a minute. But part of his mind remained on the bearded man—who had completed first-stage decompression and was literally skipping toward his distant car now—and so distracted, the attendant failed to note that the chubby twelve-year-old before him had only one chin. He took her money, gave her her map and brochure, fastened a Dreamband around her thick little wrist with something less than his usual care, and passed her through the gate into Dreamworld without a second thought. He did notice that her smile of thanks was especially incandescent.

He would have been somewhat puzzled to see it fade, thirty seconds later, as the flaw in her planning became clear to her.

There were many places in Dreamworld where a child could be alone, and there were some places where she could be unobserved. But as far as the chubby girl knew, there was only one place she could be both alone and unobserved—and if she went in there, it might be too dangerous to come out again. She had not thought Phase Two through far enough—perhaps because subconsciously she had not truly expected Phase One to succeed.

She wandered aimlessly around the Octagon—the football-field–sized commons from which all eight of the Paths of Dreamworld originated—for about ten minutes, trying to think of Plan B. The best she could do was Plan A Prime: go ahead as planned . . . and if it came apart, improvise.

Her bladder cast the deciding vote. She chose the smallest and least popular of the eight available ladies' rooms, the one way over by the path to the Bounding Main, and forced herself to go in.

No one paid any attention to her. She lingered by the sink, looking at nothing at all, until the stall she wanted came free: the one nearest the door, with only one neighbor. Once safely locked inside it, she took off her blouse, turtleneck sweater, breasts, shoes, belly pack, and forearms.

Now he was a twelve-year-old boy with makeup on. He slid his Dreamband off the wrist of his collapsed fake forearm and put it in his right-hand pocket. He opened the belly pack, took out his own shoes and a reasonably good counterfeit Dreamband, stuffed everything else into the pack, and zipped it back up. The sound reminded him of his bladder; he unzipped his fly to attend to the matter. At the last possible instant the lowered seat reminded him that girls didn't pee standing up; he was able to cut off the flow in time, but it hurt. Feeling stupid and oddly ashamed, he turned around, sat, and did his business, trying not to wonder what the napkin disposal unit was.

As he flushed, he blushed, realizing he had not remembered to make any toilet paper noises first. This was tricky . . .

Now to escape. Improvise. If he could just get as far as the door undetected, he could tell anyone who saw him emerge that his kid sister had gotten sick, and then maybe he could fade away when they went in to help. He put his belly pack back on— outside his clothes, this time—and waited, listening hard to traffic sounds outside the stall. Finally he decided there were as few girls out there as there were going to be. About ten meters to the exit. Feets, don't fail me now. He threw open the door—

—and relaxed, seeing himself in the mirror opposite. He had forgotten about the wig and makeup. He no longer looked like the chubby effeminate girl who had come in . . . but he could pass as a skinny butch girl. He ignored the two girls present and made boldly for the exit. The visual barrier that was meant to keep dirty old men from peering in gave him three strides of concealment in which to whip the wig off and wipe at his makeup with it. Rehearsing his sick-sister lines, he jammed the wig into the belly pack, opened the door, and stepped out. Absolutely no one paid the slightest bit of attention to him.

Of course. In Dreamworld, parents did not feel they had to stand guard while their children were using the toilet. Nothing untoward could possibly happen as long as they were wearing their Dreambands.

That reminded him to remove the fake Dreamband he had fetched with him from his left-hand pocket and put it on, as unobtrusively as possible. *God,* he thought, *I better steady down. Four—no, five oaf-outs already . . . and this was supposed to be the easy part!*

The hard part was coming up.

BUT OF COURSE he had to wait for Firefall. None of the rides would be running until that was over. Everything in Dreamworld ground to a halt every night while it was in progress, and just about everything else within a radius of five kilometers. People dropped whatever they were doing to watch the incredible display of pyrotechnics, lasers, holograms, and kamikaze nanobots, no matter how many times they had seen it before. You stood and stared at all that fire cascading from the sky, all those different *kinds* of fire, and your busy chattering monkey mind fell silent, and whatever was in your heart came bubbling to the surface.

He stood with the rest, and his heart threatened to boil over. There was too much compressed within it. He could not afford that, not yet. He knew how to go to a place in his mind where nothing could reach him—but it took great effort, and that particular muscle was nearly exhausted. He did it anyway. Maybe, if the gods were kind, it would be the last time for a while.

He failed to notice when Firefall ended; where he was, fireworks were still going off. He was roused from his autohypnotic trance by a minor commotion near him. The way he phrased it to himself was *a disturbance in The Force*. He scanned the crowd around him and saw three smiling Cousins in their lemon jumpsuits converging from afar like yellow corpuscles, without apparent haste or urgency but covering ground fast. Behind them came two nonsmiling Dreamworld employees in street clothes: backstage personnel. For a paranoid instant he thought they were after him, but then located their target a few meters away: an adult, who had elected to watch Firefall reclining in a chaise lounge. Two Cousins were already kneeling beside her; she must have been taken ill. One of them moved, and he got his first clear look at the elderly woman's face. Just then the lighting in the local area changed in a subtle way; within seconds they were all in shadow.

But he had seen.

He heard the nearer Cousin sigh, and murmur, "God, look at her smile."

"She doesn't have to go home, now," the other said softly. "Ever. I wouldn't mind going like that myself, when it's my time."

Then she looked up and saw him. She frowned, pasted a very good smile over it, put a finger to her lips, and addressed him in a stage whisper. "This poor lady's exhausted—let's let her nap a minute, okay?"

He kept his face straight, nodded, and forced himself to leave the area nonchalantly, as though he had bought her story. The last thing he needed was a Cousin deciding he was traumatized, putting an arm around him, asking him questions for which he could no longer remember the lies he had prepared.

He'd intended to dawdle for an hour or so after Firefall, going on a few of his favorite rides for the last time as a civilian. But all at once he felt he had been given a sign. Someone had died happy in Dreamworld. Time to finish the last detail, and then get this done.

He drifted over toward the exit, picked out an attendant who looked sleepy, and tugged at his sleeve. "Mister," he said, gesturing vaguely behind him, "the Cousin over there asked me to say he needs you for a minute."

"Thanks, son." As he'd hoped, the attendant bought it and started away, looking around for a mythical Cousin. The genuine Dreamband was already in his hand; hastily he used the attendant's abandoned wand to deactivate it, and dropped it into the bin with the rest. He had rehearsed this part many times; he was done well before the attendant stopped and glanced back for directions.

"I guess he changed his mind," he told the attendant. "Sorry."

"That's all right," the man said, resuming his station. "Thanks anyway. You leaving now or what?"

"No," he said, "not for a while," and went back inside.

He stopped at the first trash can he encountered, rummaged in the belly pack for the folded-up hat and false nose, and stuffed them into his pants pockets. He zipped the pack back up, took it off, and dropped it in the trash.

He felt an unexpected exhilaration as the lid swung closed. The last of the evidence was disposed of. The only remaining traces of his old life were the clothes he stood in. He was free as a bird . . . or the next best thing.

HE TOOK THE path for the Enchanted Forest, and when he got there went straight to the Unicorn's Glade ride. As he'd expected and hoped, the line was short, almost nonexistent. Less time to fidget and fret; fewer witnesses. Once they were inside and the cars were arriving, the crowd around him was so sparse that he was easily able to grab the seat he needed: the last one in the train. He pulled the safety bar up and composed his features into what he called his dweeb face. It worked; no one elected to sit with him. His heart began to pound with elation as the train eased into motion. This was going to work! The last hurdle had been passed, the last tricky part. From here it was as easy as falling off a log.

And so of course he did just that. He picked his moment with great care, waiting until they emerged from the dark tunnel into the first lighted section, and everyone else would be most distracted by things ahead of them. He had already weaseled out from under the safety bar, put the fake Dreamband in his pocket, and put on his elf hat and false nose. But as he slipped over the side of his car and dashed for cover, he mistook a fake log for a real one, tried to hop up onto it, slipped off, and fell headlong.

Firefall, reprised—

WHEN HE SAT up, the train was out of sight. He was not sure whether he had lost consciousness or not, or if so, for how long. With no way of knowing how soon the next train would be through, he had to assume it would be any moment.

Get up, at least to a crouch, and put on a silly leer, empty your eyes, it's okay to look at them, they expect that, but empty your eyes first, you are an audio-animatronic robot, here comes the train now, empty your eyes, here it is, shit, there's somebody in the front seat looking this way, look down, oh shit, move, cover up that shin, if she sees the blood she might report you're leaking oil, cover it with your hand while you turn that side away from her, smile, here she comes there they go MOVE! seven, six, five, four, careful don't knock over that robot, two, Safe!

—I think.

He crouched down in his place of concealment behind a pseudoboulder, and balanced risks. If the girl in the car had seen his bleeding shin—dammit, it *hurt*, now that he had time for it—she might report it, in which case he was probably screwed. How likely was it that the girl was a busybody?

Well, girls often were, in his experience. But she might simply assume that the blood was fake, part of the show. A wounded Elf for the Unicorn to heal.

The audio-animatronic robot he had dodged on his way to cover—a wizened old Elf—was coming toward him, making faintly audible whirring sounds. That was odd—he was sure that none of the robots had an itinerary that brought them through this space; he had been on this ride dozens of times, studying, rehearsing. Hell—perhaps this one *was* malfunctioning, in some way that was registering on a dial somewhere in Central Control! Time to move on. But the robot Elf stood between him and the rest of the diorama, coming closer. He backed out of its way, deeper into cover.

It stopped where he had been crouching, and crouched itself. Its faint little servo-sounds ceased. Its monkeylike face swiveled to track him.

It winked.

And said, "If you leave that bloodstain out there on the set, they'll know, and they won't rest until they find you."

SHOCK MIGHT HAVE paralyzed his limbs and tongue, but instead the reverse happened. From his hunkered crouch he exploded into something very like a Russian saber dancer's four-limbed *hah!* kick, and a shout grew in his stomach and raced like vomit up his throat—

—where he nearly choked on it, because the robot, moving faster than any robot he knew, seemed to have a hand over his mouth, and another behind his head to brace against. He tried to yank free, and what stopped him was not the futility of pitting his strength against that of a robot, but the sudden realization of how difficult it was *not*. The robot hands were strong, stronger than his own—but far less strong than they should have been. They were *warm*.

Too many urgent inputs will cause most information systems to crash, and he had been in crummy shape to start with. He went limp.

The Elf caught him under the arms, gently laid him down in a spot where he would be concealed from view, and stood back up.

Another train came through. He lay there dizzily and watched the Elf mime a plausible routine for it. The soft sounds of servomechanisms and hydraulics, the sharp sounds of clattering wheels and laughing children, and the sequentially fading series of Xerox copies that echo made of all these, all washed over him. They very nearly overwhelmed the sound of his heart banging in his chest.

"I've had my eye on you for the last week or so," the Elf murmured when the train was past, without looking at him. "I figured you were going to make your move soon. I like the way you handle yourself. You have respect, and you're not stupid."

"You're human," he said softly, wonderingly.

The Elf grimaced. "Thanks a lot."

"You're a—a—" He scrambled back up to a crouch. "—a *girl*."

"Make up your mind," she said. "Am I human or not?" She sounded like an aunt or a teacher. As old as her Elf persona looked, and sour. But she was no taller than he was. "Oh, the hell with it. Wait here."

She straightened up, making soft mechanical humming sounds again—he realized with wonder and some amusement that she was actually humming them—and walked around the boulder, out onto the set of the Unicorn's Glade and into view of its patrons. He had practiced imitating robot movements a great deal, but this . . . person . . . was *much* better. He scrambled to the edge of cover to watch her.

She walked in a seemingly random pattern that led her past the spot where he had first fallen and hurt his shin. When she reached it, she improvised a move which was in character for her Elf persona, and which brought her down on one knee. She remained on that knee until a train had passed, slid the knee back and forth along the floor, then rose and returned to his place of concealment. The blood that had been on the floor was now almost invisible on her dark trouser leg.

"Come on," she said, and continued past him.

Doing his own robot walk, he followed her . . .

CHAPTER 2

UNDER

. . . and she walked straight into a boulder and vanished.

He followed without hesitation—not because he grasped that the boulder was a hologram, but simply because he was in shock. When he passed through it himself, things changed too fast for him to integrate. Nearly at once he encountered another wall, and his knees and face proved this one was *not* a hologram. He rebounded, his vision dithering, and would have gone down again if she had not caught him. Both her grip and her arms were too strong for someone her size. *She smells like a robot,* he thought. *Like machine oil.*

"Always turn right," she murmured in his ear.

"Huh?"

She stood him on his feet, released him, and stepped back. "In Dreamworld, if you walk through something you thought was there, always turn right. It's a rule of thumb." She pointed.

Sure enough, the concealed corridor they were in now debouched to their right. He filed the information and studied her.

She was exactly his own height, which was not impressive even for a twelve-year-old, but she was unquestionably an adult. Face and voice confirmed it, as did body language now that she was no longer imitating a robot. She was a midget. Not a Dwarf, but a perfectly proportioned small person. With powerful arms and hands. Her wrinkled features, the smoky rasp in her voice, and the great dignity with which she carried herself made him think of a maiden aunt or a school principal, but somehow she would not have fit into either pigeonhole even if she were not dressed as a robot Elf. She was old enough and certainly sour enough . . . but she wasn't sad enough.

She's not lonely, he thought, and wondered how he could know such a thing about her.

"My fault," she went on. "I should have caught you as you came through. I assumed if you got this far, you knew that much."

"This is only the third time I've been all the way backstage," he said. "And I got caught right away the other times. Like under a minute."

"You're getting better," she said. "This was a good place. You'd have made it if you hadn't fallen. This far, at least."

"Yeah, I guess." He inspected his shin. "Thanks," he added belatedly, realizing he had been complimented. "Uh . . . who are you?"

"Annie."

"Oh. Uh . . . hi, Annie."

"Don't say uh—it's unbecoming. I have an excuse to grunt; you don't."

"Huh?"

"And 'huh' is even worse."

He was not prepared to debate diction. He reached, and came up with perhaps the only thing left in the world that he was reasonably certain of. "I'm Mike."

"Hello, Mike. Welcome to Dreamworld Under."

"Uh—" He caught himself. "Sorry. Thanks, Annie. Am I really here? I mean, are we safe now?"

She shrugged. "Probably safer than most of the people on this weary planet, boy. Relax. They can't see in here, they can't hear in here, they can't smell in here unless I want them to—and they don't even know *that.* And the next inspection team isn't due through this area for weeks, unless something glitches."

The knot of muscle at the base of his neck relaxed just barely enough for him to notice. "Good. Thanks, Annie. I hope I didn't, uh . . . I mean—"

"Don't mention it. Especially not to anybody else. So what's—" She stopped, frowned at something, and rephrased. "How long were you thinking of staying in Dreamworld?"

"Well . . . ," he began, so he wouldn't say "Uh," and used the tiny interval to think hard about the question. It was one he had been postponing himself, for some time now, and he knew she had not asked it casually. "As long as I can," he said finally.

Something in her serene face changed. For an instant he thought he might have offended her, or perhaps saddened her somehow, but then she said, "Good answer." She closed her eyes for a few seconds. "Okay," she said, opening them again. "You seem lucky. And clever. And reasonably polite. Here is how it will be. I will help you—but neither of us is ever going to ask the other why they came here. Ever. Is that acceptable to you?"

"Okay," he said simply.

"Here's your end of the bargain," she said. "You have to listen to me."

He nodded.

"Don't look so dismayed. I don't mean you have to hang a patient look on your face while I blather about my youth, for God's sake. I mean you have to *pay attention* when I tell you things. Talking is very hard work for me; I hardly ever do it. And if I have to tell you things twice, you're going to make some stupid blunder and get at least one of us busted out of here. I warn you: if it's *me*, this place is going to turn on you."

He digested that. "How long have you been here, Annie?"

"*Under*, you mean? What year is it?"

"Twenty-three," he said, beginning to be awed. "July something, 2023."

"Thirteen years, then." She turned on her heel and walked away.

Mike knew he must follow her, and still he stood frozen a

moment in shock. Dreamworld was only a little over thirteen years old.

He snapped out of it and raced after her.

IT WAS A little like learning that one unicorn exists. It changed everything.

Mike felt like a biochemist who has labored for years to synthesize a wonderful new drug, then learns aborigine herb-doctors have known about that one for centuries. As they moved behind the scenes of Dreamworld, he tried to pay attention to his surroundings, but had trouble keeping his mind on the task. His eyes kept being drawn to his guide. His hero, now that he knew she existed. Mike's hopeless, desperate, quixotic quest was actually possible. Someone had done it. This unprepossessing midget auntie before him had done it. Had been doing it for longer than he had been alive.

No wonder she wasn't lonely! She had the Unicorn, the Warlock, Westley and Buttercup, the Mother Thing, the Hippogriff, Wanda the Werepoodle, Captain Horatio and his crew, Master Li and Number Ten Ox, Mike Callahan and his friends, Moondog Johnny, Lummox and John Thomas, and all the countless Elves and Trolls and Leprechauns and Dwarves for her constant companions. No wonder she looked so serene! For longer than his own lifetime, she had been living not just in a, but in *the*, Dreamworld. No wonder she accepted him. They were kindred spirits, in a world of clones. He studied her with intense fascination. So that was how she walked when she wasn't imitating a robot. . . .

It suddenly came to him that he had absolutely no idea how they had gotten from where they started to where they were now—which was halfway down a long tubular shaft with a ladder on one side. There were the rumbling sounds of a ride somewhere nearby, but he could neither locate its direction nor identify it, save that it seemed to be moving too fast to be any part of the Unicorn's Glade. He glanced up, and the shaft appeared simply to end about fifty meters higher up: no access hatch was visible. He glanced down and saw only that he was lagging behind.

When he reached the bottom of the ladder, Annie stood aside and made room for him to step down onto the metal floor. She gestured at a keypad on the wall. "Do what I did up there," she said.

"I didn't see it," he confessed, reddening in shame.

She clouded up. "I told you not to make me repeat myself. What the hell *were* you looking at?"

"You," he said miserably.

She closed her eyes. "Oh, my stars and garters. 'God has punished my contempt for authority . . .' " She sighed and reopened her eyes. "At least have the wit to pay particular attention to my hands, then. I do most of my best work with them."

"Yes, Annie."

With insultingly exaggerated pantomime, she addressed the keypad and punched in a four-digit number. A door silently dilated next to the keypad. "Got it this time?"

"How do you know what number to use?" he asked.

"From this." She held up her left wrist to display a Command Band like those worn by Dreamworld's employees. It resembled a Guest's Dreamband, with pop-up monitor and keypad added. She hadn't been wearing it during her stint as an Elf; she must have slipped it on while he wasn't looking. "It also makes me invisible to three different surveillance systems—and you, too, as long as you stay within three meters of me."

She hit *clear* on the keypad, and the door winked shut again. "Seven one three nine six fourteen three point one four one five seventeen eleven-five," she chanted in a rapid monotone, and stood aside. "Now you try it."

He went to the keypad, punched four digits, and the door reappeared.

"Better," she said curtly, and shouldered him aside to step through.

At that moment he realized suddenly that he was ravenously

hungry. He decided not to mention it and followed her. He'd been hungry before. He'd never been *Under* in Dreamworld before.

They passed through a series of environments in rapid succession. Each time she let him key in the code that admitted them to the next. Some he could identify at least tentatively as air-circulation tunnels, engine rooms, repair shops, switching nodes, degaussing zones, and the like. Some were so unfamiliar he could not even guess their nature or function. Some were noisy, some as silent as a stone. All were well lit and clean. As he doggedly memorized the route, he mentally labeled such regions things like *place where it smells funny* or *room with no room* or *inside the dentist's drill*. He had the general impression that Annie and he were gradually descending below ground. At one point they heard approaching voices and footsteps, and she led him immediately and unerringly to the nearest good hiding place, where they waited together until the danger was past.

A little while later she stopped short again. Mike looked around for another hidey-hole—but instead of hiding, she went to a nearby machine, a big complex thing he could not identify. She stared at it, sniffed it, reached into it and made some adjustment, then bent and put her ear up against the side of it and listened. After several seconds had elapsed, she frowned and straightened. Taking a red marker from a pocket, she wrote something on the wall above the machine. A single rune, which Mike didn't recognize. It looked a little like the classical symbol for "male," but was subtly different. Without explanation she put away the marker and they continued on their way.

At the end of a long featureless lime-green corridor, they came to another keypad, and he automatically began to enter the access code. She stopped him with an upraised hand. "This time," she said, "punch in the date of Opening Day."

He blinked. "The whole thing?"

"If you know it," she agreed.

He punched in the six digits of the date on which Thomas

Immega had opened the gates of his mighty dream for the first time, thirteen years earlier. At once he heard the familiar, barely audible sound of a door dilating, but no doorway appeared where he was expecting it. He decided the sound might have come from off to one side, though he wasn't sure which, and glanced quickly in both directions. Still no door. But he had not heard it sigh shut again yet. Or had he only imagined hearing it in the first place?

He looked at Annie. She was trying not to smile. It made him mad. He closed his eyes, thought furiously . . . then turned on his heel and walked directly into the left wall of the corridor.

As he passed through it, he was already turning right. He was in a small room; before him was a door—a real old-fashioned door, with hinges and a knob—and in front of it lay a welcome mat. He stopped and waited for Annie to catch up.

She came through the hologram wall still trying not to smile, but having trouble with it. "Not bad. How did you know which direction to go in, back in the corridor?"

"You said always turn right when you go through a holo. If it was in the other wall, you'd have to turn left whenever you left home."

"How *old* are you?"

"How old are *you*?"

Her rebel smile disappeared. She blinked. "Point taken. I beg your pardon, and withdraw the question." She sighed, pointed her wristband at the door, and the door beeped softly. "Well, are we going to stand out here all night, or do you want supper?"

He allowed himself to become aware of the black hole at his center, and nearly fainted with sudden hunger. He turned and opened the door—

—stopped and wiped his feet on the mat—

—stepped through and turned to see her staring at him oddly. "What?" he demanded.

"This might just work," she said. "Isn't that hilarious?"

He suddenly started to see the whole situation from her point of view. He began to giggle.

To his astonishment, she joined him. She had not, until now, seemed to be the sort of person who giggled. It struck him funny. Before he knew it, all his anger and most of his tension were boiling out of him as laughter. It felt oddly like throwing up. Then his vision started doing special effects: first solarization, then color-shimmer, and finally dissolve to random vibrant pixels.

Nearly at once it resolved again. Annie's face was a few decimeters from his, taut with concern. "Don't try to get up."

"Okay," he said agreeably. He hadn't realized he was down.

He felt himself picked up and carried. He marveled at her strength: he was pretty sure he could not have carried someone his own size. She set him gently on what he could tell was a bed. He tried to toe his shoes off, but found it oddly hard to do.

"I'll get it," she said, and did. "Sleep now. You can eat later."

"Okay," he said again, and did as he was told.

THE MOMENT OF awakening can be as hard to pin down as the instant love dies. Mike's first conscious thought was that there was a spoon in his mouth. Investigating, he found his favorite food in all the universe—Captain Horatio's clam chowder—at the business end of it, and Annie on the other. He swallowed. His belly told him it was at least his third or fourth spoonful of soup. It made him think of how Mom always said he would sleep through his own hanging, and that made him want to stop thinking, so he did, and ate soup.

By the time the bowl was empty, he had become aware of his surroundings. His first reaction to Annie's home was surprise—at how unsurprising it was. Heck, it was downright boring. It reminded him of a hotel room. (A cheap hotel room, the only kind he had ever seen except in TV or films.) No entertainment center—in fact, no visible TV or stereo of any kind. No posters, paintings, or pictures. No windows. Hardly any furniture at all, really, and all of that looked old and dinky. The computer was so old it had no speakers; looking closer he saw its disk drive would accept only Stone Age floppy disks, and its monitor could not be changed in either size or aspect ratio. The bed he lay on was antique, unpowered, simply a flat rectangle: he sat upright only with the aid of a precarious pyramid of pillows. The single visible recreational amenity was a pair of bookshelves packed full with books, mostly beat-up paperbacks. Something else nagged at his subconscious, and then surfaced: there was no remote control of any kind within reach of the bed . . .

Then all at once it made sense. He asked himself two questions: *Why did I have an HEC and posters and a good PC and a real bed in my room (when I still had all that stuff)?* and *Why do most people?*— and the answer to both came back the same. *So we won't mind so much that we don't live in Dreamworld.*

Annie didn't need any of that stuff.

Besides, she'd have to be prepared to abandon everything she owned, if Security ever got wind of her and she had to jungle up someplace else . . . so why own anything much?

"You can go back to sleep again if you like," she said, setting down the empty bowl. "It's the middle of the night." She wore a dark purple silk robe and slippers. He realized suddenly that he was naked under the covers, but could not manage to work up any embarrassment over it. He had been a patient before.

He made himself take a deep breath. "H-how many of us are there?" he asked.

She blinked. "Two. How many does it look like?"

"I mean *Under.*"

"The answer is still the same. We're the whole club, boy. You and I are the only ones PWOL."

"Huh? I mean, beg pardon?"

"Present Without Official Leave. Am I coming through? No one else is Under."

"Oh."

"Dozens have tried. Well, hundreds have *tried*, maybe thousands for all I know, but dozens have gotten as far as you have. As of today, nobody but me has been Under for as long as a week. The current record is four and a half days."

"Oh." He felt sharp dismay.

"I didn't help any of them," she said. "None of them even knew I was here."

He started to answer, but the longer he hesitated, the longer he hesitated. Annie must know his obvious next question; since she wasn't going ahead and answering it, she must not want to. "What did he do wrong?" he asked finally.

"Who? Oh, you mean the record holder."

"Yeah."

"He pissed me off."

From her the expression was startling. Then the meaning sank in.

"You . . . I mean, you—"

"Got him kicked out," she agreed. "I locked a door behind him one day. He didn't belong here."

"Oh."

"Don't look so worried."

He started to relax. "I belong here, then?"

"I don't know yet," she said impersonally. "But we've been introduced. If I ever decide you don't belong, I'll tell you first."

"Oh."

"Don't look so worried, I said. Damn it, boy, you've gotten farther than almost anyone else in the history of Dreamworld: be content with that for now."

"Except for you," he couldn't help adding.

She looked amused. "I *am* the history of Dreamworld."

"Have you ever—" He hesitated. "Do you ever go . . . you know, *out?*"

"Never. And I don't plan to." There was flat finality in her voice. She got up and brought the empty bowl to the small sink at one end of the room, rinsed it, and set it aside to dry. "More soup here," she said, pointing at the microwave. "Fridge there, pantry there, dunny over there behind that door. If you want anything, help yourself: I'm going to bed." She came back to the bedside, and—to his astonishment—dropped her robe, climbed in beside him, and slid under the covers. "Don't bother trying to explore; I've locked us in."

Mike rummaged through his entire social experience in search of an appropriate comment to make to an adult female stranger who has just joined one in bed, and came up empty. By the time he came up with "Good night" as a default choice, he was talking to himself.

CHAPTER 3

SOAKING

Rather to his surprise, he was asleep nearly at once.

AND THEN, EVEN more quickly, he was awake again. Wide awake, instantly aware of who and where he was, motionless in bed, reaching out with all his senses for whatever it was that had wakened him. He couldn't identify it. But neither could he escape the conviction that something was . . . well, not *wrong* exactly, Annie was sleeping soundly beside him, so probably nothing could be seriously wrong. But something was definitely . . .

. . . different . . .

. . . happening . . .

Was there a sound in the air, behind or beneath the sound of Annie's breathing? A kind of hum? The harder he tried to answer the question, the more uncertain he became. Was there some unfamiliar smell in the room? Again he was unsure. Was . . . whatever it was . . . coming more from one direction than another? Impossible to say.

The more negative reports came in from his senses, the more convinced he became that *something* was happening, *somewhere*.

He knew the sensible thing was to roll over and go back to sleep. Even if he could figure out what was going on, and even if he concluded something needed to be done about it, he wouldn't be able to do it. His hostess-mentor, whom he did not want to piss off, was asleep next to him. He was exhausted himself and sensed he had a big day ahead of him tomorrow.

Heart pounding, he slipped from the bed, so stealthily that Annie's breathing never changed. He had no idea what kind of signal he was picking up, but perhaps if he moved his detectors around, he could triangulate on the thing. He paused for a moment, closed his eyes, and set out across the dark room.

The nameless event *did* seem to change in some way as he moved. But it did so almost at random, so that the information he gained still refused to collapse into any kind of useful pattern. He changed direction a couple of times to no avail.

"Your diet must be about fifty-fifty, carrots and locoweed," Annie said softly.

He froze.

"I can't figure out what in the name of God's labia majora you think you're doing . . . but I'm impressed by how well you're doing it in the dark. You must have eyes like a cat."

"Actually, I've got my eyes closed," he said. "I looked around before when the light was on."

"You look around a room once, and you can navigate it in pitch dark?"

"Uh . . . I mean, well, yeah. I guess. Sorry I woke you."

"What the hell were you doing, practicing square dance?"

"I . . . well, I . . . I thought I heard something. Or something."

"Oh." She sat up. "I see. Interesting. I think I'm starting to understand."

"What?"

"Why I picked you."

"Picked me for what?"

"To be my friend."

He was startled speechless.

"You're sensitive to the place," she said. "I must have known it somehow. Thank God—I was beginning to think I was nuts." She got up from the bed; he heard her start to get dressed. "Throw your pants on," she said. "We're going for a walk."

He closed his eyes and retraced his steps. His clothes were folded and stacked on a night table on his side of the bed; he was ready before Annie had finished strapping her Command Band on her wrist and beeping the door lock open.

She did not bother to turn on a light, since neither of them needed one. He followed the whisper of her clothes through the dark.

He had expected light in the corridor, but had assumed for some reason that it would be damped down to night level. It was daytime bright. He ducked and flinched . . . then hurried after her, blinking furiously.

Shortly they came to a service elevator. He made a mark on the map he had been making in his head on the way . . . and, without thinking about it, also created and stored a mirror-reversed copy of that map, so that if something went wrong and they had to come back out of that elevator at a dead run, he wouldn't have to waste half a second doing it then. Annie consulted the Command Band on her wrist, put her ear to the elevator door, and only then pushed the button; he filed that, too. The car arrived quickly, and he followed her in.

"Elevator, top level," she told it. "Lights out."

The car darkened, and they went up—slowly at first, but soon *fast.* Just as he began fumbling around for a handhold he realized he didn't need it anymore: they were there.

The moment the door opened, he knew where they were: the uppermost reach of Johnny's Tree. Its magic was not functioning at the moment—he could still see Annie, for instance, and the nets that caught you if you fell were also visible now, or nearly, gleaming translucently in the moonlight. But the spot was unmistakable. All of Strawberry Fields was laid out thirty or forty meters below them. In the distance you could make out the Bridge of Birds, and beyond that a little of Rogero's Castle, the Hippogriff asleep atop it now. It was one of Mike's favorite vantage points in Dreamworld—and only partly because during the day it conferred invisibility on all who came here. ("No one—I think—is in my tree," Johnny had said in the song for which this part of Dreamworld was named.)

Annie paused before leaving the elevator, so he did, too. He assumed she was scanning for possible observers, either up here or down on the ground, with her eyes or ears or, for all he knew, nose. But he was wrong.

"I'm rushing this," she said. "Elevator, hold."

She sounded irritated. He looked closer, squinting in the poor light, and she looked irritated, too. "What's the matter?"

She hesitated. "Do you believe in magic?" she asked suddenly. He blinked. "Of course."

She looked even more annoyed. "Let me try again. Do you believe the magic in Dreamworld is *real*, capital M magic? Or is it stage magic? Do you even understand the difference?"

"Of course I do. Jesus, Annie, I'm not a little kid."

She seemed less annoyed. "Then answer me. Is this place infested with genuine fairies and unicorns—or do they do it with mirrors?"

Mike took a long time answering. This was not a trivial question. In a sense, he was being asked whether he Believed in Dreamworld. A thousand movies and TV shows and books and comics urged him to punch his fist in the air and shout *yes* in reflex response—to dutifully support the myth, in the same way that grown-ups *would not* publicly admit to the nonexistence of Santa Claus. If this had been daytime, and there had existed even the remote possibility that another child or even grown-up might be within earshot, he would have followed that instinct unhesitatingly.

But this was not daytime, and they were not in public. The question had been privately asked. He sensed somehow that Annie wanted the most honest answer he could give. All right, then: what answer was that? More time ticked by. She waited, her face impassive.

"It's faked," he said at last.

She nodded solemnly.

"That's okay, though," he said. "I mean . . . well, it's not really *fake*, exactly, not like *cheating*. They'd use real magic if they could. They *want* there to be real magic, lots of it—so they *make* some, and give it to us, so we can carry a little bit home with us to help us recognize it." He felt himself running on, and stopped. "I mean, they're not cheats."

"Relax, I know what you mean. So you understand it's all basically a magic act? Tricks and gimmicks?"

"The best ones on earth," he said.

"Did you ever go backstage and ask a magician how a trick worked?"

He nodded.

"Did he tell you?"

He nodded again.

"Okay, here's the important part. How did you feel, once you knew? I mean, did it spoil the trick, knowing how he did it?"

The question seemed so odd he dug out the memory involved and replayed it, just to be sure. "No," he said. "Not at all. It was *more* fun knowing how. I mean, it was even more amazing, that he could do something magical like that *without* magic."

She relaxed. "Good."

"Annie, what are you asking me all this weird stuff for?"

She sighed. "Because it finally dawned on me that I can't keep you Under for any length of time without teaching you the secrets of Dreamworld. Most of 'em, anyway. And a lot of people . . . well, no matter how much they think they want to know how the magic is done, deep down inside they'd really rather not know. I didn't want to be responsible for spoiling Dreamworld for you."

He thought that over. "Well . . . thanks. But I don't think there's *anything* I'd rather not know." He frowned. "I *hate* not knowing stuff."

She raised an eyebrow. "You are a rare one. Let's go, then."

They left the elevator. Everything was at once familiar and weirdly unfamiliar. He had been here at least a dozen times in daylight. It was strange and mildly thrilling to be here at night.

The insubstantial sensation of Something Happening was back in force, intensified almost to the point of making sense.

He realized that in his previous visits, he had never noticed a second elevator. He glanced over his shoulder, and failed to find it. "How do I get back into that elevator if I need to?" he asked.

"You follow me. If I'm not around, you're SOL." She saw he did not know the idiom. "Let's just say you're 'Gully Low.' Don't worry about it, we'll get you a Command Band of your own tomorrow. Take a seat."

She had led them to a "crotch" in Johnny's Tree that happened to be his particular favorite, since it gave the best view of Penny Lane. Beneath them, the Tree—powered down or not—silently extruded gossamer safety nets. They sat together, side by side.

He gazed around at Strawberry Fields below, only half seeing it. It was all true. He was really, finally backstage, after hours. Thirty meters up in the air, he was Under. All Dreamworld was his.

The night was electric. It was too dark to make out much of the meadow below, in moonlight; he lifted his gaze, up past Penny Lane . . . to the forest that blocked off sight of the rest of Dream-world, save for the distant arch of the Bridge of Birds . . . and then higher, to the night sky. . . .

His gaze insisted on yanking itself back downward again.

There was something strange about Penny Lane. It was . . .

. . . holy shit, it was *shimmering*. Vibrating just perceptibly in the darkness. Not all of it, but most of it. He seemed to see a . . . a droplet of some kind fall from the Pretty Nurse's poppy tray to the sidewalk . . . and then another.

He leaned out as far as the barrier would let him, looked straight down at the meadow beneath his branch, and squinted hard. A scrap of cloud drifted away from the moon to help, and he cried out in spite of himself.

Strawberry Fields was *crawling*. . . .

• • •

ALL OF DREAMWORLD was crawling.

He marinated in horror for perhaps ten seconds of objective time. Is that less than a million years? Afterward, maybe. Then Annie pulled him back up into the tree crotch, squinted at his face, cursed, and slapped him hard.

It was like a cold reboot of his brain. This computer may not have been shut down properly the last time it was used; you should always shut down using the Power key. Next time I will, I promise. Now what was it that made us crash, again? *Oh!* Something to get hung about, indeed . . .

Annie was shaking him. "How old were you when you saw it?" she was saying.

Her question might have been obscure to another, but he understood it without thought and answered at once, "Eight."

"Shit," she said, with feeling. Then: "An animal? Or—"

"A cat. My cat, Smoky. I found him two days after."

She clenched her jaw and nodded. "I should have thought. I'm sorry. Mike, look at me. Stop trying to look over the side and look me in the eye." He did as he was told. "Listen hard. There is nothing dead down there. There is nothing ugly down there. Nothing creepy. I promise. What is down there is *good*. It's magic, but it's white magic. It's part of what makes Dreamworld possible. Do you understand?" She saw his expression, and with an effort made herself speak softer and more slowly. "Let me try again. Have you ever loved somebody, Mike? I mean, really loved them?"

He thought hard. "Smoky."

She seemed to wince for some reason, but pressed on. "Okay. Did you ever see Smoky shit? While there wasn't anyone else around to see you look?"

He was startled into paying closer attention. She asked the oddest questions. "Sure."

"Was it ugly?"

"Huh?"

"Everybody says shitting is gross, creepy, ugly. You hide in a closet to do it, so nobody will see. Was Smoky ugly when he was shitting?"

"No!" He pictured it. "Actually, it was kind of beautiful, if you want to know the truth. I wish I could see him do it now."

She nodded. "Then you understand. Everybody says shitting is creepy—but if it's somebody you love doing it, it's beautiful to watch. It's a part of them, so it's a gift. So then—do you see?—shitting *isn't* creepy: it's just that everybody doesn't love everybody. Enough."

"Let me think about that a minute," he said. She did, waiting patiently in her cross-legged tailor's seat. After a while he said, "Tell me if I've got this right. Stuff everybody thinks is creepy might not be creepy . . . if there's enough love around."

A full-bore smile flashed and was gone, the first of hers he had ever seen, and now he knew what she had looked like at his age. "Gold star."

He nodded . . . took a deep breath, and leaned over the side again.

He saw nearly at once this time that they didn't really look a whole lot like maggots at all, really—not if you looked closely.

For one thing, the countless trillions of swarming grains of rice below were *not* the pale yellow color his memory had imposed on them. Those near enough to a maintenance light to be seen clearly were all, he saw now, a soft pastel blue. His reptile brain relaxed a bit: almost nothing that lives is that color, and nothing dangerous.

At this distance, they must all actually be much bigger than grains of rice. He guessed them at the size of a thumb. They were *not* all the same size, either. Just most of them.

And they were not in fact swarming, technically. Not with the blind, mindless randomness of maggots; they were clearly all moving purposefully, each toward a destination of its own. Some were encumbered with things too small or shadowed to make out, either portaged on their backs or dragged behind them. In one spot he saw over two dozen of them cooperating to drag away something bulky. Someone's lost camcorder . . .

Now he understood. "They're *cleaning* Penny Lane!"

Annie's voice was serene behind him now. "Cleaning, disinfecting, polishing, resetting, reconfiguring, repairing, restocking, repainting, maintaining . . . they're *healing* it, Mike. Healing the damage people did to it without meaning to, without being able to help it. They do it every night. It's happening all over Dreamworld, right now. Robots, minibots, microbots, even nanobots, all working in harmony—billions of them. I like to come up here, or a few other places, and watch them. Everything else in the universe falls apart—but Thomas Immega doesn't *allow* entropy, in *here*. Those robots down there keep it out."

He watched them for a timeless time. "They're not creepy at all," he said at last. "They're beautiful."

"Yes."

He sat upright on the limb again. "I thought it was, like, an army of *people* that fixed everything up again at night."

She nodded. "The management do contrive to give that impression to the public, without ever exactly saying so. Some civilians who didn't know better might think little robot maggots were creepy, you know? There *is* a small army working here right now, underground—techs and engineers and set designers who forgot to go home and so on—but they're mostly not allowed up on the set. You can't trust 'em not to spill a cup of coffee or forget a power tool."

"Annie? The people that work here in the daytime . . . are they real?" He felt himself blushing. "Not the Cousins, I mean: I know *they're* real. But, like, the Elves and Trolls and Leprechauns and . . . you know, the"—he hesitated—"all the *little* people. And the big ones that are magical, like Master Li. Are they real?"

She grinned—not as good as her earlier smile, but now he knew what she'd looked like at twenty-five. "Ah—you want to learn *all* the secrets your first night. Are you sure?"

"Well . . ." As any child of four knew, if a Dreamworld character chose to touch *you*—the Mother Thing, say, or one of the little people—they certainly seemed to be real enough. But if you touched one of *them* without invitation, as often as not they were liable to vanish like a burst soap bubble. It was one of the primary mysteries of Dreamworld, a subject of endless speculation, one of the principal evidences that Magic lived here. "Yeah."

"About fifty-fifty," she said.

He did some mental calculation and was stunned. "God, there must be—"

"A significant fraction of the little people in North America work here," she said. "And more from other places. Thomas Immega is our patron saint. You must have seen the size of the employee parking zone."

"Well, yeah, but how can you tell how many of those people wear overalls and how many put on costumes, when they get inside?"

"Good point. No, the day shift is only about twenty percent Staff, twenty percent Cousins. The rest are all Cast."

"Wow." To have the knowledge felt peculiar, as if someone had given him the address of Santa's summer home. His mind skittered away. "I saw somebody die today."

The non sequitur did not throw her. "Tell me about it," was all she said.

So he did. She asked a lot of questions, and he ended up remembering it better than he'd thought he had, coming up with all sorts of details of what he'd seen, what he'd heard, what he'd felt. He decided he liked telling stuff to Annie. In the first place there was a heady quality to sitting in a forbidden place at night discussing death with an adult. This was Mike's very first bull session. And in the second place, there was something about the way Annie listened that he liked. Grown-ups rarely listened to you; they mostly just paused between their own speeches to make sure you'd admired the last one. She heard what he said: you could tell from her questions.

"I think the Cousin was right," she said when he was done.

"About her being lucky? Sure. Boy, to die in Dreamworld . . ."

"A little less than fifty people have been that lucky, since they opened the doors, and by God I intend to be one of them. But it must be a special grace to go during Firefall."

"For some reason I wish I knew her name," Mike said. "Is there a way I could find out, without taking a chance?"

"Her name was Judith Grossman," Annie said. "She was a poet from New York, and she is survived by two daughters and four grandchildren."

"You already knew about her?"

"I know everything that happens in Dreamworld. I just wanted to know about her passing. How it was."

"Well . . . I don't see how it could have been much better."

"They say the ones God loves most are the ones who die making love," she said, "but I agree, her passing was almost as good. It doesn't even surprise me anymore."

"What doesn't?"

She sighed. "Mike, I think of myself as a hardheaded realist. You have to be to live in a dreamworld. But there's a statistical anomaly that almost tempts me to mysticism. Of the forty-six people I mentioned before that have died here, thirty-five went with, as near as I can find out, an absolute minimum of pain or fear. If it was an accident that got them, they never knew what hit them; the sick ones mostly seemed to either fall down on something soft or fail to get up from a comfortable seat. Half of 'em died actually smiling. And of the eleven exceptions . . . well, at least seven of them had it coming. They were either engaged in trying to hurt someone else, or had hurt someone badly outside and come in to hide. I saw three of those happen myself, and saw convincing evidence for the other seven. The other four, nobody knows what happened. I cling to those four exceptions."

"Why?"

"Because if I ever have to concede that a benign invisible spirit is in fact watching over Dreamworld, it'll spoil the place for me. I might even have to leave."

"Huh. That'd make me want to stay."

"I understand. But I look at it this way. If there's a magic force that can help the good die happy and punish the wicked, and it's only got time to cover one amusement park, I don't think I want to have anything to do with it. I'll go take my chances on the outside with the other peasants."

Mike wondered if he were that noble. Well, he could admire it, anyway. "I see what you mean."

"Do you think you can get to sleep, now?"

He asked his body. "Yeah."

"Then let's go."

He noticed that she rose slowly from her tailor's seat, and realized she was exhausted. He pondered what, if anything, to say about that, and in the elevator came up with, "Annie? Thanks. I know I'm a pain."

She sighed theatrically. "Up all night with the baby, at my age." Seeing his expression, she sobered. "Don't worry about it, Mike. I'm glad you came. I hate like hell to admit it, and I'm not even sure I believe it, but this place was just beginning to get the tiniest bit dull." She gifted him with another of those quick smiles. "I needed to see it again through your eyes." She did an instant 180 and became stern. "Now go to bed."

He didn't know what to say, so he said nothing. But once they got back home, he fell asleep with a warm feeling.

CHAPTER 4

MEANWHILE IN MORDOR

At about the same time, at the top of a tall tower a few thousand kilometers away, a morbidly obese man named Alonzo Haines glared at his state-of-the-art executive desk and told himself for the umpteenth time that the electronic office sucked.

He was old enough and cranky enough—especially at this hour—to remember with fondness the days when people came to your office, in corpus, all the time. It was much easier to bully a live human being than any electronic avatar: a forceful personality does not digitize well. You can let your e-mail sit there in the box all day before acknowledging its existence, but the e-mail doesn't *know* you're keeping it waiting. You can't discomfit a voice-mail message by interrupting it, or letting uncomfortable silences follow statements you don't like. You can't project menace properly over even the best vidphone. Oh, there were tricks for dominating, even at such removes, and Haines had mastered them all . . . but they just weren't as intrinsically *satisfying* as seeing the other son of a bitch squirm on the far side of your desk, having him physically on your turf, *smelling* his discomfiture.

Worst of all, the electronic gadgets were so damnably simple to use now, there was no real (publicly admissible) reason to have a personal secretary anymore. There was *nobody* around the office to intimidate during the day but his three executive assistants . . . and they just weren't expendable enough for him to risk a good workout.

Ah, but tonight, at two o'clock in the morning, there was hope.

He watched it approaching on the security monitor on his desktop: Randall Conway, entering the empty office tower on schedule—*not* by way of the lobby, and *without* coming to the attention of any of the Tower Security personnel still on duty at this hour, just as Haines himself had entered ten minutes ago. As fit as Haines was fat, he moved with the graceful efficiency of a successful predator, which he was.

This might go either way. There were two possible outcomes, both good. If Conway had called this late-night meeting to report failure, then humiliating him would be not only prudent but just. If not—if he actually had something—then he would be too valuable to offend without good reason, like the executive assistants . . . but on the bright side, Haines's most cherished dreams would be about to come true.

It was a win-win situation, really. He began to cheer up, or at least sulk less emphatically, as he always did at such times.

He studied Conway's face as the man rode up in the special elevator—a longish ride even at modern acceleration—but found no clues. Well, a perfect poker face was part of what Haines was paying him for. And after all, Conway probably knew, certainly must suspect, that his employer was watching him as he ascended to the penthouse eyrie: to wear a poker face was an admission of discomfort. Or might have been, if Conway's face hadn't looked like that all the time . . .

Haines hated having to deal with Conway, for the man was *almost* as smart as he was, and just as murderous. But he had no choice. He needed someone like Conway, and Conway was the best someone-like-him there was: Haines's best and only hope of destroying the despised Phillip Avery and all his works.

He loathed Avery *far* more than he did Conway—perhaps more than anyone alive loathed anyone. Elisha Gray might have known such hatred, in his day: the man who filed his patent application for the telephone an hour and a half *after* Alexander

Graham Bell. Except that Haines was even more aggrieved—because he, God damn it, had been *first*. Thrillworld, the violent fantasy-based theme park into which he had poured several fortunes, only one of them his own—committing himself irretrievably for life—had opened its doors to the world exactly four weeks before Thomas Immega and his dog Avery had opened up their damned Dreamworld . . .

Just as the elevator began decelerating, Haines realized with a start that he had forgotten to disable the office's recording gear, and hastily did so, wiping the last ten minutes for good measure. If Conway had succeeded, there must be no record of this conversation. And if he had failed, and was here for a reaming, Haines could always turn the cameras back on.

The elevator opened, and Conway emerged like a panther from a cage. "I want a chair," he said at once in that horridly husky voice.

Haines could not be flustered by any serve, but this came close. He hated it when he had failed to think something through. "Of course," he said. There actually was a visitor's chair in the room, shoved well back out of the way, and he managed to find the button that would summon it to the proper position. Conway curled up in it without thanks. "We secure?" he rasped.

"We're not here," Haines agreed.

"I've got them," Conway said without further preamble. "I don't know exactly what I've got, yet—but I know I've got them."

Haines began the laborious task of preparing himself to be happy. Smiling, an otherwise useless grimace, sometimes helped, so he tried it. "Tell me about it. Did you find the Mother Elf?"

"I found out she really exists, yes. But I don't know where, or what she looks like, and it's not important."

Haines was surprised; he'd been sure the Mother Elf was bullshit, folk myth. But—"Okay. What is?"

"They got too many Trolls."

Haines was annoyed enough to go for the chill stare and overextended pause, which had made lesser men faint. It bounced off Conway, of course. "So what else is new?" he said finally. "That son of a bitch Avery has got practically every midget and dwarf on the planet under contract, so what? I already put lawyers on it: nothing we can do, antitrust, nothing. It's perfectly legal for those bastards to lock up a whole minority group."

Conway was shaking his head. "That's not what I mean."

"Okay. What is?"

"Every morning, four hundred and thirty-four midgets and dwarves walk into Dreamworld through the employee entrances for the day shift. Every afternoon this week, four hundred and forty walked out. Same for the night shift."

"Huh?"

"They got too many Trolls."

Haines closed his eyes. "Jesus. A dozen a day. For at least the past week."

"You see what I mean? I got no idea what it means, yet. But whatever the hell they're doing, there's no way it could be innocent. Even before we know what it is, we got them by the balls."

"But what *is* it? You have any ideas?"

"None I like much. Comic-book stuff. Some sort of fruitcake illegal immigration scam, maybe, or a new tax rip-off."

"Jesus," Haines said again. "Could it possibly be some kind of, I don't know, weird child-molesting thing? They kidnap the kids and, like, hypnotize them, and then dress 'em up and make 'em up like Elves and send 'em out to . . ." He trailed off, realizing it made no sense but reluctant to relinquish the fantasy. Avery, buggering an Elf on the *Six O'clock News*. . . .

Conway shook his head. "There are never any customers unaccounted for. I checked six ways. And it's never Elves, Leprechauns, or Dwarves. Just Trolls—at least so far."

Haines shook his own head. "I could never keep all those little bastards straight."

"There's two kinds of little people in the world: midgets and dwarves. Midgets are the ones in proportion, that look like kids with adult faces; dwarves are the ones that are built weird. Over there, nice-looking midgets play Elves, ugly ones play Leprechauns; nice-looking dwarves are just called Dwarves, and ugly ones are Trolls. They got too many Trolls."

Haines frowned ferociously. "What the hell does it mean?" He stopped. "You're right: what's the difference? It's got to be *wrong*, whatever it is. By God, I've *got* that bastard Avery."

"Yes."

"How did you happen to notice this?"

"I didn't. A computer did. I had a general analysis program running on the orbital scans, looking for anomalies, anything we could nail them on. It worked."

Something in Haines resisted being this happy; he groped for an out. "You have this documented? I mean, nailed down?"

"I can run you the orbital scans, and you can count the Trolls yourself."

"Our satellites or the government's?"

"Both. Tamperproof proof."

There was nothing for it. Haines felt his face rearranging itself in unaccustomed ways, producing the first grin it had worn since, five years earlier, an operative had brought him a photograph of Phillip Avery grunting on the toilet. "There *is* a God," he said.

"No," Conway said. "There isn't."

"Well, no. But sometimes you get lucky."

"Yes."

Haines knew his face was going to hurt in the morning, but he didn't care. "Well, sometimes that's almost as good."

Conway declined to argue the point. "How do you want to hit them with it?"

"In a leisurely manner," Haines said. "I am in no hurry at all. Avery's mine now, but I still want to know *everything* before I take him. I want to know exactly what's going on, and why, and for how long. I want to know about the frigging Mother Elf, too. In fact, I want to have a long talk with that little bitch."

"Hell for?"

"If she's real—if she's really been there all along—then she knows every single weakness of the place. Maybe some that even Avery doesn't know about. Get me a handle on her."

"It'll cost," Conway said. "She's way underground. You sure she's worth it?"

"One time I looked down at my hand and saw a straight flush, ace high," Haines said. "Hardly seemed worth it to have the waitress go peek at the other guys' hands. But there was a lot of money on the table, and what did I care if I wasted her time, so I gave her the sign again anyway. We were playing with wild cards, see, and one of those sons of bitches had five deuces. I was so happy, later that week I let her go back to being a human being again."

Conway nodded. "You can always use more information."

"How soon can I talk with the Elf?"

Conway thought a moment. "Soon."

Haines was so pleased he squirmed in his chair, and to *hell* with his hemorrhoids. No, even more pleased than that. "I'm adding a ten percent bonus to your fee," he said, not quite believing the words even as he heard them leave his mouth. "And another ten after I see the Elf."

Now Conway's face wanted to smile, too, but he managed to control his. That annoyed Haines slightly . . . and in an odd way he welcomed that small annoyance, clung to it as a lifeline back to the disposition and worldview he knew.

It made little difference, anyway. Once he had brought down Dreamworld once and for all, once he had scattered its rubble and salted its fields and pissed on the graves of its every defender, then he could afford to crush a Conway a week, for the pure sport.

Damn, now he was happy again.

He reminded himself sharply that ultimate victory was impossible. He could conquer Dreamworld, conquer Avery . . . but the Antichrist himself, Immega, had escaped him into death. Haines could—and now would—beat Thomas Immega . . . but he could never have the satisfaction of knowing that the son of a bitch *knew* it.

There. That helped. . . .

CHAPTER 5

STOOLED TO THE ROGUE

Annie was still asleep when Mike woke. He slipped out of bed, found his shorts, tiptoed to the toilet, and closed the door behind him before turning on the light.

At once he had a problem. The toilet bowl was full of water. *Full*—there was no dry land to aim for: he was going to make a loud splash. This could not be a sound Annie was used to sleeping through. He could try sitting . . . but he had done that just yesterday, in the girls' room, and it had made almost as much noise as standing up. The only other solution he could think of—putting his foot into the bowl and peeing down his leg—had limited appeal. The default choice was to hold it until Annie woke up. He turned back to the door—

—and stopped halfway. Annie must have installed these fixtures herself: her sink was set lower than usual, at a height convenient for *her*. That made it convenient for Mike . . . and a sink can be flushed clean much more quietly than a toilet.

Back outside, he catfooted around in near darkness until he understood the kitchen well enough to use it. The microwave, fridge, and coffeemaker appeared to be standard issue for a small Dreamworld food outlet. The limited selection he found in the fridge consisted almost entirely of prepared breakfasts: mostly egg rollups in assorted flavors, again clearly scavenged from restaurant supplies. The most common flavor was Huevos Jalapeños, his own favorite, so he put two of those into the microwave and set the timer, but did not start it yet. He set up coffee—Dreamworld Sulawezi, the only kind Annie stocked—but did not trigger that, either. He laid out plates, cups, and silverware for two—her entire supply, apparently—on the table. Then he sat down and waited.

As he waited, he wondered whether the second plate, cup, and silverware implied that Annie ever had other guests, besides himself. Or was it just so that, if she broke something, she wouldn't have to interrupt a meal to go get a replacement?

As soon as he heard her breathing change, he got up and switched on the coffee and oven. Annie and the coffeemaker started making burbling sounds roughly simultaneously, but she stopped sooner.

"Jesus," she said reverently, as the smell reached her.

He began serving. It took most of his attention, and by the time he had everything ready, Annie was sitting at the table in a blue robe, scowling. He poured the coffee, noting that she took hers with sugar and cream. Of course: why else would she stock them? He put plenty of both in his own.

Midway through her first sip, her scowl softened to a frown. "You put salt in it," she said wonderingly.

"Just a pinch," he said, afraid he had blundered. "It makes it less bitter."

"I know what it does," she said. "I'm just surprised that *you* know the trick." She toasted him with her cup.

He relaxed, and returned the gesture.

They ate in companionable silence, and when they were through, she got up to clear away before he could. He sat back and examined the books on the nearest shelf. Some of the titles were unfamiliar, some even inexplicable to him, but there were also a lot of old friends. Not just Dreamworld-related books like *Bridge of Birds* or *Have Spacesuit—Will Travel*, either. He'd half expected to find those, and *The Princess Bride* and all the rest. But Annie also had a lot of his favorite books that had no connection with Dreamworld. *The Flying Yorkshireman.* Edgar Pangborn's *Davy. The First* and *Second Saint Omnibus. The Little World of Don*

Camillo. John D. MacDonald's entire Travis McGee series, in sequence, in paperback. All of Donald E. Westlake's Dortmunder books, in hardcover. Theodore Sturgeon's masterpiece, *Godbody,* and some of his story collections.

And there on the third shelf, a copy of the most recent, eighty-eighth reprinting of his mother's and grandmother's favorite book: Will Cuppy's immortal *The Decline and Fall of Practically Everybody.* Mike's eyes stung. The precious tattered copy of the thirty-fifth printing Mom had given him for his seventh birthday had been the one possession he'd been most tempted to take with him when he went Under. He'd finally abandoned it only because she had used his full name in her inscription: if he'd lost it anywhere in Dreamworld it would have meant disaster, and he could not bring himself to tear out or deface the inscription.

"Something wrong, Mike?"

He smoothed his face. "Just the opposite. I like your books."

She looked pleased. "You read. Remarkable. Especially these days. Wait until you see *those.*"

He looked to the bookcase she indicated, over by the armchair, and squinted. Suddenly he was leaning forward in his chair. *"Holy—"*

Ranked in rows in uniform, like the set of encyclopedias he'd taken them for, massive gold volumes with scarlet titles.

DREAMWORLD BLUEPRINTS. DREAMWORLD SYSTEMS OVERVIEW. DREAMWORLD ENTERTAINMENT (twin volumes: PRODUCTION and PERFORMANCE). DREAMWORLD CYBERNETICS. DREAMWORLD FX. DREAMWORLD ROBOTICS. DREAMWORLD HYDRAULICS. DREAMWORLD ENGINEERING. DREAMWORLD POWER. DREAMWORLD HOLOGRAPHY. DREAMWORLD MAINTENANCE. DREAMWORLD SUPPLY & DISPOSAL. DREAMWORLD PERSONNEL. DREAMWORLD SECURITY. DREAMWORLD MEDICAL. DREAMWORLD MERCHANDISING. DREAMWORLD R & D. DREAMWORLD PUBLICITY.

The master manuals. A complete set of the Keys to the Arcana. . . .

"Close your mouth," Annie said. "I can see your tonsils."

"May I read them?"

"If you treat them with respect," she said.

He stood up, found that his knees were shaky. "I think I can promise you that." His voice came out shaky, too. He moved forward.

"But the Pageant starts in twenty minutes."

He stopped in his tracks. "Oh *gee*. We can go up and see it?"

Her eyes twinkled at his predicament—but her voice was kind. "Every morning for the rest of your life, if you want."

He was torn. The mother lode itself was meters away. But— "I only got here early enough to see the Pageant once," he said.

"That settles it," she told him. "Those books aren't going anywhere. Besides, a gentleman doesn't start reading before noon. It's the first step on the slippery slope to total degeneracy. You wind up sitting in the gutter, unwrapping wet newspaper from a dead fish to get at Continued on Page C-Twelve. Get your shoes on and we'll go."

"Okay."

She frowned. "Wait. You have a bogus Dreamband?"

He rolled his eyes. "Of course." There was no way you could last more than ten minutes in Dreamworld without one, without being noticed.

"Let me see it."

He showed it to her. "You make this yourself?" she asked, and after some hesitation he nodded. "Nice job. I had one I was going to give you, but this is almost as good." He felt himself grow slightly larger as he soaked up the praise. "Okay, saddle up."

By the time he was ready to travel, she had worked a magic transformation on herself—he almost cried out when he first saw it. She was now Mike's own age. It wasn't a mask, it didn't seem to be makeup. She was just—somehow—a child. The skin of her face was as smooth and unwrinkled as his own, even on her neck.

His astonishment must have showed. She grinned—and there wasn't even a smile wrinkle on that face yet, now. "Trust me, those are not attractive tonsils," she said.

To his obscure relief, her voice came out the way he remembered it, husky and *old*. He closed his mouth.

"That's better," she said, and held up her left wrist to display a fake Dreamband of her own. "This way I don't have to be Cast. We can both be Guests, and walk and talk together without drawing any attention. I've got my Command Band in my pocket, in case we need it."

He nodded. "That's good." He decided to ask. "Will you tell me how you did that? Changed the way you look?"

She grinned again. "Before or after you dig into those manuals?"

He thought hard. "Before."

"Good instincts," she replied. "It's one of the deepest darkest secrets of Dreamworld. But we'll have to wait till we get back here. It isn't something you can talk about Topside, where Guests might overhear."

"Okay," he said.

"Come on, we better hurry."

Halfway to the door he stopped, suddenly too happy to walk. "Annie?"

"What?"

"This is gonna be really *great*, isn't it?"

She understood at once. "Yes, Mike," she said, nodding slowly. "I think it is."

LOOKING BACK ON it in later years, Mike would conclude that this was probably the happiest day of his life.

The Pageant was even better than he remembered; the state of the art was always improving, and today's Cast were really first-rate. When it was over, he and Annie simply let their feet guide them away from the Plaza, critiquing the newest effects together too intensively to care where they walked. As they passed through Florin, they were politely accosted by one of Mike's favorite characters—and for the first time in his life he succeeded in beating Fezzik at rhymes, winning a holocaust cloak from the giant and a look of respect from Annie.

More than once a passing child greeted Annie by name, and Annie introduced Mike to all who did. One or two he had seen around before; regulars like himself. He even saw one grown-up nod and smile at Annie, who waved back.

They turned east, wandered down Route 25A with the sun in their eyes, had a Coke in Callahan's while listening to Fast Eddie play "Small Fry." He was a very good Fast Eddie, too, the best Mike had ever seen—even better than the one on the old TV series. When Mike smashed his glass in the fireplace, his toast was "To freedom"—and behind the bar Callahan said "Amen" and added his own glass, triggering a barrage from all around the room. Mike was grinning proudly when they left. Annie had let him pay for the Cokes—and had flattered him by not even checking first to make sure he intended to pay with cash rather than traceable plastic.

They turned north on Penny Lane by tacit mutual agreement. There they did all the usual things—said hello to the Barber, bought a poppy from the Pretty Nurse, laughed at the Banker— but today they were somehow even more fun than usual for Mike. To his surprise, Annie let him have a four of fish, and the *hell* with spoiling his appetite for lunch; he had not realized there was an adult female alive who could countenance such a thing. She had two finger pies herself. This time she paid, using plastic. He sneaked a look; it said her name was Agnes Meade. The wiper accepted it without a hiccup. She disposed of it with the napkin, a few minutes later. He had been wondering what he would do when his small supply of cash was exhausted; now he stopped worrying about it.

When they finished eating, they wandered over into the Fields—pausing to use the Fields WC—and took the conventional, public elevator up Johnny's Tree together. Annie held his hand the whole way, so they wouldn't get separated when they became invisible, and he found the sensation interesting. It was *not* as weird and embarrassing as he'd always imagined holding a *girl's* hand would be . . . but it wasn't at all like holding your mother's hand, either. Actually, it felt kind of good—like when your best bud punched you on the shoulder and made your arm go numb. Mike hadn't had a best bud in some time.

When they reached the top, he found that now, in daylight, he could just barely make out the edges of the hidden elevator door. He was careful not to stare at it. They were able to get the same spot they'd had eight or nine hours earlier, out on the branch. He looked around, briefly pictured everything out there *crawling* in the moonlight, and found nothing repulsive in the image. Because of that, this was now as beautiful as it was. He wished he could tell Annie . . . then realized she already knew. He could tell by the way she was holding his hand.

It was, in short, a perfect day. Even more so than a normal day in Dreamworld, enhanced by three powerful spices: he was here illicitly, and he didn't have to leave at closing time, and he had a friend.

By midafternoon, after listening to Master Li give a riotous lecture in drunken verse to Number Ten Ox, Mike had reached a state of happiness overload and heard himself ask Annie if they could go back Under again for awhile. She understood at once and slipped her Command Band onto her wrist. They made sure they were unobserved, walked straight into a dragon's mouth, turned to the right . . . were back at Annie's place ten minutes later.

Where, impossibly, it got better.

ALL RIGHT, BOY. I'll tell you the secrets of Dreamworld. Ask me anything. Want to know why it's so hard to have a bad time here?"

Mike hesitated. It would be easy to just say *yes*. But this was a day for taking risks. "I . . ." He caught himself before he could say, "uh," and pressed on. ". . . think maybe I know that one."

She lifted an eyebrow. "So? Interesting. What's your theory?"

Now he was committed. "Well . . . I'm really into music a lot. And I read once in a book about the notes that people can't hear, that are too high or too low. You can only hear from twenty cycles a second up to about twenty thousand, you know. Dogs and cats can hear some of the hypersonics, the ones that are too high. But the subsonics, the ones that are too low . . . I read there's this one note, fourteen cycles a second, and if you play that note real loud, nobody can hear anything, but they start to get, like, nervous and uptight and scared, and if you keep it up they freak out—no, really," he said, seeing Annie's face.

She smoothed it over. "I wasn't arguing. Go on."

"Well, it just stands to reason. I think if there's a note you can't hear that makes you feel real lousy, there must be another one that makes you feel real good. There's speakers everywhere you go in Dreamworld. Once I came here with a Walkman, and I just didn't have as much *fun* whenever I had the ear things in my ears. And another time when I had a cold and my ears were stopped up . . . what?"

Annie was looking at him funny again. "Mike," she said slowly, "that is one of the *lesser* secrets of Dreamworld. At least four national governments and perhaps twenty private individuals have figured that one out. It took all of them a great deal of time and effort and a lot of other people's money to nail it down; I watched most of them do it. You aren't old enough to shave, and you cracked it with a Walkman. Is there any chance I could rent that brain whenever you're not using it? Or do you have such times?"

"I really figured it out?"

"In the Far East, there is a temple with only one entrance. You have to stoop to go in. Everybody who does so, without exception, the moment they get inside and straighten up, they burst into tears. Subsonics. The building's architecture and acoustics combine perfectly to produce and sustain just the right tone. Thomas Immega figured that out and got to experimenting on a computer."

He was thunderstruck. "What's the note?" he asked excitedly. "What frequency?"

She gestured toward the shelf of master manuals. "Look it up."

Somehow he had known that was what she was going to say. "I will. Tell me something else. A big one. How . . . I know: how do they make you see stuff that's not there, and sometimes not see stuff that is?"

Again she raised an eyebrow. "The Black Bird!"

"Hu . . . beg pardon?"

"That's the biggest big one of all. The main secret. Nobody on earth who isn't loyal to Dreamworld knows that one, Mike. Are you sure you want to know?"

"Absolutely positive. I'd keep the secret under torture."

She didn't smile. "I believe you really would. Okay, sit there a second—"

Dynamite could not have removed Mike from his chair. Annie rummaged, returned with a camcorder. She powered it up, held a fingertip just in front of its lens, and fiddled with the focus. "Okay, look right into it," she said, and held the camcorder about a decimeter from his right eye. He obeyed. "Look straight ahead; try to keep your eye absolutely still. Hold it . . . hold it . . . hold it steady . . . don't blink now . . . fixed stare . . . good." She stopped taping, shifted her aim from his face to the monitor across the room, and tapped keys to send it the file. The screen lit and began replaying what she had just taped, in slow motion. "Come here," she said, and led him closer to the monitor. "What do you see?"

He watched it through in silence. "Can I see it again?"

She put it on a replay loop. He watched it all the way through twice more.

"Well?"

"My eye never totally stopped moving. Not once. Not for

more than, like, a split second. I thought I was holding it steady, but I wasn't."

"You can't. Nobody can. Eyes hop around all the time. The hops are called saccades."

"Sick odds?"

She corrected his pronunciation and spelled it for him. "It's a good thing eyes do saccades, too. Do you know about your blind spot?"

"Sure. We learned about it in school. *Oh.* Now I get it. I could never understand how come you don't *notice* your blind spot unless you do the experiment about it. But it makes sense. If your blind spot is always moving, your brain can just paint in the missing part. What it shows you there might be wrong—but never for more than a second. Cool."

She was looking pleased with him. "All right. Now you know that gadget the superstars use, the Pap-Zapper?"

"The thing so you can't take their picture?"

"That's right. It constantly scans the environment, looking for anything that might be a camera lens, and if it finds it, it blinds it with a low-power laser. The car-rooftop model can handle fifty pap-rats at once, and the home-defense model can deal with over a hundred. The inventor was inspired by Princess Diana's death, and he made a *fortune.* Do you know who the inventor was?"

He started to shake his head—and the penny dropped. "Thomas Immega!"

"That's where he got the money to start building Dreamworld. The real-life heroes and princesses didn't *want* people loving them so much anymore . . . so he gave people ones they can come visit and talk with any time they want."

"Wow." He thought hard. "I still don't think I get it. What's that got to do with saccades?"

"If a Pap-Zapper's targeting vision system can pick out and lock onto a camera lens at five hundred meters . . . how much trouble do you think it'd have locking onto your pupil?"

"*Oh.*" Suddenly it all fell into place, with an almost audible *click*. He sat up straighter. "So when we're up Johnny's Tree—"

"—the system tracks your saccades, knows exactly where you're looking at all times, and uses tricks to make sure the right photons are waiting to meet them there. You look at me, and it's like I'm a large Annie-sized blind spot, and the holographic system helps your brain paint in different information there, so you can't see me no matter where you look."

He began to hop up and down in his chair. "And that's why we can both look at the same spot in the Warlock's Keep, and each see different things! Whatever I'm seeing isn't really there—except for the split second my eye happens to point in that direction—and it follows my eye around as it saccades. If you and I ever really *do* happen to be looking in exactly the same direction, it can't be for more than an instant—"

"—and our brains both ignore the garbled frame," Annie agreed.

He began to beat out a rhythm on his thighs with his fists, unconsciously. "Oh, that's so *cool*. But how does—"

Annie held up a hand. "Enough."

It was as hard to stop babbling questions as it would have been to stop peeing in midstream. "Okay, but just tell me—"

She expanded her Command Band's keyboard to useful size, tapped a few keys, and shrank it again. At once, her face changed—back to the real one, the one she had started with that morning. She was Annie again. Old. And tired. He trailed off in midsentence.

"Boy, you cannot have any idea how *exhausting* it is, being around someone as happy as you are. Everything you want to know is in those books over there: do your own homework."

"Oh." He started to apologize, but something told him that would be a further mistake. "Thanks, Annie. You've really been swell."

"Yes, I have," she agreed. "And now, because I'm swell, I'm going for a walk, so you can wallow in those master manuals to your heart's content. I'll be back with supper in a few hours.

Everything in the manuals is in the computer as well, by the way; you'll see the folder. Just for heaven's sake don't send or receive any data without me here. And don't go wandering outside, either."

"I won't."

"If I were you I'd start with . . . oh, cancel that; start wherever you please." Frowning, she turned on her heel and left without another word.

Mike knew Annie was upset about something. It was even possible she was angry with him for some reason. But he also knew there was nothing he could do about it right now . . . and the master manuals of Dreamworld were waiting.

He stopped halfway across the room, torn between the bookcase and the workstation. As a general rule, he preferred words on paper to words on-screen—even a "smart paper" screen. But in this case a sophisticated search engine was an irresistible advantage; he sat down at Annie's computer.

Its exterior might be quaint, but the moment he hit the power key he knew its innards had been modernized: it booted instantly, like a proper machine. He found and opened the Master Manuals folder, located the Dreamworld Overview subfolder, selected the Read Me First and FAQ files, opened both. Words came up and sucked him into the screen. His body and the world ceased to exist, and Mike entered Nirvana.

HE WAS SO absorbed he did not even realize Annie had returned, until suddenly the computer receded from him and spun away to his right. He just had time to realize that she had grabbed his chair from behind and yanked him away from the screen . . . then the careening chair caught a wheel on one of his discarded shoes and nearly dropped him onto the floor. When he got his balance, Annie was in his place, crouching over the keyboard, typing so fast her fingers seemed to blur.

He was unhurt, and too startled to be angry. Slowly he worked out that something must be seriously wrong. "Are they onto us?" he asked.

She failed to hear, kept on punching keys and mousing. A succession of windows appeared and disappeared. Then the screen filled with an aerial view of Dreamworld, from an apparent height of about two kilometers. Mike saw the letters in the lower right-hand corner and realized Annie was accessing a GPS satellite in real time: an expensive operation. She zoomed in rapidly until she had a view of the employee parking lot, seemingly only a few hundred meters below. Firefall was obviously long over by now, and Dreamworld closed for the day: the lot looked like an ant farm, crowded with Cast, Cousins, and other employees going home, and a few night-shift staff arriving late. Annie panned around until she found what she was looking for.

"Gotcha," she muttered, zoomed in again, and tapped out a command.

Now they were tracking a specific Cast member, a dwarf, from a height of only about twenty or thirty meters. It would have been difficult to get a sense of his face from almost straight over-head, even if he had not been wearing a large floppy hat. Mike could see nothing especially remarkable about him—for a dwarf, at least. Since he was not in costume now, it was hard to tell, but Mike felt somehow that he played a Troll. He walked with a troll's usual stoop, made more pronounced by a large, heavy-looking backpack, and he seemed to wear the characteristic scowl—from force of habit, Mike guessed.

As the software's virtual camera continued to track him, Annie opened up another application in a small window at the lower right corner of the screen, typed rapidly, and straightened up to wait. After a while she said some words Mike had never heard before but correctly interpreted as a horrible obscenity.

He looked closer. The small window now read, *404: File not found.*

"What does that mean, Annie?" he asked. "Are we in trouble? Is something wrong?"

The urgency in his voice finally reached her. She took a deep breath, squared her shoulders, and turned to face him. "No, Mike," she said gently. "Nothing you need to worry about. We're fine."

Mike was thoroughly sick of grown-ups telling you everything was fine when it obviously wasn't. "Right."

Annie was instantly apologetic. "No, really. There's no danger. I'm sorry I crashed in on you like that. I haven't had much use for manners, the last thirteen years. And I was in a hurry."

"How come?"

"Just something I don't understand. A little thing. Nothing important—I think. It's just that I like to understand *everything* about this place." She cleared the screen, returning it to the file he'd been reading when she arrived. "I imagine *you* can understand that. How's it coming along?"

It all came back in a wave, and he forgot the Troll. "*Awesome,*" he admitted. "It's just—I mean, it's all so—I'm, like, just—"

"Incoherent," she finished for him. "If I were you, I'd knock off after another hour or so. You don't want your brain to explode."

"I'll risk it," he said.

She suppressed a smile. "Want to come topside with me for dinner, first? Take a break?"

"I'm not hungry."

"Of course not. All right, I'll bring you back something in an hour or two. And now that I think of it, we're going to need to get you some clothes—so we can wash the ones you're wearing." She stepped away from the keyboard and gestured him to return. The screen he had been reading when she arrived called out to him. . . .

He never noticed her leave. Nor did he notice falling asleep in his chair, two hours later. Nor, an hour after that, Annie returning and putting him to bed. The typing sounds she produced for the next hour or so, he took to be his own; his fingers flexed in his sleep, and his eyes saccaded ceaselessly across screens full of information so astounding and wonderful that a tiny part of him vaguely wondered why Annie kept cursing.

JUST AS HE had the previous night, he woke instantly in pitch darkness, with no idea what had woken him. He was no more aware of having dreamed than he had been, hours earlier, of falling asleep. From his point of view, he simply scrolled down a screen . . . and found himself sitting up in bed in the dark with Annie——in her arms, sobbing his heart out.

Mike was *not* a crybaby. He had no conscious memory of ever having cried so hard in his life before, and had no idea why he was doing it now. All he knew was that he could not stop. He was embarrassed, and afraid that some passing nightshift worker out in the hall might hear, that he might give Annie away . . . but he couldn't help himself. It was terrifying. Like vomiting a snake: it was awful, but to try and stop halfway through would be much worse.

"Harder," Annie murmured in his ear. "Get it out. As much as you can."

". . . don'teven . . ." he managed, ". . . evenknow . . . whatitis . . ."

"Doesn't matter. Let it out." She rocked back and forth with him and patted his hair. "Let it go, boy."

He tried crying even *harder*, and it helped somehow. His fear began to ease a little.

"It'll be all right," she told him, and kept telling him until he began to believe her. He surrendered totally, let her rock him in her arms and let his tears do with him what they would.

In the end, he cried himself right back to sleep again, falling asleep without realizing it for the second time that night.

CHAPTER 6

TOO MANY TROLLS

This time he woke slowly, grudgingly, in fits and starts. When he finally had the job done, he found himself alone in bed. He was in his underpants, with the covers over him. The aroma of coffee was in the air. And rollups—ham and cheese, it smelled like. He opened his eyes, saw Annie sitting at the table, which was set. Yesterday morning in reverse. He was so hungry his mouth watered.

"It's hot," Annie said.

"In a minute."

After a little longer than that, his boner subsided enough that he was able to slide out from under the covers and get to his pants without mortifying himself. Then it was necessary to detour to the bathroom . . . where, after some thought, he decided that with Annie awake and listening, it was less embarrassing to pee in the toilet and put up with the splash, than to pee in the sink and not make one. Then he made himself mime washing his hands, because even though he was not in the habit of peeing on his fingers, he knew women were sometimes funny about that. When he came out he found three complete sets of clothing piled on the bed, all in his size. A maintenance coverall, an Elf costume, and another outfit like the one he was wearing, appropriate to a Guest. He chose that one, started to put it on, and stopped when Annie pointed out that he ought to shower first. By the time he got to his breakfast and coffee, he had to renuke both.

Despite his hunger, the food tasted rather flat, even when he salted and peppered it. Even the jelly donut, his favorite snack, was unexciting. The coffee had no kick.

Annie made herself another cup and sipped it in silence while he ate. From the way she held her other hand, he could suddenly tell that she was a reformed nicotine addict, who still missed it. Why did people ever start something whose only promises were death or endless yearning? He thought about asking her, then changed his mind.

Instead, when he was finished eating, he asked, "What happened to me last night?"

"Equilibrium."

"What do you mean?"

She made no answer.

"I mean, all of a sudden I was crying like crazy, and I still don't even know *why*. And now I just feel . . . I don't know, wrung out. Dull. Like I've been sick."

"Balance," she said.

He shook his head. "I don't understand."

She sighed. "Think, boy. Forty-eight hours ago, you were in total despair. You must have been, or you wouldn't have done what you did. I *know*. And yesterday, I'm betting, was the happiest day of your life. You think you can do an emotional bungee-jump like that without a cost?"

"Oh. *Oh*." It started to make sense. She was right. He'd gone from feeling as lousy as he'd ever felt in his life to as happy as he would probably ever be, in a single day. No wonder he felt so weird. "And the crying helped?"

"Without it you'd probably be sick with a high fever about now," she said.

He nodded. "I bet you're right." Suddenly he frowned. "Did you know this would happen?"

"I was pretty sure."

"Then why didn't you—"

She was grinning at him. "And spoil the happiest day of your life?"

Even in his torpor, he had to grin back. It took a startling amount of energy. "So what do we do *today*?"

She reverted to her default scowl. "You stay in bed today and read—books—and if you have any sense, you'll read anything *but* those damned manuals. Leave them for another day." She got up and went to the bookshelves, picked a book. She started to toss it to him, then changed her mind and brought it to him. "Here, read this." It was *The Decline and Fall of Practically Everybody*.

He blinked at it. "What about you?"

"I've got some errands to run. Nothing fun. Routine maintenance. This place is much too important to be trusted to the staff. Read whatever you please, boy—or watch videos if you must. But nothing more exciting or ambitious, today. Leave the rest for later. There'll be plenty of time." He started to protest, but she held up a hand. "I'm too damned old to keep getting up in the middle of the night."

"Okay, Annie," he said humbly.

She got something and brought it to him. A Command Band, just like hers. "I'm not going to activate this until I've checked you out on it." She frowned fiercely. *"Rigorously."* The frown softened. "But in the meantime, if you need me for anything . . . even just to help you cry some more . . . push this." She pointed out a stud. "I won't be far, and you won't be interrupting anything."

He nodded, and she left at once.

After a while, he opened the book at random, and read about Nero. Soon he was giggling.

AS ALWAYS, READING Will Cuppy's whimsical biographical sketches restored him. Even the great names of history were revealed to be as goofy, fallible, and human as anybody else—a great comfort to someone as self-conscious as Mike. He allowed himself three chapters, his customary maximum, then put the book aside. He decided he no longer felt tired, and was tempted to return to the computer for another installment of what he was coming to realize would be an ongoing lifetime project. There was so much to understand about Dreamworld! But Annie had advised him not to . . . and so far, all her advice had been good. He went to her fiction shelves, browsed until he found an author he didn't know, one named Thomas Perry. He selected one at random, titled *The Butcher's Boy,* sat in Annie's computer chair, and opened it to page 1. . . .

Timeless time later, he heard Annie come in, and hopped up from the chair just in case she might feel like dumping him out of it to get at the computer again. Instead, she tossed something at him, which turned out to be a packaged sandwich. "Lunch," she said.

"Hi, Annie. Thanks—listen, I found the most—"

"Feel like doing a cloak-and-dagger job for me?"

"Huh? I mean, 'Excuse me?' "

"Are you available for undercover work?"

He studied her face, convinced himself she was not kidding. His pulse rate rose. "*Sure.* When? What's up?"

She came and stood beside him, tapped commands into the computer. "Study this layout while you eat," she said. "Pick out a good spot to loiter and keep an eye on *that* for an hour or so without drawing attention."

He studied the screen. *That* turned out to be the area where Cast members clocked out for the day, on their way to the employees' locker areas and the exits beyond. A row of poles, still called turnstiles although nothing about them turned anymore, constrained both departing and arriving employees to pass between them one at a time, for accurate counting in either direction. Mike was looking at the area from a camera perhaps fifty meters distant. At this time of day the area was all but deserted; the morning shift would not be leaving for another hour or so, and there was only a single guard at the desk beside the turnstiles, idly reading his wrist. Mike turned to ask Annie a question, but she was deeply engrossed in one of the master manuals. He returned his attention to the screen, figured out the camera controls, and panned around until he had located a vantage point he liked: a row of nearby ATM booths that commanded a view of the area. If he could manage to get the last booth in line, the one closest to the turnstiles, its one-way security glass would allow him to observe them from relative concealment.

He remembered a chart he had seen in one of the master manuals. If he had it right, a big ventilation tunnel went right past that area on its way to the outside world. He changed the computer display, checked the relevant chart, and found that not only did the tunnel pass within twenty meters of those ATMs, there was an inspection and maintenance access hatch at just that point.

"Find a good spot?" Annie asked.

"I think so. If you can get to it." He showed her what he had in mind.

She understood at once. "Good. We can make that work. But you're going to do it, not me."

"I am?" His pulse went up even further.

"Pay attention: here's the plan. First, we costume you and make you up to look like an adult little person, like me. You're a midget who works as a tunnel rat, got it?" He nodded. "Then we send you down that tunnel, wearing your new Command Band—" He began to object, but she overrode him. "I know, you don't know how to use it yet—but I do. We'll insert you at a point where all you'll have to do is go straight ahead until you get my signal." He nodded again. "When you reach that hatch, your band will blink white three times. Then you wait."

"How long?"

"That'll depend on what's waiting for you outside that hatch," she said. "I'll be monitoring the area from here. If we get you down there fast enough, and there's still only the one guard to worry about, it won't be any time at all. But if other people start wandering through leaving work early, or other guards show up, I might have to wait for just the right moment. Whenever it comes, your band will blink *red* three times—and on the third blink, an electrical panel behind that guard is going to fail, in a gaudy and spectacular way. Hit that hatch release the instant you see the third blink, and you should be able to make it to the booth while his back is turned. Understand?"

"Sure."

"Can you do it?"

He reviewed it in his mind. "Sure."

"Good man. Let's get you made-up."

Annie worked *fast*. It took her less than five minutes to alter a maintenance uniform until it appeared to fit him, and another two to alter his features until he appeared to fit the uniform. She would not let him talk during the process. Soon Mike blinked at himself in the bathroom mirror, and by God, he was a grown-up midget. "They have little people working in those tunnels?"

"Sure. And other tight spots in and under Dreamworld. Most of them are friends or relatives of Cast who can't act worth a damn, or just aren't pleasant-natured enough. That's why I'm guiding you with blinking lights instead of audible directions. You may run into one or two real tunnel rats on your way."

"Shit—what then?"

"You either bluff or hide. I recommend hide."

"Hide *where*?"

"A branch tunnel, if there's one near. If not, wherever you can. There's machinery all along the length of that tunnel: impellers, precipitators, scrubbers, ionization units, fire-fighting gear, lots of things to condition all that air. Be creative. And if you have to bluff, remember to deepen your voice and say as little as possible."

"Okay."

"All right. Are you ready?"

"Well . . . two more things," he said reluctantly.

"If they're quick: we're running out of minutes."

"What am I supposed to *do* once I get into the ATM?"

For a moment she froze, expressionless . . . and then she burst out laughing. "Oh, *that*."

He grinned himself, in relief. He had not known many grown-ups who could laugh at themselves.

"I beg your pardon, Mike. First signs of senility setting in. What you do is count how many people clock out this afternoon." She took a pair of clickers from a drawer and gave them to him. "I need *two* counts: total employees, and total Trolls—can you handle that?" He nodded and tucked a clicker in each shirt pocket. "I need both as accurate as possible, so you can't take your eyes off those turnstiles for a second, okay? They should all be through in twenty minutes or so; you'll know it's over when they go back to just one guard again."

"What do I do then? Wait for another panel failure and run for the tunnel?"

"No. You just leave the ATM and walk away, bold as brass. You make like you just came on shift a few minutes ago, and head back inside to The China That Never Was. You know how to get back here from there; we did it yesterday."

"Sure. But Annie? If all you want to do is count little people going off shift . . . why not do it from *here*, over that camera, both of us? We could play it back to check our count—I mean, why?"

She nodded. "Fair and intelligent question: is this trip necessary? I think so. Mike, cameras can be fooled, easily and cheaply. So can eyeballs, you know that now . . . but it's difficult and ex-pensive, so people generally only bother to fool the eyeballs they expect to be looking. I need that count as accurate as possible."

"Who's trying to fool us? What's going on?"

She glanced at her wrist and grimaced with exasperation. "Mike, we're out of minutes. I'll tell you as much as I know myself when you get back, I promise. Do you trust me?"

"Of course," he said at once.

She blinked. "All right, then. Something *wrong* is going on in Dreamworld. I don't know what. I need you to help me find out. Will that do for now?"

"Let's go."

She grinned. "Good man. Come on, I'll take you to the best spot to enter that tunnel."

Outside the access hatch she had him repeat back his directions and instructions. "Don't jump the gun. Those last three red blinks may never come. If there are too many eyes around by the time you're in position, we'll have to abort and try again when the night shift leaves. In that case you just retrace your steps back to here again."

"Through the tunnel? Couldn't we just wait until it's back down to one guard again, and then . . . no, I get it. Then you wouldn't be able to use the same gimmick again when we try tonight, to get me out of the tunnel again. It'd look funny."

She was looking at him oddly. "Mike?"

"Yes, Annie?"

"If anything goes wrong, I will get you out of it. If I have to bust you out of a Security holding cell. Do you understand?"

"Sure."

She frowned ferociously. "Well, go on, then. Don't take dumb chances." She opened the access hatch, and air escaped with a *chuff.*

"I won't," he said, and entered the tunnel. He heard her say, "Good luck, boy," and the hatch closed.

THE TUNNEL CEILING was just high enough for him to stand upright; an adult of normal height would have had to walk stooped over.

He walked into a constant stiff breeze. It had no odor, no temperature, and kept whispering nonsense, gently but insistently. Lights every ten meters or so gave adequate illumination. The walking was tricky at first. There was no flat flooring to the tunnel; it curved up on either side, and he found he had to keep exactly on the centerline as he walked, or he ended up veering all over the place. There was indeed gadgets and gizmos and widgets of all kinds and sizes installed every hundred meters or so along the length of the tunnel, and he could see that some of them did offer shadowy places of potential concealment; he started keeping track of how often those came along. At irregular intervals he came to places where branching tunnels departed; most often they were half the size of this one, less than a meter in diameter.

It came to him all of a sudden that he was enjoying himself.

Then he heard the approaching voices ahead.

He took hasty inventory. The nearest full-sized intersecting tunnel was about fifty meters farther ahead, toward the voices— indeed it must be where they were coming from, since nobody was visible straight ahead for a long way. The nearest full-sized tunnel *behind* him was *way* behind—long before he could reach it, the maintenance crew would have entered this tunnel and seen him. That left two possible places of concealment: a small tunnel, just beside him on his left, and a large piece of hardware about halfway between him and the cross-tunnel the voices were coming from.

He squatted and stared down the small side tunnel. More of a tube than a tunnel. It ran straight as a die for several hundred meters until it reached another large tunnel parallel to this one, and was absolutely devoid of machinery or cover of any sort. He could fit into it easily, crawl on all fours without difficulty . . . but if anyone happened to glance into it as they walked past, they could hardly miss him.

The voices were getting closer. A man and a woman. He straightened and sprinted toward them, hampered by the need to avoid scuffling his feet.

The big gadget, whatever it was, was about the size of a desk. Mike noticed a mark chalked on the wall above it, one he almost recognized—a capital letter Q with an arrow through it—but most of his attention went to a lovely recess on this side of the gadget, a splendid recess, a shamelessly shadowy recess that was, in Mike's hasty estimation, *just* large enough for him to fold himself into.

But as he began to try, his nose warned him. The harsh bright stink of burnt wiring. The maintenance crew were coming here . . .

Oh shit oh shit oh shit . . .

Mike's life had prepared him to accept what could not be helped. Without hesitation, he spun on his heel and made for the small tunnel. It was not possible to be *both* fast *and* quiet, and neither was optional. He did his best, flung himself halfway into the hole without looking back to see if he was in time, and humped himself the rest of the way inside in a single convulsive wormlike movement. Then he *froze*, like a Mobile Infantryman in Heinlein's *Starship Troopers,* controlling his breathing with an effort that made his head swim.

Behind him, in the main tunnel, a male voice said, "Hell was that?" He had the high voice of a dwarf.

"Come on, cut it out," said a female voice. "I'm not buying it. Do I really look that gullible?"

"She's real, okay?" The man sounded offended.

"I didn't hear a thing, and neither did you."

"Well . . . maybe not. I don't hear it now. But Goddamn it, the Mother Elf is real."

"You know, Max, you don't *look* like a druggie."

"Yeah, well, you don't look like a jerk. It's this one here."

"How the hell do you know? Oh, what, because of *that*? Anybody could have done that."

"It's this one." There were sounds of metal being tapped. Somehow the sound was easier to localize than voices, and it helped Mike confirm that the two mechanics were in fact at the housing he'd almost chosen to hide within. If he hadn't been in freeze, he'd have sighed with relief.

"This is the one, all right," the woman conceded reluctantly. "Arced all to hell."

"Hold the light."

"Let me get it," the woman said. "I got the spare thing right here, all ready to go."

There was a clattering sound.

"Hey!"

"Listen to me," the man said heatedly. Then he was silent for some time, choosing his words. "While you're workin' with me, as long as you don't believe in *her*, you get to hold the Got-damn light. If you don't like it, file a beef with the shift supervisor and see what *she* says. Is that understood?"

The woman paused for nearly as long as the man had. "Max, come on. A phantom fixer? An invisible magic midget that watches over Dreamworld and fixes our mistakes? Everybody has to believe *that* to work here? Give me a break."

"To work with *me*," he corrected. "Other people . . ." He grunted. "That's between you and them. You'll find out. Now hold the Got-damn light higher."

"Where does she sleep, Max? A flea couldn't hide in this place overnight. Hell, we got over a hundred *ghosts* in the joint, and *they're* all accounted for, every night. No wait, I get it: she just beams back up to the mother ship—"

"Amparo."

He said it very softly, so softly that even from a few meters distance Mike almost missed it amid the sound of her talking . . . but she shut up in midsentence.

"One more word and you can give me the light. And get your ass back to the shop. You aren't screwin' up my luck—we clear on that?"

Silence.

After that, there were tool sounds, and barked-knuckle noises, but not another word was spoken by either mechanic until, an endless time later, there came the blessed gentle hum of the whatever-it-was powering back up. Then there was a pause, and she said "Well," and another pause, and he said, "I don't think you're gonna make it around here," and a third pause, and then finally Mike heard them both walking. *Away.* Away from him, back in the direction they'd come from.

He waited until he couldn't hear their footsteps anymore. At last he relaxed his rigid muscles, allowed himself a long noisy sigh, and squirmed backward out of the coffinlike tube. Max and Amparo were gone.

He wanted to stay where he was. He wanted to go back the way he'd come. But he knew time was short: shift change was coming. And Annie was watching him from back at her place.

He moved forward as quickly as he dared.

As he went past the machine he'd almost hidden behind, he noticed that one of the mechanics had left a candy bar on top of it. He was tempted to swipe it, but decided it would be stupid: when they came back and found it missing they would know someone else had been here, and there couldn't be very many people who were supposed to be.

He also noticed that the chalk mark on the wall was now erased.

From that point onward, everything went exactly as planned. As far as he could tell, nobody spotted him leaving the tunnel; nobody challenged him while he was in the ATM; he had no trouble getting what he was sure were accurate counts of both total employees and Trolls; he left the ATM booth unremarked and made it back to Annie's without incident.

GOOD WORK, MIKE, were her first words.

Now that it was over, he was fiercely proud of himself. Not to miss counting a single departing employee had been a challenge for him. "Thanks, Annie."

"What are your counts?"

He told her, and she frowned. "You're sure you didn't count anybody twice?"

"Positive," he said happily. Then, "Why? What's wrong?"

She was silent for so long he was about to ask again. "I don't know," she said finally. "But now I'm sure something is wrong."

"Why?"

"Because six more Trolls just went off shift than came on shift eight hours ago. And I think it's been going on for days. Maybe longer."

"Huh? I mean, how can that be?"

She sighed deeply. "Mike, I haven't the faintest idea. Yesterday I happened to see a Troll I didn't recognize leaving the place. I found him on the orbital scan—you saw me—and confirmed that he's not on the personnel roster. Then I searched the *entire* departing crew . . . and found five *more* ringers. I pulled up yesterday's scans—as far back as I can go without leaving a spoor—and got the same result: six shills. And I haven't been able to ID *any* of them through public records. They seem to be nonpersons."

"How can that be?" Mike asked again.

Four or five questions later he realized she was not going to say anything more to him that night. Eventually he went back to the book he'd been reading.

CHAPTER 7

DEBUGGING DREAMWORLD

The next morning after breakfast, Annie cleared away the table and said, "We are now going to hold a conference of war."

"War on who?"

She nodded. "Exactly."

Mike must have looked as confused as he felt.

Annie sighed. "This is my home, Mike. Somebody is messing around with it. I won't tolerate that. I have to find out who's doing it, what they're doing, and why, and then stop them."

"Just because too many Trolls left yesterday?"

She gave him a withering look. "They keep *close* track of numbers around here. First, to make sure there are no lost or hurt or, God forbid, snatched children. And second, to catch people like you, trying to sneak Under, or even just to sneak in for the day without paying admission. Posing as an employee is a standard tactic, so they monitor staff just as closely. Alarm bells should be going off . . . and they're not."

Mike was scandalized at the notion that anyone would try to sneak in for free, for a single day. To want to *live in* Dreamworld he could understand—but to *cheat* it? The thought was intolerable; he turned his mind away from it. "Maybe they're slipping in inspectors, like, to check up on the rest of the staff?"

"I've checked Security's and Management's files. No, there's something funny going on."

"But what? Why?"

"I don't know. That's why I'm worried. But 'when you have eliminated the impossible . . .' "

" ' . . . whatever remains, however unlikely, must be the truth,' " he finished the quote. "Sherlock Holmes."

She smiled for some reason. "You've got it," she agreed. "Weird as it seems, more people are leaving the grounds than are entering."

"How?" Mike asked again.

Again, she nodded as if he had said something intelligent. "Exactly. That's our only angle of attack. If we figure out how they're doing it, perhaps that will give us a line on who it is."

"Have you got anybody in mind?" Mike asked. "Any suspects?"

"One," she said, "but I don't understand what he'd expect to gain—and he never does *anything* unless he expects to gain."

"Who?"

She shook her head. "I don't want to direct your thinking in any one direction just yet. No preconceptions."

Mike thought about it. "So what do we do?"

"We try and think like them."

"But we don't know who they *are*."

"But we know something they're doing. Forget why, for a moment. Suppose we—you and I—made it our mission to do what they've done. How would we go about it?"

Mike tried to think, but swiftly realized he lacked tools. "I don't know, Annie. You know this place a million times better than I do."

"True," she agreed, and frowned ferociously. "And I confess that, so far, I come up empty."

"Huh? I mean . . . really?"

"To smuggle people *out* of here, you have to smuggle them in, in the first place. As you well know, there are upwards of half a dozen weak points to this place, junctures at which it's possible to slip a person into the system without them being tagged right away."

Mike only knew of three weak points. "Okay. So we—"

She frowned even harder. "I told you when you came here you would have to *listen* to me. I said 'a' person. There is *no* point I know at which you could possibly introduce half a dozen people a day . . . much less outfit them in genuine Dreamworld Troll costumes. We know at least six got through today. I'm pretty sure yesterday's satellite photos show six ringers leaving the parking lot. That many, day after day . . . no, even with infinite resources, it's just out of the question. For a start you'd have to alter either the incoming or outgoing totals, and you know yourself how hard that is to do. You'd have to steal Troll suits wholesale, or make your own and smuggle *them* in, too. On a daily mass production basis, I just can't see it." She shook her head. "No, it's up to you."

He was horrified. "What do you mean, it's up to me?"

She started to cloud up—then got control of herself with a visible effort. Her voice came out calm. "I will *not* repeat myself again. You know what all four of those words mean."

"Why *me*?"

"Mike, I know all there is to know about Dreamworld—and I say what's happening can't be happening, so I'm no use. But you broke in here more recently than I did. I'm soaked in thirteen years of indoctrination. My opinions about the security of this place are nearly identical to those of Phillip Avery and his Security staff—and clearly, all of us are wrong. If anybody is qualified to spot the flaw in our thinking, it's someone who recently outwitted the system."

Mike was almost in despair. "But I don't know *how*!"

"Close your eyes." He did. "Now remember how badly you wanted to come Under." Again, he obeyed. "You're right back where you started—outside, wanting in. Only now imagine this— you have two brothers and three sisters, and it's just as important to get all of *them* Under, too. All at once."

Mike did his best. He thought of all the weak points he'd

identified in weeks of careful study. Nothing came to him. Two, maybe; three, conceivably—six, impossible.

"Hurry," she said softly. "There isn't much time. Your little sisters are depending on you."

Damn it, it wasn't fair! The safety of Dreamworld on his back, and the welfare of five imaginary siblings—why was it up to *him*?

And then suddenly insights started going off like a string of firecrackers in his mind.

First, he thought of a reason why it might be his responsibility. He was Under. Annie was, too, but she had spent most of the last thirteen years paying her ticket. Mike hadn't paid a thing, yet.

That triggered insight number two: the "Mother Elf" those two mechanics had been discussing in the tunnel was Annie! Mike had almost known that when he heard them, he'd just been too busy and too scared to think about it. Who else could Max have meant? Mike suddenly recalled his first hour Under—remembered Annie stopping at a machine, frowning, and marking it with a curious symbol on the wall, just like the one he'd seen over the defective machine in the tunnel. Annie looked after this place, backstopped the people who kept it in good running order, directed their attention to developing problems, fixed little things that failed to show up on an alert-board before they became big things. She wouldn't be able to help herself. And she'd be careful, very careful, but still, over thirteen years, the crew—all the crews—would come to sense her existence, and half believe in her and half not. Maybe they left her cookies.

That was the example he had to live up to. And all he owed her was everything, and she wanted his help.

So he thought twice as hard as he had so far.

He pictured a small group of dwarves, dressed as Trolls, suddenly materializing in some unnoticed corner of Dreamworld. . . .

And all of a sudden it was as if Firefall had suddenly gone off behind his eyelids, the whole thing in that enclosed space. The thought train went by so fast that the shock of slamming to a halt at its conclusion drove most of it from his head—but he never doubted it for an instant. Before he could start to doubt, he opened his eyes and spoke.

"I think I know how it's being done," he said. "And you're right: that tells us a lot about who's doing it."

Annie was already grinning. Somehow she'd known he had the answer before he did. "*Good* man. I knew you could do it. Tell me: who are the bastards?"

"Aliens," he said. "The outer-space kind, I mean."

SHE FROWNED FEROCIOUSLY and opened her mouth, and he was quite certain she was going to tell him he was *crazy*, or a dumb little kid, or at the very least that he was wrong. But what she finally said was, "Tell me why you think so."

Dimly grasping the extent of the implied compliment, he pressed on. "Dreamworld can make fake people appear out of thin air. But even Dreamworld can't make *real* people appear out of thin air. Well, somebody else can. Forget why for now—whoever's doing it has better technology than Dreamworld, *and* zillions of dollars to spend, right? Okay, who's on that list? One of the other theme parks? If they had better technology than Dreamworld, they'd be using it to make half as much money for once, not to play games. Some giant multinational? Same thing. The FBI? You told me they can't even get agents in here without asking permission first—and where would they get all the dwarves? The Chinese government? I don't believe it—if they could do it, they'd do it at the Pentagon, not here. I keep striking suspects off the list, and pretty soon I've eliminated everybody on the planet." Annie opened her mouth again, but then closed it. "There just *isn't* anybody with better technology than Dreamworld. Nobody on Earth. We've eliminated the impossible."

Annie kept her mouth closed.

After a while, Mike said. "You asked me the other day if I believed in magic. Do you believe in life on other planets?"

She glowered.

"The thing I always hate about movies where the ETs come here," he said, "is how *stupid* they always are. They come all this way, and then they aren't smart enough to observe us without getting caught at it, and then there's a big stupid fight 'cause they scared us."

She said nothing.

"So suppose you're an alien, and you're pretty smart. Smart enough to come light-years. You've already seen years of our TV, on the way, so you know a lot about us. You want to send down some observers—not an army or anything, just half a dozen a day or so—without causing a fuss. And you all look like trolls. *What spot on the surface do you pick to beam down to? Where do they already have a lot of trolls?"*

This time Annie's mouth *fell* open.

"They're going Under . . . on Earth, the way we're Under in Dreamworld—" Mike kept on talking for a while, but he had the idea Annie wasn't listening anymore, and shortly she proved him right by interrupting him. "How do we *know* it isn't a fucking army?"

"What?" He was shocked; he had never expected to hear Annie use that word—when she knew he was listening, anyway. "An army? Six or seven soldiers at a time?"

"Suppose you have alien technology, beyond the ken of mere mortals. How many Terminators do you need to take a planet?"

Guerrillas? Invading through *Dreamworld*? Mike had been thinking of them as explorers. Annie's notion was horrifying. "They're *dwarves*—," he protested, and broke off, flustered.

"Ever see a Ghurka?" Annie asked coldly. "Do you think Darth Vader could take Yoda in a fair fight? Do you think there's a Security man in Dreamworld who could take *me*?"

"I'm sorry," Mike said. "I wasn't trying to put down little people, okay?" Dumb, tactless and dumb, to tell a midget that little people could never pose a serious threat. And wrong, too— he could see that, Annie was right about that: size was irrelevant if you had advanced technology. Yet he still instinctively resisted the idea of an invading troll army—so he searched for a better argument against it. "Look . . . what do you think is the longest they could possibly keep this up before somebody else notices? I mean, *we* did. How long before Dreamworld does?"

Annie looked surprised. "Why . . . you're right, of course, it can't go on indefinitely. Avery isn't stupid. I guess I would say . . . on the order of a month. A month and a half, at the outside."

"Okay. If they're smart enough to dream this up in the first place, they're smart enough to know that. Let's say they're averaging five beam-downs a day. Thirty-five a week. The *most* they can reasonably expect to get through before being spotted is two hundred and ten guys. And that's only if they don't make a single mistake, or have any bad luck—like you."

She nodded. "So?"

"If you had weapons so good that two hundred of you could beat a planet . . . why would you bother sneaking in through an amusement park?"

Annie's face went through interesting changes.

It was a novel and heady sensation for Mike, being taken seriously by a grown-up, having his opinions listened to and deemed intelligent. He wished he had time to appreciate it.

"I think they're here to study us," he said. "Like Sir Richard Burton sneaking into Mecca. They've seen TV—probably even enough to know that's not what we're really like: now they want to find out what we *are* really like. Two hundred of them *isn't* enough to whip us; that's why they're sneaking in. That and to avoid freaking us out and messing us up—you know: like the Prime Directive on *Star Trek.*"

He'd had her up until then, but the last two words brought her up short. She made a sour mouth. "Oh, this is ridiculous. I can't believe I'm sitting here seriously discussing the motives of spacemen. I accept that I am compelled to, since I can't think of an alternative explanation for what's going on—but let's keep television out of it, all right? The Prime Directive is wishful thinking."

"What do you mean?"

"Advanced technology does *not* imply advanced ethics."

"Why not? Smart is smart."

She hesitated, then continued. "Look at us humans. We're not a particularly ethical species. Outside of Dreamworld, anyway: that's why this place is so *special*. And yet *we* very nearly have star travel—we could probably do it now, if we really wanted to. Instead we have nuclear weapons. How ethical has our sophistication made us?"

"We're more ethical than we *used* to be," Mike said. "We've had nuclear weapons for more than seventy-five years . . . and we've only used two. Did we do that good with gunpowder?"

She blinked. " 'That well,' " she corrected absently.

He ignored it. "Just as we got smart enough to make factories, we invented liberty. You know? The smarter we get, the smarter we start acting. We can afford to, 'cause we're not starving."

Annie blinked again, leaned forward and stared at him closely, then shook her head vigorously. "You are the *damnedest* little boy."

"I know our society isn't very smart, or kind. Believe me, I know. But it's the smartest, kindest one that ever was on *this* planet, so far—from what I learned in school, anyway. Maybe by the time we're smart enough and rich enough to send two hundred guys to Alpha Centauri and beam them down to a planet there, we'll be smart enough to be doing it for a good reason. Just to *learn*, maybe. It's possible, isn't it?"

She still did not look convinced, but he had her thinking, he could tell. He had himself thinking, too.

"Think about this," he tried. "Is this the only place they could have picked?"

"Huh?" Annie actually blushed. "I mean, come again?"

"They could have beamed down to any remote spot. In the mountains somewhere, in a desert. Any dark street at three A.M. If half a dozen aliens materialized in a crack house, they'd get a round of applause. Or if it had to be someplace with a lot of little people, they could have used any big school yard, or Thrillworld or one of the other big theme parks. Of all the spots on Earth they could have picked . . ."

"They picked Dreamworld," Annie finished.

"That's gotta mean something."

She frowned and chewed her lip. "Yes. But what?"

"Well . . . maybe they just *like* the place. Like me. Like you. Like everybody with half a brain."

Annie got a real funny look.

"Why wouldn't they?" he went on. "How many places are there in North America where you can be absolutely sure there isn't anybody carrying a weapon around? Where you couldn't cause a riot if you tried? You know Dreamworld, Annie: if an angry grizzly bear came roaring down the street, half the kids would run to it and try to pet it, feed it candy. And their parents would let them. It's not like Thrillworld, where stuff's getting blown up or killed all the time, and you have to sign a waiver to get in. It's a *nice* place to be."

She got up from the table, walked over to her computer and then back again. "Then why do these aliens keep *leaving*, every night?"

Mike shrugged. "Same reason kids do. They have to go to school the next day."

She walked back to the computer, spun the chair to face it, and sat. She fiddled with the keyboard, but did not boot up. Mike resigned himself to a long silence, and suddenly she whirled the chair back to face him and yelled, "I cannot *believe* I am talking as if I *believe* this! *I don't believe things like this.*"

"You think we're alone in the Galaxy?"

"Of course not," she said impatiently. "I've always believed there's life out there somewhere. But damn it, boy, this is just like all the stupid flying-saucer stories, with exactly the same logical problem. Intelligent life does not cross light-years to play hide-and-seek!"

"This isn't like flying saucers at all," Mike said stubbornly. "These guys didn't get spotted by some airliner pilot, or a farmer in a cornfield, or a cult. *Nobody* saw them . . . except you. They play hide-and-seek *good*."

Annie clouded up. For a second he thought she was going to erupt, and flinched. She saw that . . . and got control of herself with a visible effort. She took three deep breaths, each longer than the last, and her features became serene.

All at once it seemed totally clear to Mike that she was right and he was nuts—that his ingenious theory was nonsense, childish, fantasy bullshit. His conviction evaporated, and he was ashamed. He felt his cheeks grow hot, groped for words with which to backtrack—

"I have to admit I have no better explanation for the facts," Annie said slowly.

Again, Mike did an emotional instant-180. "Holy shit—"

She held up a hand. "I am going to think now. Very hard, for a long time. You will be as quiet as possible while I do." She got up from the computer, went to the bed, and lay down. "Think yourself, or read, or play games with headphones on, or go Topside if you like." She clasped her hands on her belly, closed her eyes, and appeared to go to sleep.

Mike was too excited to read or sit quietly, but reluctant to leave. How could he just walk around Dreamworld like a tourist, knowing there were *aliens* in it somewhere?

After some contemplation he slouched in his chair, put his calves up on the table, folded his hands in his lap, and did some thinking himself.

AN HOUR OR so later, Annie suddenly got up from the bed, went to the computer, and sat down. "If you're right," she said slowly, staring at the blank screen, "and if they're as smart as you think they are . . . and assuming their luck holds . . . then at some point, the tide will turn. School will be over—this semester, anyway. They'll start coming *back in* again, sneaking in with the morning shift and then beaming up to the mother ship or whatever." She spun away from the keyboard and faced him, but she was still talking to herself. "The longest they could plan on is a month or so . . . so the turnaround point can't be later than the end of the second week . . . and for all I know, they could have been doing this for *days* already . . . haven't been paying as close attention as usual, these last few days, what with a houseguest . . . so we may have no more than a week to work with. . . ."

"What do you mean?" Mike asked. "To do what?"

"To *catch* the sons of bitches. And kick them the hell out of Dreamworld. I'm going to find out what they're up to, boy. If I like it, I'll let them continue—but somewhere else! And if I don't, I'm going to kill every last one of them."

ANNIE, THAT'S CRAZIER than my whole idea!"

She nodded.

"I mean . . . look, you're pretty smart, but there's no way you're gonna beat an alien civilization by yourself."

"Of course not. I have you. A godsend, just when I needed one."

"Jeepers—"

"You can say 'Jesus' in front of me, boy. You can say anything grammatical, if you—"

"Jesus, Annie, we can't do this. We just—"

"They want quiet," she said, smiling dreamily.

"What?"

"Whatever they're doing here, they don't want it on TV. That gives me a lever."

Oh. That was certainly true. "But how do you *use* it? If they catch you spying on them, they could—"

"You've read it at least a hundred times, boy. The hero must deal with a criminal too powerful to threaten. So what does he do? He lets the criminal know he's left a sealed letter with a third party, with instructions to open it if he doesn't report back by a certain time. You're the sealed letter, Mike."

He began to see how it could work. "I get it. And then you tell them what your price is, to not let me be opened and read."

"Good boy." She was looking as serene as a nun, her gaze on the middle distance. "And my minimum condition is, get the *hell* out of my home, at once! After that, we can negotiate. If they convince me they're as benign as you think they are, we can work something out."

Mike grimaced. "What if they won't go that high?"

Her eyes refocused on him, and all at once she looked a thousand years old. "Then you get opened and read."

"Oh."

Several minutes of silence went by.

"If you decide they're Bad Guys . . . how are you gonna fight 'em?"

"Good lord, how should I know? At this point I don't even know what star they're from, or how to kill one of them. But anything that lives can die, and anything that can die can be killed."

"But there aren't any weapons in here, Annie."

She sighed. "There are weapons *everywhere*. I'll improvise. If I have to."

More silence.

"So where do you start?" Mike asked finally.

She nodded. "That's the next question, all right. I'm making a list now."

She fell silent again, and although her words had answered nothing—a list of *what?*—he kept silent and waited for her to finish her list.

"I make it somewhere between twelve and fifteen," she said at last. She saw his incomprehension and explained. "I said before there were six possible points where someone could break in, unnoticed. I've been working out how many points there are where one or more persons could—I suppose I might as well use the expression—'beam down' routinely, with zero chance of being noticed by Staff or Guests. Tricky, since I don't know if beaming down makes noise or not. I come up with at least a dozen, and a few others I'll have to check."

Mike thought of a few such sites himself. "Which do we check first?"

She pursed her lips, like a teacher who just heard you say, "Jesus." " 'What you mean "we," paleface?' " she said dryly.

He didn't know the joke, but he took her meaning. "Well . . . shit, Annie, what am *I* supposed to do?"

She glanced around. "The dishes and the laundry, for a start."

He said a word he was almost certain she would find objectionable, albeit softly; she ignored it and went on.

"After that, you sit down and type up an e-mail containing everything we've been talking about, in as much detail as you can. Avery's personal private address is in my file. I've fantasized using it a billion times in the last thirteen years. Never thought I ever actually would." She shook her head. "Anyway, you address that message to Avery, with a copy to Security, and you place the cursor over Send Now, and then you spend the rest of the day no more than a second's jump away from that mouse button. I'll report in by voice if I see anything worth reporting—if I can— but if your Command Band lights up red, you go straight to the mouse and wait. If it starts to blink or goes dead, hit the mouse . . . and then run like hell."

Mike was too dazed to take this all in at once. *"Where?"* he asked, to be asking something.

"Out from Under," she said. "Someplace where there are a lot of people. Yell a lot. Draw a crowd."

"But what do I *say?*"

"Tell them about how I died," she said. "Tell them to get out their cell phones and call CNN."

He started to cry silently. It shocked him; there was no warning. Tears simply started leaking down his cheeks.

She saw the tears and frowned hugely. "Don't worry, boy: it

isn't going to *happen,* for God's sake. You're the backup letter, remember? Ever read a story where one of them got opened and read?"

He shook his head no in agreement, but the tears kept flowing. He wanted to stop them, but couldn't. He wiped them away with his arm. "Okay," he said. "This sucks, but okay."

Her frown went away. "Any questions before I go?"

He nodded again. "Where's the goddamn laundry machine?"

She smiled faintly and pointed to the sink—then smiled bigger at his expression.

Mike took a long slow deep breath, and then another. How else could she do laundry regularly without getting caught? What else did he have to do while he waited to find out if he needed to run for his life or not? "Aw . . . okay. But this *really* sucks. The big one."

"After you finish your chores, read Thomas Perry."

"Yeah, yeah."

Her smile waned. "And Mike—"

He held up his hand. "Annie," he said angrily, "if you tell me to be real careful not to hit the mouse by accident, you can get yourself another sealed letter."

Her face went blank. "I was going to say, 'Wish me luck,' actually."

They both knew she was lying. "Good luck, Annie," he said.

They both knew he meant it. She got up and left at once.

HE WAS HALFWAY through typing the letter before it occurred to him that if this letter were ever actually sent . . . he and Annie wouldn't be Under anymore.

He had no idea exactly what would happen, couldn't envision the consequences in any detail, save that he was pretty sure Dreamworld would never actually have anybody put in *jail*—certainly not for warning them of alien invasion. But it seemed a safe bet that when it was over, he and Annie would at best be . . . Out There, somewhere. In the world.

It seemed . . . well, drastic. What did Annie care if some space guys snuck through Dreamworld undetected? She and Mike did the same thing themselves every day. He did not know the word "territorial" yet, but he wondered if Annie was just being jealous. Like she had to be the Boss of Under, even if she got herself thrown out proving it. And him.

On the other hand . . . what if she were right to be suspicious of the intruders? Maybe it *didn't* necessarily follow that traveling between stars made you a nice guy. Maybe it was just like all the stupid movies Mike had ever seen, and they wanted to conquer Earth, for no good reason.

Something suddenly occurred to him. If that were so, if something ever happened to Annie and he actually had to send this e-mail message he was writing, the act of doing so would make him—really and truly and no shit—the Boy Who Saved the World.

He finished the letter.

As he was addressing it, something else occurred to him. If he sent that message, one of the first things Mr. Avery would do was call the army guys—he'd have to. And what would the army guys want to do to the aliens' landing zone?

Nuke it! Or come in in armor with guns blazing . . . gunships swooping down out of the sky on Dreamworld . . . paratroops drifting down onto Strawberry Fields . . . Firefall come early to the Octagon . . . horror unimaginable, ultimate obscenity. . . .

A two-for-one bonus: the Boy Who Saved the World could also be the Boy Who Destroyed Dreamworld Doing It.

For a moment he was so angry at the aliens, he wanted them dead as much as Annie seemed to. The very reason he'd come Under was because Dreamworld was a place where you wouldn't ever have to make decisions like this.

Maybe there was no such place. He saved the message, placed

the cursor over the "Send Now" button, took his finger carefully off the touchpad, and got up from the desk.

As he did the dishes he kept pausing after rinsing each item and turning to stare at the computer, rehearsing the leap that would take him to the mouse button in the shortest possible time if the alert came.

Doing laundry by hand required closer attention; he glanced toward the computer only once a minute or so. Thomas Perry proved *too* interesting; Mike tried to train himself to pause and rehearse his leap at the end of every other page, and failed often enough that he reluctantly put the book aside. He traded it for the DREAMWORLD SECURITY master manual, and that was just right: it held his attention without imprisoning it.

A couple of hours later, he suddenly had another of those internal-Firefall realizations, a thought so powerful the manual fell from his lap, unnoticed even though it landed on his foot. It was one of those lovely, rare double epiphanies, combining an "oh wow!" with an "of course!" The kind where the instant you saw it, you couldn't believe you hadn't thought of it hours ago, but it was so lovely you forgave yourself.

Mike was going to get to do him some alien hunting after all. Annie was going to *have* to let him.

"Do you read?" his wrist said. "Come in, over."

He jumped half a meter in the air and almost hit himself in the teeth with his Command Band. "Are you okay, Annie?" he yelled at it, and then felt stupid, blurting out her name that way like a kid.

"Answer, dammit!"

He felt even stupider. Annie had only had time the night before to teach him a few of the Band's myriad functions, but enabling its mike had been one of the first. He got a grip on himself, switched the thing on, and said, "Read you. Status?"

"We got troubles," she said.

CHAPTER 8

IGNORANT ARMIES

Not quite believing he was doing it, Mike got up and went to the computer. "Where are you?"

"Hold your fire!" she said urgently, ignoring his question. "Don't do it yet. In fact, wipe the damned thing: we'd look like idiots."

"What?"

"No, don't do that. But go through it now and take out every reference to ETs. They're human beings, lad."

He felt an odd mixture of relief and disappointment. If they were only human, he had no doubt Annie could handle them. But now his brilliant spaceman hypothesis was as dumb and child-ish as Annie had originally thought. He was just a dopey kid who'd managed to talk a smart grown-up into believing in fairy tales for a few hours. Impressive, by his usual standards . . . but a major comedown from being the Boy Who Saved the World.

"Who?" he asked automatically as these thoughts and others tumbled through his head.

"Beats me. I've spotted two so far, maybe a third—and this is *in addition to* costumed Trolls. These are goons, in civilian clothes. While you're editing, put this in: they're carrying *guns*. I don't know how, but they are, no mistaking it. Can't tell what kind. Are you typing?"

After all that rehearsal, he tripped and fell on the way to the computer. "I am now," he said when he got there. Taking great care not to touch the mouse button just below it, he used the touchpad to move the cursor from the Send button to the text area, clicked there, and began scrolling and editing. "Where are you now?"

"The Warlock's, heading in. They're running some kind of search pattern. Don't know what for."

"Are they all little people?"

"Affirmative. We knew that."

"Who could they *be*?"

"Insufficient data."

"But—"

"I don't know, all right? I'm going to go silent now: getting hard to keep them in sight without being in earshot too. *Do not* take any action without my signal."

"Be careful." The line went dead.

He finished editing the message to Mr. Avery, doing the best he could, removing all references to extraterrestrials. And then he waited, for a million years, in an agony of suspense and indecision.

He thought he knew—at least in theory—a way to interface his Command Band with the computer, and then use it to physically track Annie's Band, plotting its location against a map of Dreamworld. But he might be wrong—and if he opened up the necessary application and experimented, it would take him precious seconds to get back to the e-mail application if the alert came. Worse, he might hang the system and have to reboot.

But he hated not knowing exactly where she was.

AFTER AN ENDLESS time, he reached the horrid conclusion that something had gone wrong.

Annie was not going to come back online. If she could, she'd have done so by now, if only to reassure him. There must have been a fourth one she hadn't spotted. Or one of the bogus Trolls had seen her, or perhaps there'd been a second search team backstopping the first—it didn't matter how: she'd been caught, and Mike had to *do* something.

But she had not sent the signal.

The very last thing she had said to him was, "Do not take any action without my signal." All he could do was sit here and do nothing, while the fate of Dreamworld was decided somewhere else by people he'd never seen.

With all his heart, Mike wanted to leave—race to the Warlock's Keep, pick up Annie's trail, and rescue her somehow. But even assuming he was actually competent to pull it off—defeat several grown-ups in combat and rescue another—he knew it was the one thing he must not do. Now of all times. If Annie *was* in trouble, had been captured, then the only card she had left to play was him, the only weapon she owned was the sealed letter he represented. The worst possible thing he could do was risk getting himself captured too. Nothing dumber lay within his power.

To be doing something, he tried his idea for interfacing his Command Band with the computer, and it worked. There were some keyboard functions he couldn't figure out how to duplicate with the Band, but basically it was now a remote terminal for the computer. Shortly he had a fix on Annie's carrier signal. She was in a large vehicle depot about halfway between the Warlock's Keep and The China That Never Was, two levels underground. Her position was unchanging.

With a little fumbling, he managed to bring up readings from her Band's medical monitor. It said she was in stress. High pulse, blood pressure, and blood oxy.

Something within Mike fractured.

He returned to the mail program. Leaving the Avery message carefully undisturbed, he opened a second message box on top of it. After some thought, he addressed this one to "John@aol.com"— there *had* to be one—and limited the message to two blank paragraphs, even though Annie had assured him this account had no official existence and could not be traced. He placed the cursor on *this* message's Send button. Then he stepped back a few paces, took a few deep breaths, held his breath, and poked at his Command Band.

On-screen, the cursor turned into a spinning ball, and the blank message vanished, on its way through cyberspace. He stepped forward and confirmed that the cursor now rested on the Avery message's Send button. With his Command Band, he had just proven, he could send that message to Mr. Avery from anywhere in Dreamworld.

The fractured thing within him snapped clean through.

He made a slow circle, but the most lethal portable object in the room was a steak knife. Those six seconds were all the time he wasted before racing out the door. He knew of places along the way where tools were stored . . .

THREADING THE MAZE through the underside of Dreamworld was a challenge. Despite his newly acquired working knowledge of the basic layout, he got lost and had to backtrack twice. The second time, he even needed to briefly go Topside and reorient himself. This was his first time in this particular part of Dreamworld—underground, anyway—and his grasp of geography was largely theoretical. He wished he were more sophisticated in the use of his Command Band as a computer remote interface: he suspected it was possible to use it not only to track any changes in Annie's location, but to monitor his own progress, let him know when he was drifting off course. But even if he knew how to do that, he might not dare. At all costs, he must keep the Command Band and computer ready to send that message at the press of a stud.

At last he recognized landmarks that told him he was approaching his goal, and slowed his pace drastically, lest he blunder into a trap. He'd decided on tactics along the way, while choosing from among the tools he'd found available.

According to the records, the depot where Annie was now

located housed assorted floats and other vehicles used during the Firefall Parade. In theory, it was accessible only from the surface, via a large freight elevator or an emergency stairwell. Obviously it would be stupid to go anywhere near either of those. A pity there were no internal-combustion mobiles in Dreamworld, or the depot would have had huge ventilation shafts. But even modern vehicles implied drains. Vehicles always leaked oil and other fluids, and had to be washed and hosed off. Beneath that depot would be unusually large drains and catch basins—and Mike believed he knew how to get into the drainage system.

Sure enough, the access hatch was just where he'd hoped it would be. The lock yielded to the same code that had let him into the maintenance tunnel system yesterday. The drainage tube was much smaller than that one had been—but no smaller than the branch tunnel in which Mike had hidden then. Of course, this one had no lights at all in it . . .

He climbed in without hesitation. It was clammy inside and damp at the bottom, but there was no actual standing water in it. He sealed the hatch behind him and began crawling as fast as he could through total darkness, ignoring damage to knees and elbows and trying to build three-dimensional maps in his head with insufficient data.

He did this to keep his mind off his fear. Annie's captors, whoever they were, very badly wanted their existence kept secret. There were only two ways to do that: take her out of Dreamworld against her will—a much bigger technical challenge than sneaking in in the first place—or kill her.

God, it stinks in here. Getting slimy, too.

If they knew that she was Under, that there was no record of her existence here, they'd almost have to be crazy *not* to kill her and put her corpse into the outgoing sewage system.

Should be a left coming up soon . . . ah, there! Turning was harder than expected, but he managed at the cost of some skin. *Straight shot from here . . .*

There was a theoretical third possibility: terrifying her into silence. But Mike didn't think anybody could look at Annie and believe she could be threatened.

He was distracted from distracting himself by the sight of what appeared to be pale hexagrams, hovering in the darkness ahead of him. At first he took them for optical illusions, hallucinations produced by his brain in response to total darkness, like the paisley swirls of color he'd been seeing all along. But these enlarged as he moved forward. All at once he realized what they were. Each "hexagram" was bars of light filtering down into the tube through a large rectangular grate overhead. He was nearly under the depot . . .

When he was five meters from the first grate, he slowed his crawl to a crawl and listened as hard as he could. It was difficult to hear anything over the hammering of his own pulse.

Voices. Indistinct male voices.

Silent and inexorable as old age, Mike moved forward.

When he reached the second grate, he could tell he was as close as he was going to get to the voices. He rolled over onto his back and went into freeze.

"I'm not sure, Boss," a man said.

Something about his voice told Mike he was talking to someone elsewhere by phone or radio. Sure enough, there was a buzzing-bee sound that had to be the reply, though Mike couldn't make it out.

"How the hell should *I* know?" the speaker went on. "I'm no doctor."

Another reply buzz.

The man overhead sighed deeply. "What can I tell you? She looks like she's having a heart attack. Her bracelet says she's having a heart attack."

Mike was in freeze; he did not cry out. But there was a buzzing in his ears he knew had nothing to do with any reply. God, he'd never thought of this! Annie was *old,* and old people weren't built for adventure.

"Sure, I can strap a doctor on her arm and take her anyway. Maybe she'll be alive when you get her."

Buzz. Pause. Buzz.

Mike left freeze, reached up with a pair of needlenose pliers and began untwisting the screws holding the grating above him.

"An hour, maybe hour and a half, depends on traffic."

First screw unscrewed as far as he could get it from beneath, no problem. Second, the same. Third one stuck a little—back off the pressure the instant it gives so it won't squeal—

"So what do I do? Take her, leave her where she is . . . or lose her?"

Short two-syllable buzz. But *which* two?

"Okay, Boss. Out."

Third screw all but out. Nobody up there had noticed the screws unscrewing themselves. Yet. Mike attacked the fourth and last fastening—

"What's the story, Tom?" a second man asked. The first speaker seemed to be standing a few meters to the left of the grate, this one to the right.

"We're taking her," Tom said. "Life support unit'll meet us out in the parking lot. Ape, you and Tom go Topside and get that powered chair—and make it quick! I'll have Little Miss Muffet ready to transport by the time you get back."

"Shit," said the third man—located with Tom to the left of the grate. "She gon' die, you watch."

"What do you care? You're still getting paid."

"I know. I'm jus'sane. Nome sane?"

"Waste of energy and risk," the second man said.

"Thassumsane," Ape agreed.

"Go," the leader ordered, and Mike heard the two walk away at a fast clip.

He set the pliers down silently. The grate was now held in place by no more than a thread or two of each of the four screws. If he slammed it suddenly with both hands, it would pop off.

Damn, if he'd only looked in Annie's bathroom he might have found one of those little mirrors, and he could sneak a peek before committing himself. His fix on Tom's voice was not precise.

He heard sounds that had to be an elevator closing its door and beginning its ascent.

Well, the odds would never be better. And he didn't have much time.

He took the weapon he'd chosen from the tool locker out of his waistband and fitted it to his hand. A nail gun, roughly the size and weight of an old .45 automatic. He set it alongside his hip and rehearsed his moves. Slam the grate with both hands, then flip it sideways and out of the way. Retrieve weapon with right hand, grip edge of opening with left hand, and pop up firing. Okay, *go*—

He could not do it.

At close range, the nail gun might well be lethal. Indeed, part of him was counting on it, for Tom sounded dangerous. But Mike had never shot anybody before.

Even if he had the stomach for it—even assuming he could pull it off—what the hell did you do with a corpse in Dreamworld? The lid would be off . . . of everything.

Oh, what difference did it make? The lid was off anyway. Maybe Annie was dying while he dithered.

Just then, he heard Annie groan.

A compromise plan came to him, one that seemed unlikely to work but was better than nothing.

He raised the nail gun to one of the openings in the grate, tilted it in what he prayed was Tom's general direction, pulled it back away from the grate as far as he dared, and fired. Luck was with him twice: the nail went through the opening cleanly, and the gun made less noise than he'd feared.

Quickly now. Set down gun. Pop grate. Success! Flip aside. Recover gun. Stick head up—

Everything working out great so far. Tom three meters distant, facing the other way. Most of the gun's *poot* had stayed in the pipe, so the first sound Tom had heard was the nail landing some-where beyond him. Mike got his arm out, took dead aim at the back of Tom's head, flung the solid nail gun with all his strength at point-blank range—

—missed—

—and Tom spun and drew down on him with one of those new vibrator guns that jellied whatever their beam hit.

Mike got ready to die. It wasn't as hard as it had been the first time.

Tom's eyes widened as he grasped that his antagonist was a child, and raised his gun. "Jesus Christ, she's got a kid!" he said. "Show me your other hand, kid—*now*."

Numb, Mike obeyed. At Tom's feet, he could see Annie, lying on her back, face gray and eyes closed. A first-aid unit was strapped to her upper arm but not yet activated.

"All right, come on up out of there—slow and careful."

Mike eased himself up into the room. *Blew it, blew it, blew it*—

"Anybody else down there?"

He shook his head miserably.

Tom shook his head, too. "Now what the hell am I gonna do with *you*?" He produced a roll of duct tape from his coverall. "Call in again, I guess." He stepped over Annie and yelled, "SHIT!" when she yanked his ankle out from under him. As he was falling she was rising; there was just time for his face to hit the floor before she kicked him in the groin from behind, a beauty that curled him up like a bug and left him gasping for air that wouldn't come. His gun slid across the floor to Mike, who picked it up automatically. Annie stepped around Tom, studied him, and care-fully kicked him again, behind the ear. He made a rattling sound and went limp.

Mike thought about joining him.

"Nice work, boy," Annie said. She no longer looked like she was having a heart attack. She wasn't even breathing hard.

He snapped out of his trance. "Yeah, right."

"Let's go home. I could use a nice cup of tea."

Mike blinked. "What about *him*?"

Annie glanced down at him. "Not our problem," she said. "He can take care of himself . . . or not."

"Okay." Mike started to make for the stairwell at the far end of the depot.

"Wait," she said. "Leave that here with him."

He turned, and she was pointing at the vibrator gun, forgotten in his hand. He looked down at it, then at its former owner. "Annie—," he began.

"Listen to me, Michael," she said softly, holding his eyes. "I will not tolerate guns in Dreamworld. And *especially* not in my own house. No matter what. Put it down."

He nodded slowly. "Yeah. Okay." Sigh. "But *gee*—"

"Take the charge out of it first. And wipe the handle."

He did so, then put the gun at Tom's feet.

When they reached the stairwell, she stopped. "You go on ahead. Give me that charge pack."

"But—" he began, handing over the cylinder.

"Wait for me halfway up. I'll be right along."

He did as he was told. He waited on the second landing, fretting, for something like a minute before she appeared, looking very pleased with herself. "Home, Jeeves."

Mike was numb by this point; his "Very good, Mr. Wooster" was automatic.

Just as they began to climb up the stairs, they heard the sound of the freight elevator carrying Ape and the other man and their wheelchair down. Annie chuckled. "See? Plenty of time."

THERE WAS NO conversation on the way home. As soon as they conveniently could, they went back Under, and laid a complex meandering trail that crossed itself more than once. Twice Annie paused and simply waited in silence for a few minutes before continuing. By the time they got back to her place, both were sure they had not been followed.

The moment her door closed behind them, Annie whirled on him and snapped, *"What the hell did you do that for?"*

He was beyond being startled or defensive. "To save your life."

"That was more important than saving Dreamworld?" she blazed.

He thought for a moment. "I guess so," he said simply.

All the wind went out of Annie's sails. Her face smoothed over, became unreadable. She turned, walked to the kitchen table, and sat down. Mike sat on the side of the bed.

"The heart attack was saccade tricks and acting, you know," she said after a while. "I could have taken them. All three of them."

"I know."

There was an even longer pause, and then she said, "Thank you, Mike."

He nodded. "You're welcome. What did they want?"

She frowned. "I don't know. Oh, me, obviously—but something else, too. Information, but they wouldn't say what it was. Something they thought I could tell them once they got me out of here."

"What?"

She shook her head.

Mike nodded again and lay down and stretched out. It occurred to him that a little nap before dinner might not be a bad idea, but by then he had already been asleep for several seconds.

HE WOKE AN indeterminate time later with a terrible sense of urgency. Something was wrong, something needed to be fixed so badly that he had to remember what it was even before opening his eyes.

Right. He'd left the message to Phillip Avery on-screen, where a careless elbow might accidentally send it.

He opened his eyes and looked. Annie was at the computer,

typing away. She had put a blanket over him. He snuggled into it and went back to sleep.

AT DINNER ANNIE caught him being depressed, though he was being quiet about it. "Why the long face?"

He did not answer.

She sighed. "Mike, your alien hypothesis made sense. I believed it, didn't I? It was the *only* hypothesis we had that made sense. In fact, it still is."

He was stubbornly silent.

"So now we'll just start over, with newer and better data, and develop a *new*—"

"I missed him!" Mike blurted.

"Pardon?"

"He was two meters away and I *missed* him. Totally."

Her face went smooth. She said nothing for a moment, then picked her words with obvious care. "Mike, *anybody* can miss even an easy throw. That's why they invented guns. Professional pitchers throw wild all the time, under pressure."

"Two lousy bastard meters," he said, but he knew she was right.

"Consider this," she suggested. "At the angle he presented to you, there was exactly one place you could have hit him and disabled him at once. And it was about the size of a poker chip." She pointed to a spot behind her own ear. "*Anywhere* else you could have hit him, he'd simply have turned and shot you before I could stop him."

He thought about that. Vibrator guns were pretty awful.

She spoke even slower. "He was well trained and alert. If you had not diverted his attention, I don't know if I could have taken him. You saved my life, Mike. And even if you had failed utterly and we both had died or been captured, you would still be the bravest boy I have ever known."

He felt his cheeks grow hot. No, his whole face. And his ears.

"And if you ever take a risk like that for me again, I'll slap you cross-eyed."

He drew breath to defend himself—and let it out.

"Do you understand me?"

He looked stubborn.

Annie studied him and sighed. "I can't give you orders, can I? Much as you respect me. You'll do what you think is right."

He looked at her eyes, saw she wanted an honest answer, decided to risk giving one, and nodded.

And to his utter astonishment she grinned hugely and said, "*Good* man."

In spite of himself, Mike burst out laughing.

ANNIE? HE ASKED as he was washing up.

"Yes?"

"I could have *shot* him. Instead of throwing the nail gun, I could have shot him with it."

"And got yourself killed, like I said."

"Yeah, maybe. I guess. But that's not why I didn't. *I couldn't!*"

"Ah."

When she made no further comment, he asked openly. "Well, what do you think about that?"

"Look at me," she said.

He stopped washing dishes and did so. Her eyes bored into his and held them. "This is what I think you are asking me. You want to know if I think you less than a man should be, because you cannot bring yourself to kill, even to save your friend's life. Am I close?"

He squirmed under her gaze. "Well . . . yeah."

Very slowly and solemnly, she shook her head from side to side. "No. I would think you less than a man should be if you found it easy to kill a stranger, in cold blood, with a gun, from ambush. Okay?"

He nodded, but must not have looked convinced.

She sighed. "Mike, murder has nothing to do with manhood. Finding me, in time, thinking up that brilliant drainpipe entrance—all that was more than most grown men could have done. And it was enough. *And*, for what it's worth, it is more than any *other* man has ever done for me."

He felt his face get hot again, and returned to his dishes. "Okay," he said after a while, and when next he snuck a peek at Annie, she was busy straightening the covers on the bed.

SO WHAT DO we do now?" he asked when the morning chores were all done.

"Now we defeat the bastards," she said cheerfully.

He nodded. "Cool. How? We still don't know who they are or what they're doing or why. Do we know *anything* more than we did yesterday, except that they're not Martians?"

"Yes," she said. "Some of it even mildly useful."

"Like what?"

She sat across from him. "The man we took down together is named Thomas McAnaly, a private-security thug with a police record that took twenty seconds just to download. He's supposed to be unemployed and on benefits at the moment, but his last employer of record was an outfit called RTC Security, owned by one R. T. Conway. *His* record took over two minutes to download, and there were at least eight nations and three governments among the complainants. It is alleged that Conway worked for the American NSA once, and *they* found him too treacherous. A real piece of work. If you want a small country overthrown or a Supreme Court justice murdered, and you can afford the best, you hire RTC."

"How do you know all this stuff?" Mike asked.

"McAnaly handled my Command Band when he was trying to see if I was really in cardiac arrest. Maybe you noticed, he wasn't wearing gloves. After you fell asleep last night, I ran the

Band through the scanner. It turns out Photoshop can be tweaked to bring out a fingerprint, if you play with it a little. The rest was just hacking."

He grinned. "Way cool." He thought about what she had learned. "So who hired Conway? To do what?"

She sighed, slouched in her chair, and put her feet up on the table. "Here we enter into guesswork. I didn't even try to go *near* RTC's own data. And the same with the guy I suspect is Conway's client. The best I could probably accomplish is to give them one of my bogus e-mail addresses."

"I see that," he agreed. "So who do you suspect?"

"What do you know about Thrillworld?"

He shrugged. "I've never been there. People say it's almost as fun as here." He shrugged again. "Different, though. My cousin Magdalen said some of the magic was, like, creepier. And there's a lot of gross stuff: blood and guts, and shooting and stuff. I hear more people *go* to Thrillworld, but they don't keep *coming back* as often as Dreamworld fans do."

She nodded. "A fair summation. It is owned and operated by a man named Haines. He is a toad, and richer than even a toad should be, and he probably hates Dreamworld more than Satan hates Heaven. He has been trying to close this place since it opened."

"I heard about that," Mike agreed.

"Up until now, he has used lawyers and money and political leverage—and hasn't succeeded, because Phillip Avery is smarter than he is, and has just as much of all three. But Haines has come very close, once or twice, because he's more unscrupulous. It would be absolutely in character for Haines to give up on legal means and try some kind of direct sabotage. It's how he operates in most other areas of his business. Until now he hasn't quite dared with Dreamworld, because . . . well, because it's *Dreamworld* . . . but he has tried to pressure others into wrecking the place for him, more than once. I think he finally ran out of patience, good judgment, or both, and decided to do his own dirty work—or at least hire it done. RTC's corporate headquarters are in the same city as Thrillworld."

That certainly made sense. "But I still don't get it. How does it help him wreck Dreamworld to smuggle five or six little people in and then back out again every day? They don't seem to *do* anything while they're here."

"That we know about," Annie corrected. "For all we know, they're mining the place."

Mike was horrified. "Jesus, we have to start tailing them."

She shook her head. "Two people can't follow six. And they may not know anything useful about what they're doing. And we *still* don't have a clue how or where they're getting in. We need to talk to Haines himself."

His jaw dropped. "How?"

The corners of her mouth turned up, but the result could not have been called a smile. "We call him up and invite him over for a chat."

And after looking at his expression, her own did become a smile.

CHAPTER 9

ONLY A MOTHER

Haines hated having to come to Conway.

But it was his own fault. No one could approach him in his headquarters during daylight hours without being seen by others; Haines himself had planned it that way. And he must not be seen with Conway. And he needed to see Conway, *right now*.

Back at his office, of course, many minions were no doubt buzzing over the Old Man's first unexplained, unplanned departure from his office during business hours in longer than anyone could remember. But as long as they were buzzing, it meant they didn't know anything that could hurt him. Haines rather liked his ant farm agitated.

His second in command had tried to have him followed, of course. Haines had spotted the tail in the first six blocks and pointed it out to his driver, who said only, "Crash him or lose him, sir?" When Haines decided, "Crash," the driver had nodded and touched the dashboard, and there had been loud sounds behind them briefly. Damned airbags. . . .

Now he said, "Hold on, sir," and suddenly they were exiting the highway—from the left lane, and at the last possible second. Haines turned and watched carefully. No other car took that exit; none braked or changed lanes in an attempt to. He grunted in satisfaction and faced forward again, making a mental note to ask the driver his name, someday.

If only Conway had proved as reliable!

Most infuriating of all, Haines had no idea exactly what had gone wrong, or how badly. Only that it couldn't be anything minor. Conway would not have called a secret emergency face-to-face to deliver good news.

Still, the thought of the reaming he was now entitled to give the man was considerable consolation. He dwelt on that for several kilometers.

A deserted road eventually brought Haines and his driver to an abandoned, fenced-off factory. The locked gate unlocked itself for them. They drove around behind the main complex, out of sight of the road, and stopped. Haines saw no signs of life. After a pause that he knew represented an ID check, a man stepped out from behind a Dumpster and directed them with gestures down an alleyway between two warehouse outbuildings. At the far end another man gestured to turn left. The doors of the warehouse on that side were open. The driver drove them inside and shut off the car, leaving one hand on the dashboard.

Haines waited until he saw Conway approach, then got out. He had given his opening line some thought, and delivered it as soon as his target was in range. "How bad did you screw up?"

Men like Conway do not flinch, but a vein suddenly stood out on the right side of his forehead. "The Mother Elf exists. My men had her and lost her."

Haines nodded. "Brilliant. Did they blow their cover?"

"No, they all got clear."

He relaxed a bit. "Thank God for small favors. Tell me about it."

"She faked a heart attack. She shouldn't have been able to fool them, but she did somehow. And then it turned out she's got a son."

"Jesus," Haines said in spite of himself. "So that's why they call her the *Mother* Elf—"

"Yah. Midget in his twenties. My man says he mistook him for a normal-size kid until the little bastard sucker-punched him and kicked his nuts in."

"Your man was alone?"

"The rest of his team had gone to get the wheelchair they were going to take her out in. They took him out in it instead."

"Two men on the chair, one on the victim. Shrewd," Haines said.

"An old lady, having a coronary. Who knew there was another one? There aren't any legends about *him*."

"Professionals should be prepared for anything."

Conway said nothing at all.

Haines frowned. Conway was an unsatisfying man to ream. "Did your men get any information out of her?"

Conway shook his head.

"Did they accomplish anything useful at all? Aside from not getting caught by Security?"

"We know for sure she exists now," Conway said. "I say that makes her a lead pipe cinch to be the one smuggling Dwarves in and out. I never did believe it could be Avery—not without one of our spies getting at least a whiff of it—but it's nice to know for sure."

One of Haines' favorite bullying tactics was the sudden, unexpected explosion; he used it now. "It would be nicer," he began mildly, bursting into an earsplitting bellow only on the last word, "to know *WHY!*"

Conway gave no sign of noticing. "Yes," he agreed.

Haines gave up. Conway was no fun. "And so now you will . . ."

"Go back in again—and get both of them."

"Now that they're forewarned and expecting trouble."

"Yes."

Haines closed his eyes and nodded. The hell of it was, he believed Conway could do it. Maddening as all this was, it was, in the end, only a temporary setback. "Very well. I want at least one of them alive and talking. Don't screw up this time."

Conway turned and walked away.

Haines stared after him. When the man was out of sight, he shook himself slightly, and got back into his car.

All the way back to the office he replayed the conversation, trying to understand what had gone wrong with the reaming. An employee who apparently could not be humiliated, even by the knowledge of his own failure, was a curiosity of great professional interest to Haines, like a woman who could not be frightened, or a politician who could not be bought.

He was still puzzling over it as he seated himself again behind his desk. When the phone rang, he was more startled than angry, for he had not yet indicated to his electronic secretary his willingness to accept calls again. Furthermore, it was so late in the day that nearly everyone had gone home by now. But it was not his official line, he saw, but the private one. No more than a dozen living humans had that number, and he was certain it would be Conway. He picked up the phone, hoping the man had some new screwup to report, so he could try out an experimental approach he had thought up in the car. "Haines."

"You sound just as ugly as you look in your pictures, Alonzo," somebody's grandmother said pleasantly. "A remarkable accomplishment. Congratulations."

Haines knew he had never heard this voice before in his life. He drew in breath for a snarl—and held it. His pulse began to hammer. He was not an intuitive man, but suddenly, somehow, he *knew.*

"You."

"Me," she agreed. "The Mother Elf her own self."

He glanced at his call display and cursed silently. She was calling from a pay phone. Doubtless in Dreamworld. Big help. He triggered the recorder. "How's your heart?" he asked sarcastically.

"How's your soul?"

Haines had absolutely no reply to make to that.

"We should talk," she went on.

"Go ahead."

"No, it's got to be face-to-face or nothing."

"I'll tell the doorman to expect you," he said. "You be bringing your kid along? I'll lay in some lollipops."

She chuckled grimly. "Don't bother. *I'm* not going anywhere."

Now he was getting pissed. "You actually expect *me* to come to . . ." He couldn't even say it. ". . . *there?*" If she said yes, he was going to say two words of his own and slam the phone down.

Instead she said, "Avery only knows about two of your spies, fat man. I know about all eight."

The two words trembled on his lips, but he forced himself to swallow them. "Not *there*. Anywhere else."

"And I know who tried to crash the Hippogriff," she went on inexorably, "and how . . . and who pressured her into it . . . and how."

Haines swallowed a lot more than two words then. He nearly choked on it, and his voice came out strangled when he finally said, "Okay. When?"

"Tomorrow morning, during the Pageant."

"In broad *daylight?*" he groaned. "No way in hell. If anyone ever saw me there—"

"Wear a disguise if you like. I'll know you."

"No, God damn it, forget it. You'll just have to—"

"I have her suicide note. It's very detailed, Alonzo."

His head spun. "Tomorrow's no good," he insisted, desperate to retain some shred of control, salvage *something* from this disaster. "Make it the day after if it's gotta be daytime. I can't just drop everything and get on a plane."

"Fine. There'll be a message for you on the Big Board in the Octagon, telling you exactly where to meet me. And Alonzo?"

"Uh huh."

"You will suspend all operations here between now and then. Nothing more happens until we talk. Right?"

Stop trying to kidnap her, in other words. "Sure," he lied. "Hey, tell me something. The kid is Immega's, am I right?"

He was talking to a dead phone.

He sat there with it in his hand, unmoving, for several minutes, not even hearing the recorded voice that kept telling him to please hang up. In the game of manipulation, he did not often lose. Twice in one day was a record—and all at once he realized the day was not over yet.

Finally he accepted his fate, broke the connection, and called Conway to tell him they were going to have to meet *again*. Strike three.

YOU'RE GOING? WAS all Conway said.

Haines looked around the airport parking lot. "I have to. Never mind why. And you're coming with me. I want you on the scene, directing this personally."

"She's got something on you."

He ignored that. "I don't intend to go in there with nothing in my hand but my dick. I need some leverage. An edge. As of now, I want you to pull your men off her and the kid. I want a couple of those bogus Trolls instead. As many as you can get me. Do it right away, at tonight's shift change, in case they take time to crack."

Conway shook his head. "It takes time to set up even one extraction."

Haines was in no mood to be argued with. "I don't care if you chloroform 'em in the parking lot and pepper spray all the witnesses," he roared. "I want some Trolls, and I want 'em tonight!"

Conway merely shrugged. "Okay. But they're foot soldiers; they may not know much."

"They'll know more than I do now. Even if they don't, they'll make good hostages. Come on, we've got a plane to catch."

CHAPTER 10

INTO THE TOILET

"I'm not going to tell you the specifics of what I threatened him with," Annie said. "You have no need to know, and it would only upset you. Just take my word for it: he'll be here the day after tomorrow, on time. And between now and then, he won't make any further attempts to kidnap me. Haines knows I'm dangerous, now."

Mike nodded. "Okay. Do you think he's really going to stop sneaking fake Trolls in and out, in the meantime?"

She looked pained. "There, I'm not sure. I don't think he will. The way I read him, he always feels he *has* to cheat on any deal at least a little, as much as he thinks he can get away with: it's the way he's built. He may gamble that I won't take the final step of blowing my own cover unless he takes another shot at me personally. And he's right." She rolled her head to relieve a crick in her neck. "And on the other hand, he might stop, at least until we meet and he has half a chance to kill me. I'd have a better idea if I had a *clue* what the hell those fake Trolls are all *about*. Maybe I was stupid to insist he stop. For all he knows, I already *know* what's going on—and now I've thrown away my best chance to find out." She frowned and rolled her head the other way. "But I couldn't help it. I don't like strangers traipsing through Dreamworld."

Mike came over and stood behind her chair, began massaging her neck, gently at first and then harder. She made a sound somewhere between a groan and a purr, tilted her head back, and rolled her eyes up until she could see his face. "Why didn't you *tell* me you could do that?" she asked.

"I didn't think of it. Lean forward."

She did. After a while he widened his attentions to include her shoulder girdle. She guided him with little moans whenever he hit an especially good spot . . . then stopped when she realized he didn't need to be told out loud. Minutes went by.

"Annie?"

"Okay, Mike."

"Huh? I mean—"

"Whatever you're going to ask me for, okay. That was the first neck rub I've had in thirteen years."

"Oh. Well, I wasn't going to ask you for anything, exactly. It's just I was thinking—"

"Yes, I could smell it. And you thought—"

"And I thought, even if Haines decides to keep his word, stop whatever he's doing with the Trolls until you guys talk . . ."

"Yes?"

"Well . . . today's load are probably already *here*, right?"

Annie sat bolt upright, spun her chair to face him, staring. For a wild instant he wondered if he had offended her somehow, so intently was she staring. And then she smiled.

"By all the gods," she said softly, "I wish he was right."

"Who was right?"

"Haines. He thinks you're my son."

Mike was struck speechless.

"You're a genius. Of *course* today's Trolls are in. And even if Haines pulled the plug as soon as he hung up the phone, the smartest and safest time to move those Trolls out is still tonight as usual, at shift change. I have at least one more shot at figuring out what they're up to!"

"We," Mike corrected.

She frowned. "Are you speaking French?"

"I'm going too, this time."

She stood up. "In a pig's eye."

"You *said* anything I asked for—"

"Mike!" she said in her stern-aunty command voice.

He shrugged it off. "Annie, I *have* to go."

"I have already explained why you *mustn't* go—the sealed-letter principle, have you forgotten?"

"Bullshit," he insisted. "I figured out how to set up a remote terminal on my Band. Either of us can send the letter, from anywhere—we can be *each other's* deadman switch."

"Mike, listen to me. The *only* way Haines knows of getting leverage back over me is to kidnap *you*. We have to keep you out of the line of fire at all costs—"

"I'm telling you we can't," he said. "This might be our last shot, right? So we want to be as sure as possible we find at least one fake Troll, right? *So what if none of 'em are girls?*"

Annie blinked. "I don't follow."

"Exactly. I know where they hide during the day, okay? While they're waiting for the shift to end. At least some of them—they must: it's the perfect place! Nobody notices that you're hanging around not doing anything for hours, nobody talks to you, nobody even looks twice at you—"

Her mouth fell open as realization dawned on her. "Oh my God—"

"The bathrooms. Employee bathrooms, with no security cameras, no parents waiting outside."

She was staring at him again. "And all the ones I've spotted so far were male," she breathed.

"I thought of it while you were out having your heart attack this morning," he said. "I was thinking of it as a great place for Mr. Spock to beam down to . . . but it still works for a hiding place for humans."

She kept staring. "I have *got* to stop underestimating you. Or is it overestimating myself?"

"I can pass for either a man or a woman, with you to make me up," he said, pressing his advantage. "But you'd have a heck of a time standing at a urinal."

She snapped out of her trance. "Sit down."

"Why?" he asked warily.

She pointed to the chair beside her. "Sit *down*."

He sat.

"Now turn around. *I* am going to rub *your* neck."

"I'm going?"

"Yes, you're going, damnit, now turn around."

His smile hurt his face. "Cool."

For the first neck rub she'd given anyone in thirteen years, it was pretty good.

SEVERAL HOURS LATER, Mike was getting tired of looking at washrooms.

Sixteen, so far, and he'd seen a grand total of two Trolls. Each time, he paid no attention, pretended to pee, and left, then loitered outside . . . and each time the suspect Troll left the washroom shortly after he did. Each time, he called Annie by Command Band nonetheless and gave her coordinates to feed the satellite tracking program . . . and each time, she reported that they checked out as genuine Dreamworld Trolls.

It had been fun at the start, being taken for a grown-up by everyone he passed, but that had worn off, too. Also, his feet hurt. As he approached his seventeenth employees' men's room, in a service corridor between the Enchanted Forest and Chip's Backyard, Mike was strongly tempted to goof off, take at least a short break.

Glancing at the time, he realized he might as well: it was nearly time for Firefall, and any seeming Dreamworld employee found in a washroom during Firefall *would* excite suspicion. Now, if ever, was when they would leave their hiding places and mingle with the crowds, working their way toward the employee exits while everyone else was staring at the sky.

But he kept going. If it was nearly Firefall, it was nearly time for the shift to end—and tonight might be his and Annie's one and only shot. Maybe he'd catch one coming out, and tail him to wherever they rendezvoused for departure.

No such luck. He approached this washroom as slowly as he dared, but nobody emerged before he'd reached it. He debated whether to bother going in, and realized he actually did have to pee.

Nobody inside—not even an Elf or Leprechaun or Dwarf. Not even a Cousin or other normal-sized employee. This was not surprising: both the Glade and the Backyard had other employee facilities more conveniently located than this one; Mike had already checked both. The room was so empty he could hear the echo of his own breathing. He remembered his space-aliens fantasy, reflected that here and now would be a smart place to beam down, and then was annoyed at his own childishness. To compensate he did a thorough job of searching the room, opening each stall door to confirm that nobody was hiding inside, perched on the crapper. He urinated then, zipped up, and began to leave. But as he was opening the door, an odd thing happened: the sound of his breathing got louder. He stopped in the doorway, and it got even louder.

But it should have *diminished* when he'd opened the door. . . .

He stopped altogether—stopped breathing, stopped moving, stopped everything but thinking. The sound continued to swell, a susurration without a sibilant, like a hundred whispers overlaid with the treble control spun all the way to minimum, its volume still slowly increasing. Mike could feel the air itself roiling, feel it against his skin, and the noise wasn't anywhere near loud enough to do that. There was a funny smell in the room now, one he didn't know—

He moved before he understood why, was still thinking it

through as he stepped out into the hallway, let the door *almost* close behind him, stopped it with his toe and put his ear to the crack.

At once he heard a sound like the cracking of a whip played through a guitar amplifier, at low volume but with way too much reverb and flanging—then, a second later, another one just like it—then utter silence.

"Jizz," a hoarse dwarf's voice said in hushed tones. "Like something out of a story-bead it is." His accent was barely understandable, and unlike any Mike had ever heard.

"Something out of a bead it is," said a second, even more liquid voice. "And we the editors are. Come." This one's accent was worse.

"Pause. A minim I need."

"No—hurry is!"

"Oh, *crot!*"

On the other side of the door, Mike came close to fainting, grabbed the wall to steady himself. He had just begun to grasp the enormous realization that somehow he had been right all along, that aliens *were* indeed beaming down into Dreamworld—and now almost at once he knew he had to cancel that idea and start over.

If an alien beams down to Earth, it either arrives speaking Alien . . . or, if it is planning to pass as human and wants to stay in character for practice, it arrives speaking unaccented English, in correct local contemporary idiom.

These were not aliens. Their true nature burst over him all at once, he knew what they *had to be*, and he was simultaneously stunned and furious with himself for not having thought of it sooner. He clenched his teeth so hard he saw sparks behind his eyes.

He heard the sound of a urinal being flushed. "Unbelievable," the first voice said. A faucet was turned on and off, and the same voice said, "The arrogance!" A stall door banged open—

"Zhin, *come!*" the second voice insisted. "Later futz."

Zhin grunted a reluctant assent.

Two sets of heavy footsteps sounded.

At once Mike let go of the door, sprinted ten paces—turned on a dime, and began walking, slowly, back *toward* the washroom. As the two newcomers emerged, he strolled past them and on down the hall, giving them only the casual and disinterested flicker of a glance any employee would give two others he passed in a corridor.

Two dwarves costumed as Trolls. Exceptionally ugly even for Trolls. Bad skin. Deeply sad eyes. Both of them rather on the large side as dwarves went, but somehow frail-looking just the same. The taller of the two Mike guessed to be Zhin; he was the more indignant-looking.

Mike looked away at once, but kept his peripheral vision working. Both Trolls flinched slightly when they saw him, but both recovered smoothly when they saw he was ignoring them, and walked away in the opposite direction. He listened to their footsteps recede behind him, calculated that they were going as fast as they dared. He took the first turn he could, put his Command Band up to his ear and signaled Annie.

"Red alert," he said softly.

"Report," came the reply nearly at once.

"Two bogies."

"Where?"

"Number—uh—forty-seven, between—"

"I know where it is. On my way."

"Wait!"

"Go ahead."

"Look, I know this is gonna sound stupid. But I'm *sure*, okay? Absolutely sure. And I want to say it now, in case some more come before you get here and I get caught or something."

"Slow down. Say it."

"They're time-travelers."

There was no reply at all for a long time. Then Annie said only, "I'm on my way. Watch yourself! Out."

· · ·

HE WAITED FOR her in the corridor just outside the washroom. After some thought he had decided that more time-travelers might arrive at any moment. By loitering in the corridor, he would know that any Troll walking out of that washroom was one who had not walked into it first . . . but they would not *know* that he knew that.

It half killed him to wait outside; with all his heart he yearned to *see* a time-traveler materialize. But he knew he couldn't afford the risk of being caught watching. The only hiding place in there was the stalls, and he'd heard Zhin look into one of them. Besides, for all Mike knew, their time machine had some kind of fail-safe that kept them from arriving when anyone else was in the room—hadn't they only arrived when he was halfway out the door? Better not to chance it. He consoled himself with the thought that there hadn't seemed to be any interestingly gaudy visual effects involved—none that showed through a crack in the door. Just weird sounds. Probably they'd simply . . . flicked into existence, like on a TV show with no budget. Boy, Annie was going to—

Two more Trolls emerged from the washroom.

Mike nearly panicked. He had neglected to prepare a cover story, to explain what he was doing there loitering outside a washroom. Somehow the same instinct that kept him from flinching warned him not to try and improvise one now. Damnit, *they* were the ones who needed a cover story! Instead of looking for a way to melt into the scenery, he simply stood his ground and stared right at the two Trolls, as if at any moment he might decide to ask them a question or a favor.

However instinctive, the strategy worked. The instant they became aware of him looking at them, both Trolls visibly ceased to be aware of his existence, walked past him with the sublime disassociation of a cat walking away from a turd on the rug.

Mike was momentarily tempted to make up a question and hurl it after them, just to see how they'd handle it. But he suppressed the urge; he had more important things to think about.

Such as whether to wait for Annie or follow these two bozos. He could probably come up with some kind of equivalent to a trail of bread crumbs to leave behind. Come to think of it, he could just call her on his Command Band and *tell* her what he was doing, and let her track him herself, with her own—

While he dithered, Annie arrived.

Seeing her expression, and knowing how little time there was, he chose his words carefully.

"Listen to me," were the first three, and only when he was sure she would did he continue. "I'd just checked this bathroom out. I was in the doorway, leaving. Two Trolls materialized out of thin air. They didn't see me. They spoke English—but in weird accents, with words and expressions nobody uses even in old books. Guys from outer space wouldn't do that. Guys from the future probably would. They came out of the can and left. I called you and waited right here. A few seconds ago, two *more* came out. I'm going after them." He turned to go.

"Mike!"

"There's no *time*, Annie, there might not *be* any more of them coming—but there might be, so you gotta wait."

She took a deep breath that lasted a hundred years, and held it, frowning, for fifty more. "Be careful," she said at last.

He spun and ran after the second pair of Trolls.

CHAPTER 11

OUT OF KIN TROLL

At first Mike ran as fast as he could, conscious of the long lead they had on him. But he didn't want to attract attention . . . and he knew *they* wouldn't be running because they didn't want to attract attention, either . . . and the more he thought about it, he was pretty sure he knew where they were going anyway. They would be taking the most direct route toward the employee area, since every minute they loitered in Guest country increased their risk of being accosted by some child who wanted to play, and if they were like the first pair, they probably didn't speak contemporary English well enough to pass. Also, he was afraid they might spook if they heard him come thundering up from behind. So he gradually slowed his pace, first to a trot and then to a fast walk, and by the time he left the staff corridors and entered Dreamworld proper, Guest country, he was moving at almost normal pedestrian speed, which turned out to be a good thing.

Otherwise he might have failed to notice until too late that he was not the only one following those Trolls.

He spotted the followers before he saw the Trolls—knew them for what they were the instant he saw them, even from behind. They were a pair of thugs, just like the ones who'd tried to kidnap Annie except that both of these were of normal adult height and costumed as employees, one of them a Neanderthal and the other a Centurion. Each moved like a panther and kept his right hand in a pocket. Mike could not have said just how he knew they were following the Trolls—like him, they were trying *not* to look like they were following someone—but from the moment he saw them he never doubted it.

Sure enough, just then the crowd ahead parted and he got a glimpse of the two Trolls in the far distance. So did the thugs. They picked up their pace slightly and began to close the gap. Mike kept pace, frowning.

Until that moment, he had assumed these two were escorts, in league with the Trolls, following them to make sure nobody else was doing so, ready to move in fast if anybody tried to stop them. But now their body language told Mike they were *stalking* the Trolls, just like him. They were Conway's thugs, working for him and thus for Haines and Thrillworld—and they were *not* allied with the time-travelers. They meant to follow these Trolls until they reached some out-of-the-way spot, and then grab them, the way they'd tried to grab Annie.

Mike felt immediate panic, and a strong urge to intervene, quickly.

It took him a few moments to work out why. He had absolutely no idea what was going on here, no clear idea of which side he was on. Perhaps these were *not* thugs but Good Guys, trying to neutralize invading time-travelers—

Either they succeed or they fail. If they succeed, I don't get to learn anything more about those particular time-travelers, who may be the last ones I'll ever see. If they fail, there's liable to be a fight gaudy enough for other people to notice and alarms to start going off. If that happens, Dreamworld Security will not *fail: they'll move in from all sides and snatch everybody up, and interrogate them. And if they do—*

—oh holy shit, if they do—

The whole universe—everything—could end.

Anyone who'd ever seen a Star Trek movie knew that time travel *had* to be kept secret. Changing history was supposed to be major-league Bad News. Time travelers from the future would not have tried to enter the year 2023 by stealth if the record of history said they were doomed to fail. So if the Trolls' cover *was* blown, if they were revealed as time-travelers, they would enter public record, become a part of history—would *change* that history—creating a paradox that could tear the universe apart.

MIKE WALKED AS fast as he dared now. Good Guys or not, those two clowns had to be stopped. And soon—ideally, well before they could make their move.

Where would they do that? He thought hard.

The two Trolls were already leaving the Heinlein section, just entering the outskirts of Strawberry Fields. The two goons were closing the gap—Mike estimated that if nothing happened to slow them up, they would overtake their quarry just about the time they all crossed Penny Lane. . . .

Something clicked in Mike's memory. The Fire Engine on Penny Lane only actually got used there once an hour, in the show. The rest of the time it pooted randomly all around Dreamworld—and four times a day it actually left the grounds and took a swing around the parking lot, exiting and reentering via the large-vehicle gate near the Main Gate. If you could get a Troll into one of the many alleyways off Penny Lane, render him quickly unconscious, and somehow load him inside the Fire Engine, you could get him out to the parking lot without having to go through the turnstiles!

Mike was just leaving Heinlein's Centerville now. As he approached the tunnel he nodded automatically to Oscar the Spacesuit . . . and as suddenly as that, the germ of a plan was born in his mind. No time to examine it for flaws. He slowed, stepped out of the traffic, and stopped beside Oscar, doing an elaborate pantomime of nonchalance. At the last possible instant he remembered that he was dressed and made up to look like a midget maintenance worker, and he deepened his voice what he hoped was appropriately as he murmured, "Trouble in the house."

The man playing Oscar answered at once, just as softly. "What's the problem, brother?"

"Two gorillas about a hundred meters ahead," Mike said without moving his lips. "Caveman and Roman soldier. I think they're bogus."

Oscar's opaque helmet did not turn. "The dirty blonde and the one with the shoulders?"

"Yah. Little girl about eight, fifty meters farther on. They've both been following her since she left the Enchanted Forest, and I think they're moving in on her. I smell a custody snatch. At least, I hope that's what I smell."

"Okay, I'll call Security—you try and get between them and her."

Mike nodded. "Thanks."

He continued on his way, starting off slow but picking up speed as he went. By the time he got out of the tunnel, he had taken his shirt off, used it to wipe off as much makeup as he could, and wrapped it around his left forearm like a bandage: he entered Strawberry Fields as a child.

Maintenance men were not supposed to run in Dreamworld—you could start a panic that way—but kids in T-shirts did it all the time. Paradoxically, Mike became invisible to the two goons by approaching and then passing them at a dead run, grinning like a fool and humming a little tuneless song.

He timed it so that he seemed to run out of steam and slow to a fast walk when he was well past them, and about ten or twenty meters behind the two Trolls. He kept station there until he heard the commotion behind him—angry voices, shouts. Without looking behind him, he picked up the pace. Without looking behind themselves, either, so did the Trolls. Even so he overtook them almost at once. Too quickly to suit him: the problem of exactly how to approach them was one he could have used more time to ponder.

When he was right on their heels he thought of a way that might work. He stopped muffling his own footsteps, let the Trolls become subliminally aware of him behind them, and then insinuated himself between them—just another impatient kid overtaking some grown-ups in Dreamworld. As he passed between them, without looking at either he said softly, "Don't stop walking. Welcome to 2023."

TO HIS RELIEF, both Trolls were good. Of course they reacted—but no more than any adult might when suddenly jostled by a rude child in a hurry. Both had finished flinching before they had passed out of Mike's peripheral vision . . . and they proceeded to do what any startled adult might do in such a situation: speeded up their pace slightly to catch up to the rude child and give him a piece of their mind.

As they pulled up even with him, one on either side, the one on the left said, "How do you know about us? Who are you?" His voice sounded as if he'd been gargling broken glass.

Like any lectured child, Mike answered him but would not look at him. "I'm the guy who just took out those two goons behind you. They were going to jump you on Penny Lane and smuggle you out of here in the Fire Engine. Their backup could be along any minute. Follow me and I'll get you to a safe place; then we can talk."

The one on the right glanced over his shoulder and then quickly back again. "Crot!" he said softly but emphatically. The one on the left gave Mike the indignant glare of the adult whose kindly intended advice has been rejected by the rude child. "Why should we trust you?"

Mike shrugged. "Don't. See how that works," he said, and picked up his pace.

A good ten seconds later, just as he was about to turn around and go back and try reasoning with them, they finally caught up with him. He sighed with relief and slowed down to normal walking pace again: the rude child who has decided to relax to the inevitable and let the indignant adults lecture him.

"Where do we go?" the spokesman said. "We schedules have, and keep them *must*."

Mike glanced at him for the first time. Like the first pair he'd seen: exceedingly ugly even for a Troll in costume. Nose bristling with hairs, skin like rice puffs, rheumy cataracted eyes, wrinkles deep enough to conceal small change, and an apelike protruding lower lip. "What's your hurry?" Mike asked him. "We're about ten minutes' walk from the employee area, and the shift doesn't end for another hour at least."

Hairy Nose and his companion exchanged a sharp glance. It was not lost on Mike. He knew he was on the verge of over-playing his hand: by trying to impress them with how much he knew (because he knew hardly anything), he had succeeded in alarming them. They were both mentally debating whether it might not be better if this rude child had an accident and fell down, and didn't wake up until they were both far, far away. He addressed the one on his right, who had not spoken so far except to curse. "You saw those guys get taken down back there, right?"

This one was, if anything, even uglier than the first, with a nasty squint that made him look as paranoid as he sounded now. "Yes. Hunters they were."

"And you know it's you they were after."

Squinty nodded. "Even as with the guards they argued, at us they kept looking."

Mike nodded back. "Okay. Two groups of people know about you. There's me and my friend Annie, and there's those guys and their pals. They want to kidnap you. We don't. You can spend the next forty-five minutes running, and leave here knowing no more than you do now—if you're lucky—or you can hang out in a place where they won't find you, and spend the time finding out whether or not it's safe for me to know what I know, and how I found out. You pick."

They walked together in silence perhaps ten paces, before Hairy Nose said, "Who is Annie?"

That one gave Mike pause. How could you explain Annie to a stranger—much less one from another century? Any capsule description of her seemed inadequate. So many things about her were unique, special, and right now these nervous time-travelers needed to understand *all* of them. It took a surprisingly long time for the words he needed to come to him, especially since they were so few.

"She's the Mother Elf," he said.

For only the second time since Mike had overtaken them, the Troll flinched—and then he stared intensely into Mike's eyes, and slowly his face changed a little in some indefinable way, became infinitesimally less ugly. "We will go with you," he rumbled. "Where?"

"Do you guys know about Johnny's Tree, in Strawberry Fields?"

It turned out that they did not. He explained the salient fact: as they all entered the elevator and the door slid shut behind them, they—and everyone else—would seem to become invisible. They could touch each other if they wanted, but all any of them would see was an apparently empty elevator, with not even their own reflection visible in the mirrored walls. From that point on, the rule was to keep to the right, so you wouldn't bump into people coming the other way. "But you don't have to worry about that," Mike added. "Once we get off at the top, I'll make us *really* disappear."

"How?" asked Squinty.

Mike started to answer—and suddenly wondered if some distant listener had a shotgun mike trained on them. "You'll see," he said evasively, and Squinty seemed to accept that.

As they waited for the elevator, he unwrapped his shirt from his left forearm, tied it around his waist, and offered each of them one of his hands. They looked at them. "So we won't get separated when we get invisible," he explained. They exchanged a glance and took his hands. The elevator opened, and they all entered together, along with two other kids and a grown-up with a beard. Mike was a little worried that one of them would notice he was wearing a Command Band on his wrist instead of the Dreamband a kid should wear—but it was awkward to hold someone's hand with a shirt wrapped around your wrist, and he was going to need to get at that Command Band soon, and besides, the risk lasted only a few seconds.

Both Trolls squeezed his hand as they all went invisible. He was glad he'd warned them to expect it. He squeezed back, and discovered an odd thing: he was stronger than either of them. With his hands, anyway. It was so unexpected, it took him the whole ride up to be sure of it. Every time one of the other kids in the elevator spoke—which they of course did the entire trip—both of the hands Mike held tensed, giving him a chance to measure their grip. These guys were candy.

He confirmed it when they reached the top, by tugging them both gently but firmly out of the stream of traffic without difficulty. He led them silently to the inconspicuous alcove nearby. "Leggo of me for a minute," he whispered, and after a moment's hesitation both hands released his. He had a bad moment then. He had failed to anticipate how tricky it would be to operate a Command Band he could not see. But after a little fumbling, he was relieved to see the employee elevator door smoothly and silently slide open.

Almost at once he became alarmed again, as he thought it through. The service elevator was here, at the top, because the last time it had been used had been by . . . the Cousin presently on monitor duty up here! The monitor was as invisible as everyone else, circulating through the crowd watching for problems. If the monitor passed this way and happened to see the employee elevator door standing open, all or part of hell would break loose.

Mike groped on either side of him, reacquired his time-traveling Trolls, and hustled them into the elevator.

As soon as the door closed behind them, they all became visible again. Both started, and instinctively tried to break his grip. He allowed them to succeed. At once he untied his shirt from his waist and began putting it back on. "From this point on," he told them, "we're kind of safe. I mean, no goons can find us. And we'll all pass for employees as long as nobody looks too close at my face. But in five minutes we'll be *really* safe. In a place where we can talk and everything."

Hairy Nose pushed his lower lip out even farther as he thought. Finally he took a deep breath and nodded. "Good."

"My name's Mike."

"We are Edward and Francis."

"No, you're not," Mike said positively. "Those are your cover names. People from the future aren't named Edward and Francis."

The Troll frowned ferociously—then sighed and relaxed to the inevitable. "Hello, Mike. I am Hormat."

"Durl I am," Squinty said, looking more paranoid than ever.

"Hi, fellas," Mike said. "Welcome to Dreamworld Under."

"We . . . go . . . under the ground?" Durl asked.

An odd little nonverbal communication took place then. This was the first time Durl had put the verb anywhere but at the tail end of his sentence, and something in his voice and expression made Mike realize suddenly that it was a small strain for him. He knew people talked that way here, he must have been briefed, but where he came from (no, *when* he came from) it must be so odd to speak that way that he felt silly doing it. Mike imagined how he would feel himself if he were someplace where everybody spoke Pig Latin. Sure he could do it . . . but he'd feel really stupid the first time he tried it, even if everybody else was doing it. In that moment, Durl was vulnerable: Mike could have laughed at him. And their eyes met, and they both knew it.

"Yeah, a couple of levels," Mike said.

"Thank you," Durl said.

The moment passed.

"But don't worry, it's perfectly safe down here."

He caught a flicker of expression on Hormat's face, then, and sensed that he'd made some kind of small blunder. He'd revealed ignorance of something Hormat had thought he knew. He thought about it. He had expected the Trolls to find being underground a little scary. He should instead have expected the Trolls to find being underground reassuring. What did that tell him?

Nothing—and he was busy. "Excuse me," he said, "I've gotta call Annie." He put his Band to his mouth. "Do you read? Over."

To his relief, she responded almost instantly. "Roger. Report."

"I'm with my two. Two of Conw—of that guy's goons tried to jump them in the Fields. I put Security on them and we got clear."

"Jesus."

"It's okay, I tell you. There was no fuss. We're Under. I'm taking them to where we met those other guys before. Can you meet me there?"

"That's brilliant, lad. Yes, I can."

"How did *you* make out?" he asked her.

"Not as well as you. There were *three* goons after my pair. I managed to neutralize all three—but I lost my quarry in the confusion."

The elevator was slowing. "I gotta go."

"ETA six minutes," she said, and the Band went silent just as the elevator opened.

The trip went without incident. They passed only one other employee, who spent too much of his brief glimpse marveling at Hormat's astonishing ugliness to notice how young Mike looked for a maintenance man. Mike spent part of the time savoring the word Annie had used. "Brilliant." Secretly he didn't see what had been so brilliant. He'd needed a place where they could all be alone and talk in safety and privacy—and of course he dared not take the enormous risk of letting the time-travelers know just where he and Annie lived, or the secondary risk that they might be followed there by more of Conway's thugs. The underground vehicle depot was the only handy place he could think of that would serve. But if Annie thought it an inspired choice, who was he to argue?

THEY HAD TO briefly go above ground again, to get to the stairway that was the only practical entry to the garage. Mike looked around carefully during the brief interval of exposure, but saw no one who was paying the slightest bit of attention to them. Not surprising: Firefall was in progress, and everyone was looking up. He yearned to stop and watch it himself. Nonetheless, he felt safer when the stairwell door closed behind them, and they were Under again.

He was also a little relieved that neither Hormat nor Durl had taken the opportunity to try and bail on him. For the life of him he couldn't imagine how he might have stopped them if they had—he wouldn't have dared to so much as yell after them as they faded into the crowd.

The garage was empty of thugs this time. The thought made Mike squirm just a little inside. Everything that was about to happen now would depend on convincing these time-travelers that he and Annie were the Good Guys . . . and here he was only meters from the very spot where he had almost shot a man, and where Annie had beaten and humiliated the guy.

He went over and checked, and the grille he'd used to enter the room the last time was still the way he'd left it: in place, but with its fastening screws missing. Good to know there was an escape hatch in case of need. When he turned around, the two Trolls were walking down the middle of the vast room, staring around as though it were interesting. They seemed to be muttering to each other under their breath. He had the odd idea that there was something odd about them, something strange about the way they walked, but he couldn't figure out what. Trolls always walked funny.

Mike studied the available vehicles, picked out a huge Glory Road float from Heinlein's Worlds that had three seats up front to accommodate the performers who played Scar, Star, and Rufo. He went to it, climbed up into Scar's seat, and waved the Trolls over to join him. After some hesitation, they did. Hormat chose Star's seat in the center, and Durl took Rufo's chair at Star's left hand.

"So," Mike said, "what year are you guys from?"

Durl made a strangled little groaning sound.

"We do not use your numbering system—," Hormat began.

"Of course not," Mike said, "but you must *know*. Jeez tell me how many years you came back and I'll do the math myself."

Hormat sighed. "We will not reveal that information."

Mike nodded philosophically. "Yeah, that's what I thought you'd say. You've got to avoid paradox."

Hormat's eyes narrowed, and Durl made another of those little gargling sounds. "The danger you *understand*?" Durl said.

Mike rolled his eyes and grimaced. "No. I'm like totally four-oh-four, and I want you to tell me which stocks are gonna go up next week so I can be the first child billionaire." He saw their expressions. "Jesus, don't they have sarcasm in your time? I know all about time paradox, nimrods! For your information, I've been reading science fiction since I was a little kid."

This time there was nothing strangled about Durl's groan: he just let it out. Hormat coughed into his hand suddenly and got all red in the face.

"Why us?" Durl moaned. "The worst *possible*—"

"Who were those two men," Hormat interrupted. "Why were they trying to capture us?"

Just then footsteps sounded in the stairwell. Durl sprang to his feet and jumped down to the ground, then stood uncertain which way to flee. Hormat didn't appear to move, but suddenly he was alert as a cat. Mike had been expecting footsteps, but his heart hammered nonetheless. Were these the *right* footsteps?

"It's me," his wristband said, and he let out his breath.

"Relax, guys," he told his guests. "It's Annie."

They did not relax until she appeared alone in the doorway, and didn't relax very far even then. They watched her very carefully as she approached.

Mike got down from his seat and waved Annie to take it, rolling a nearby battery-charging unit over to the float and perching on that. As she passed him, she caught his eye and slipped him a wink. Durl waited until she was seated before reseating himself.

Mike was terribly relieved to have Annie with him again. He had been doing a solo for too long, juggling heavy responsibility with no backup. Just the sight of her serenely twinkling eyes was enough to begin unknotting the muscles at the base of his neck. "Hormat and Durl," he said, pointing out each as he named them, "this is my friend Annie."

Somehow the way she was sitting made Mike think of a queen. She inclined her head to each of the Trolls in turn. "Hormat, Durl, I bid you welcome. Welcome to 2023, welcome to Dreamworld, and welcome to Dreamworld Under, my home." She offered her hand.

Durl began to speak, but Hormat restrained him with a glance, took her hand, and clasped it formally. "Thank you, Annie." Mike noticed he had begun to sit up straighter himself as soon as Annie had started speaking. "We are pleased to be here, but regret that our time is short. If you permit, let us speak at once of urgent matters. There are things my friend and I *must* know."

She released his hand and nodded. "Of course, Hormat," she said imperturbably. "What things?"

The Troll closed his eyes a moment in thought. He was much uglier with his eyes closed; something about them helped take a little of the sting off, it seemed to Mike.

"First," he said, "do you understand the danger, if what we are were to become public knowledge?"

"Or even *private* knowledge," Durl couldn't resist adding.

Annie looked grave. "I do. All of history, perhaps all of reality, is at stake. Forgive me if I say that I suspect I may understand the danger better than *you*. In your place I don't know that I would have made the trip."

Hormat and Durl exchanged a glance. Mike couldn't read it.

"You said time is short," she reminded them. "Can you prioritize the rest of your questions?"

Hormat turned back to her and nodded. He closed his eyes again. "How many know about us?" he began slowly. "*How* do you know about us? Who are those others who stalked us? What do they know? What do they want?" He opened his eyes. "Who are *you*, and Mike? What is your position here at Dreamworld? What do *you* want?"

Mike realized Hormat thought he and Annie really worked here, on the Dreamworld Staff, and he did his best to keep his face blank.

"Is that everything?" Annie asked.

Hormat gestured Durl into silence. "The important ones," he agreed, and seemed to inspect one of his fingernails. Mike saw that there was a little digital display on his fingertip. "And I hope you can answer them all in fourteen minutes, for we *must* leave by then."

"That will depend on how much of those fourteen minutes get used up first in answering *my* questions," Annie said.

Hormat's face did not fall, having nowhere to fall. But he looked unhappy. Durl's squint became pronounced enough that he appeared to be trying to retract his nose. "Please list them," Hormat said.

"I already tried asking them what year they're from," Mike said. "They won't say." He half expected to be glared at for interrupting the grown-ups' palaver, but he'd felt she needed the information.

Annie apparently did not classify him as a child. "Thank you, Mike," she said politely. "But that would not have been on my list. I can't think of any good it would do me to know that."

Hormat looked mildly surprised.

"My list is much shorter," she told him. "I have only two questions for now." She held up a finger. "One: what is wrong with you?" She held up a second finger beside the first. "And two: what is wrong with you?" Both fingers went down. "If you don't mind my asking."

The two Trolls exchanged a long glance. Finally Hormat

shrugged and turned back to Annie. "I do not understand your question . . . or questions. Can you expand them?"

Annie nodded with grave dignity. "Certainly. First, what is wrong with you two—physically? Are you ill?"

For a moment Mike still didn't get it, couldn't see what she was talking about. And then all of a sudden he remembered his earlier, half-grasped intuition that there was something elusively wrong with the way Hormat and Durl walked, and understood what it was.

Trolls *always* walked funny. That was how you could tell them from Dwarves, even at a distance. They walked in a heavy slow shamble, bent-backed and weary, shoulders bowed and arms swinging of their own weight, like bears just awakened from hibernation and beginning to think about breakfast. They walked funny, and they moved ponderously, as if each move cost them an effort. That was the proper way to walk, if you were in character as a Troll.

But Hormat and Durl had walked and acted that way even after they were Under—even after they reached the garage, where there was no one to see them. Mike himself had stopped projecting *I am a grown-up midget maintenance man* the moment they'd arrived, without even thinking about it. But now that Annie called his attention to it, the Trolls, even sitting still, looked *old*, somehow . . . or sick . . . or maybe just very tired.

Even as Mike was grasping that, Hormat answered stiffly, "And your second question?"

"Is more general," Annie went on. "It applies not just to you two but to all of your companions, and I don't believe I can make it any clearer than that. Perhaps emphasis would be of some help." Suddenly she was roaring at the top of her voice. *"What the hell is wrong with you idiots?"*

Each Troll, on either side of her, recoiled slightly from the whiplash of her voice. Mike flinched, too.

Annie spoke directly to Hormat. "You have risked every hope and dream there ever was or ever can be; you are gambling with a *universe*—with *my* universe—and you have the colossal effront-ery to ask *me* if *I* understand the dangers? Ever since I learned what you are, I have racked my brains, trying to conceive of any possible purpose you might have that could justify such a mon-strous irresponsibility, such criminal optimism, and I come up with nothing. I think there *is* no sane purpose for time-travel. I think you are all either nitwits or fanatics, and I am asking you which."

Durl's face had gone pale as she spoke, but Hormat's had red-dened; by now he was purple. He opened his mouth to speak.

Annie interrupted him. "I warn you in advance, if I don't get an answer that satisfies me, I'm going to stop you. I'll screw up your whole operation and send you all back home."

Mike wondered if she was bluffing. The more he studied her, the less sure he was.

Hormat closed his eyes, seemed to count to twenty, and tried, "Please . . . accept my assurance, on my word of honor, that if I *could* explain our purpose in your time, you would wish to help us. Any healthy mind would."

Durl nodded vigorously. "Truth he speaks! But explain we dare not."

Annie shook her head. "Not good enough. See here: you've been in operation less than two weeks, and already *two different groups* know about you—and you know *nothing* about the second group, wouldn't know them if you walked past one of them. You don't even know how lucky you are that we got to you before they did. You're walking on the edge of utter disaster and you're trying to be coy. I say you're not bright enough or not adequately prepared to do what you're doing. You need help from a local of demonstrated goodwill."

Hormat clenched his hands, squeezed until the knuckles whit-ened, and bowed his head in thought.

"I have all the answers you need," Annie lied, "and my min-imum price for them is all the answers I want. Starting with why I should lift a finger to help you. Ante up or get out of my time. I believe you have about seven minutes left."

Hormat glanced involuntarily at his fingertip, and then his massive shoulders slumped.

"Tell them, Hormat," Durl blurted.

Hormat sat up straight, very straight. "I *cannot* tell you what you want to know. I do not have the authority."

Annie nodded. "All right. But there is *someone* on this planet in this time who can. Tell your principal to post a message on the Big Board in the Octagon, from Hormat to Mother, proposing a time and place for us to meet and settle this matter. I'll reply the same way if necessary. Until he or she comes and speaks to me, face-to-face, *don't try to bring any more shifts through.* You don't know how to protect them. More important, you don't have my permission to try. I'll wait to be contacted until Closing tomorrow night. After that, all bets are off. Good day, gentlemen. Mike will see you back Topside if you wish. Thank you for your time."

Hormat stared at her for a long moment. Then he sighed and got wearily to his feet. "Thank you for yours. We will find our own way." He climbed down from the float with elaborate care, looking oddly like an outsized infant making his way down his first staircase.

Durl made an involuntary little squeak sound, barely audible, and heaved himself erect as well. "Hormat—"

"Durl."

Durl glanced at his own fingertip and got down from the float without another word. The two Trolls trudged away as if they were on their way to their own execution. Mike felt like saying something, but didn't know what. Annie merely watched them go in silence.

Halfway to the stairwell door, Hormat turned and called back to her, spacing his words so the echo wouldn't obscure them. "In your place, I would bargain just as hard."

She nodded.

"I wish you were stupider," he added, and continued on his way.

Only after he and Durl had gone, and only just loud enough

for Mike to hear, did Annie say, "I've often had that same wish, sonny." She got down from her own perch, and said, a little louder, "Oddly, right at the moment I wish I were smarter."

"I don't," Mike said. "That was great."

She smiled. "It wasn't bad, was it? Come on down from there, and let's head for China. We'll go by Callahan's Place and get some really good coffee." She frowned and slapped her hip. "Oh, shit. It's after Firefall. We'll have to drink *my* coffee."

Mike broke up. After a minute, she did, too, and they were still chuckling when they reached the stairs.

He stopped on the second stair—climbing and chuckling both. "Annie?"

"What is it, Mike?" She picked up on the uneasiness in his voice and stopped climbing, too.

He hesitated before replying. He was tired, both physically and emotionally—it had been a very long day, and all he wanted in the world was to go back to Annie's and read in bed for an hour or so, to let the events of the day sort themselves out in his subconscious, then go to sleep. But the question would not stop nagging at him. "Why were they in a hurry?"

Vertical wrinkles appeared between her eyebrows. "Hormat and Durl? Why, it's closing t . . ." She trailed off.

"It's closing time for *Guests*. They're supposed to be Staff. They can't leave for at least another hour."

Now the vertical wrinkles had horizontal ones above them. "What the *hell* are they all going to *do* for an hour, the six of them, without a crowd to hide in? They have to go to ground somewhere until it's time to clock out—but *where*?" She sat down on the step, scrunched her eyes shut, cocked her head at that odd angle people use when they're retrieving memories from deep storage, and concentrated.

Mike waited confidently. Nobody knew Dreamworld like Annie. Nobody. To fill the time, he checked his appearance. He was going to have to play a grown-up midget maintenance man again, all the way back home. And without the help of Annie's makeup job, which he'd wiped off—good thing the light Topside was poor now—

"Oh my," she said softly. She opened her eyes and stared at nothing. "Oh my," she said again, louder. Then she sprang to her feet. "*Cushlamachree*," she cried, and started up the stairs at high speed.

Mike stared after her, caught by surprise.

"Come *on*, boy," she snapped over her shoulder. "We've got to hurry!"

He shook off his stasis and scrambled up the stairs after her, his calf muscles complaining bitterly. This hero business sucked big rocks.

CHAPTER 12

LIARS' POKER

Conway was pleased. After a disastrous start, the day was improving. Things were working out, if anything, even better than he had planned. So much so that he decided he could afford the luxury of improvising a little. The bogus Trolls were exactly where he'd guessed they must be: in the Employees' Lounge, mingling with the forty or fifty other genuine workers fortunate or industrious enough to have completed their shutdown responsibilities early. Or rather, the Trolls were *not* mingling: again, just as he'd guessed they would be, they were pretending to play cards for matches—the most plausible way to keep to themselves for half an hour or so, until the exodus to the parking lot began.

The interesting part was, there were only four of them tonight.

Conway had been planning simply to keep them under covert but close observation here, and then have his men take them on their way out—as many of them as he could get without raising a disturbance. If they'd been the usual half dozen, the same as the previous days, he would have done just that: kept an eye on them and kept his distance until they left, then followed them out and fingered them for his men.

But you could ask to sit in, at a table with only *four* card players. . . .

The impulse was irresistible to him. He went to their table, pulled out one of the empty chairs, and waited with a politely raised eyebrow. They broke off their muttered conversation and stared up at him. Nobody said a word.

"Okay if I sit in?" Conway asked, pitching his voice and body language to indicate that a positive answer was expected. When there was still no reply, he picked out the tallest Troll, one with an expression of permanent indignation who happened to be closest to him, and locked eyes with him. "Or is that a problem?" he asked.

One of the others started to say something, but the indignant one silenced him with a sharp gesture. "Not at all," he said. "Join us."

Conway sat beside him at once, on his right, and studied the cards on the table. "Five-card draw, huh? Is anything wild?"

Again there was silence. He looked up to see poker faces. "No," the indignant one said, sounding somehow as if he were guessing the answer on a multiple-choice quiz.

Conway nodded. "Fine. Whose deal?"

"Mine." The Troll gathered in the cards and began shuffling.

"Are we, uh, playing for anything besides matches?" He let his voice and expression suggest that if they were secretly playing for real money—gambling on company property in violation of policy, and settling up in the parking lot later—he was willing to play along and wanted to be included.

The dealer's face turned to stone. Conway looked at the others, saw nothing but blank stares. He put on his *Come on, do I look like a stool pigeon?* face and waited.

The dealer glanced around at his mates and cleared his throat. "We play for Dreamworld," he said.

Conway had recourse to his own poker face. He could tell everyone was studying it. The dwarf had spoken firmly . . . but his body language as much as his incomprehensible answer told Conway plain as day that he was bluffing—bravely and hopelessly. Somehow he had failed absolutely to understand Conway's question, and so had everyone here, and none of them wanted to admit it.

Something very funny was going on.

What kind of people were unfamiliar with the concept of playing cards for stakes?

This had been a bad idea. If he spooked them now, they might bolt early, before his men were in position out in the parking lot.

All this went through his mind in the time it took him to draw breath; he had begun nodding the instant the Troll had finished speaking. "Fine," he said, as though the Troll's answer made sense. "Let's do it." He took out a pack of matches and began pulling out individual matches to bet with.

The dealer looked even more indignant than ever, and began passing out the cards. In Conway's professional estimation, he had been playing poker for a maximum of a week, and had learned how from a video. Conway carefully kept this awareness from showing on his face.

"My name's Scotty," he said while the hand was being dealt.

The dealer said his name was Al. The one next on his left was Bob. The third was Carl. The fourth one visibly hesitated, rejected his first choice—which Conway was certain would have started with *D*—and picked Robert.

By now Conway's expression had petrified. He simply acknowledged each name as it was given. Nor did he appear to notice that none of the other players sorted their cards after picking them up. But by now he was thinking so hard and fast that he might as well have been in combat.

His own hand, he noted, was one of the worst he'd ever been dealt. No pairs, all suits represented. When the time came, he took three cards. He ended up with a hand that was, if anything, even worse: a bogus straight, jack, queen, king, ace, two.

He followed his hunch and bet heavily.

Nobody raised; everybody called. "Carl" had the winning hand: two pairs, kings high. Conway put down his own cards with a triumphant smile, said, "I win," and started to rake in the pot.

Nobody objected.

Even Conway was having trouble keeping a poker face by now. Eskimos knew how to play poker. Cannibals in the Micronesian Islands knew how to play poker. What *planet* were these guys—

The thought detonated in his brain, and quite involuntarily his fingers clenched tightly around the double handful of matches he had just collected.

"Why don't you quit while you're ahead?" said a rumbling voice at his elbow.

Matches went flying.

In his defense, it had been a long time since anyone had successfully sneaked up on Conway. And it had never been done by a dwarf before: having the sudden voice come from that close to the ground was unnatural and helped to spook him. Even so, he managed to refrain from going for his weapon. His head snapped around so fast he heard the tendons crack.

The missing two Trolls had finally arrived. "Ed" and "Frank," no doubt. One with thundercloud eyebrows, a hairy nose, and a pendulous lower lip; the other one a bit shorter and afflicted with a terrifying squint. Hairy Nose seemed to be the one who had spoken. "We're Hormat and Durl, and we usually play with these men," he went on. "Sorry we're late."

"Certainly," Conway said smoothly. "I hope you don't mind me keeping your chair warm." He began to rise.

"Oh, don't get up." Hairy Nose laid a heavy hand casually on Conway's right shoulder—Conway permitted this, since he did not shoot right-handed—and sank into the empty chair on that side of him. "At least you can watch the game."

The squinty one pulled up a nearby chair and sat on the other side of him. Conway spun his head that way and met one of the most skeptical gazes he had ever seen. "Hello," the dwarf said, and squinted even harder. His voice was a little higher than the other one's, and less hoarse.

"Durl is just learning the game," the one behind him said. "Perhaps you can coach him."

Conway started to turn back to the speaker, but got sidetracked on the way. All four original Trolls were *staring*, card game for-gotten. Not just at him, but at their two late-arriving buddies as well.

He realized suddenly that Hairy Nose still had a hand resting on his shoulder, and completed the motion of turning his head to face him. He found the dwarf's index finger scant centimeters from his face, approaching fast. "Something on your upper lip," the dwarf said.

Conway knew at once what the dwarf intended, held his breath, and prepared to start pretending he was inhaling whatever was on that finger. But instead of hovering below his nostrils, the damned finger thrust itself insolently up the left one! Startled, he still managed to keep from inhaling and yanked his head away at once—but it didn't matter: instant spreading numbness in his face explained to him that the drug was not an aerosol but a grease of some kind that worked on contact with mucous membranes. He had to admire the dwarf, even as he tried to curse him and failed to make his mouth obey.

Already he was reaching for his hip pocket—but as he did so the weakness came on so fast he knew he'd never get the gun out before he lost the strength to grasp it. Better not to try. He took his right hand back out of his pocket empty, managed to get a weak grip on the wrist of the squinty dwarf beside him with his other hand, and then lost consciousness. His last coherent thought was that the squinty dwarf had a strikingly slender, almost childish wrist for a Troll.

CHAPTER 13

HUNTING TIGER

Mike couldn't keep from grinning, even though it threatened to crack the heavy brows of his Troll makeup. Annie sure knew how to do some cool stuff. He freed his wrist from Conway's limp fingers, slid his chair sideways, and leaned in to keep Conway from falling over.

Annie wiped her finger off on Conway's upper lip, wiped it off again carefully with his shirt. Her movements were unhurried, methodical. From a breast pocket she retrieved the little vial she'd dipped her finger into a moment ago, replaced the cap, and put it away. Then she pulled up a chair and sat on Conway's other side, positioning herself to help Mike brace him upright.

"I'm Annie," she said to the tableful of gaping Trolls, "and this is my friend Mike. *This* guy," she went on, pretending to give Conway's slack cheek an affectionate squeeze, "is bad news—or rather, was. He doesn't know what you are, but he and some powerful friends want to find out very badly."

" 'What we are . . .'?" the Troll who had dealt the cards repeated, frowning. Karf, Hormat had said his name was, the team leader.

"When you're from, Karf," Annie said quietly.

Everyone at the table became as still as Conway.

"Don't worry. The real Hormat and Durl will be along in a second; they can tell you all about it."

They came a few seconds later, arriving just as Mike and Annie had perfected the combination of chair placement and elbows necessary to keep Conway upright inconspicuously.

"Pull up a chair, fellows," Annie said to them.

Karf said, "We should go now." It was clear to Mike from his voice that he was on the verge of panic. "Right now. Family illness we can claim—"

"Pardon me, but that's exactly what you shouldn't do," she told him. "Tell him, Hormat."

The team leader's eyes widened.

"Truth she speaks," Hormat agreed quickly. "Hunters for us outside wait."

Everyone at the table flinched in sudden panic.

"Relax," Annie said. "Keep your cover. Without this fellow here to spot for them, they have no way of knowing which Dwarves are you . . . *unless* you call attention to yourselves by leaving before the crowd. Just stick to your original plan, play cards for another twenty minutes or so and leave with the rest, and you should get clear. We'll take care of this one after you're gone."

Karf and Hormat exchanged several thousand words by eye contact, and Mike had the feeling the team leader was considering some sort of drastic action. Apparently Hormat had eloquent eyes; Mike saw Karf reluctantly change his mind.

The card game resumed.

Mike glanced surreptitiously at Conway, wedged between himself and Annie, and saw that he was doing an absolutely splendid job of seeming to be conscious. His sunglasses and baseball cap helped a lot, he was so fit that his spine and neck seemed to *prefer* being upright, and he slept with his mouth closed. It even seemed to curl in a faint feral smile. His own personality conspired against him.

Mike put his attention back on the game. At first he made a point of pretending to kibitz, to keep any outsiders from trying to strike up a conversation with him. Then as boredom set in, he began to watch in earnest—and realized the Trolls were rotten poker players. He caught Annie's eye after he saw Durl fold a flush. She kept her face straight and pointedly looked away after a moment.

The lounge gradually began to fill with chattering employees from two directions: early-arriving employees, who mostly passed right on through on their way to the locker rooms, and departing employees, who remained here to wait out the final minutes of their shift. Soon the room was crowded with milling people of all sizes and shapes, some still in costume and some in mufti, most displaying the weary exuberance of those about to leave work. The card game formed an unnoticed island in the midst of the commotion.

Mike found it fascinating to study Karf's face. Once, years ago, at a time when Mike had been just dying to pee, but was blocks and blocks from anywhere he could possibly do so, he had caught a glimpse of his own face in a store window. Karf looked like that now. He must have had a million questions for Annie, or at least for Hormat, and he was obviously *burning* to ask them. But he was *not* going to ask a single one of them here and now, while there was the slightest chance that some passing stranger might overhear something compromising. Not even in a murmur, for Hormat might well whisper back something that would cause him to raise his own voice involuntarily. Mike was impressed with Karf's discipline.

Karf looked up from his cards and met Mike's eyes for a long moment. Mike did his best to send the nonverbal message *we mean you no harm*, but the squad leader looked dubious. Mike realized his own Troll makeup probably wasn't helping.

"Any you happena know how the Giants done?" came a booming voice from above and behind Mike.

Karf covered quickly and well, glancing down at his cards. Because Mike happened to be staring directly at his eyes, only he of all of them instantly understood that Karf's brain had just over-loaded and crashed. Karf had absolutely no idea what the question meant, had no clue how to answer it, and had far too many urgent things to think about already: all his circuits were fused. All the other time-travelers would wait for their squad leader to take the lead; by the time they realized he was frozen, and manufactured some response, a most suspicious hesitation would have occurred. Annie couldn't know anything about sports—hell, she didn't even watch the news. Mike craned his head around to face the newcomer, for the first time in his life wishing to God *he* followed sports.

Inspiration came to him in the time it took him to turn his head: he grimaced and, remembering at the last microsecond to deepen his voice, growled, "Christ, how do you *think* they did?"

"Shit," the man said, and let his shoulders slump slightly. He was of taller than normal height, which must have helped confuse Karf as to what he'd meant by "giants." He was a Cousin, already changed into street clothes.

"You got that right," Annie said. "I don't even watch anymore."

Still craning his neck to look up at the tall Cousin, Mike kicked Karf's foot under the table. "Me, either," Karf blurted.

"I also stopped," Durl said, and a few of the other Trolls had the presence of mind to mumble agreement.

The Cousin looked mournful. "If only they got rid of you-know-who. . . ."

"Not much chance of that," Mike hazarded.

"Why not?" the man asked argumentatively.

Mike was lost now. He put on a knowing look, winked up at the guy, and said, "Think about it."

There was a pause, and then the Cousin said, "Oh, I get you. Yeah, sure."

I bluffed him, Mike thought. *He has no idea what* I'm *talking about, but he doesn't want to admit it and look dumb.* Mike's neck was getting stiff from looking up and over his shoulder at the man. He decided there was no reason to hide the fact, reached up, and began massaging his vertebrae.

The guy took the hint. "Didn't mean to hold up your game, guys. Catch you later."

"Later," Mike agreed, and a ragged chorus of muttered "Later"s came from several of the others at the table. The man left and headed for the exit.

"Nice work, Mike," Annie murmured.

He had completely forgotten about Conway the moment the Cousin had spoken, had ceased to do his half of holding Conway's sleeping body upright. He saw now that Annie had picked up the slack for him: she had an unobtrusive death grip on Conway's belt. "You, too," he said, and leaned back inward and braced himself so she could let go.

Karf was staring at him. "Thank you," he said, meaning it.

Mike blushed. "My pleasure," he said.

Karf stared even closer. Suddenly Mike understood. Karf was trying to figure out how old he was. Mike was presently in character as an adult midget maintenance man, using the adult voice and mannerisms that had been fooling other adults for days now, but something had cued Karf that he was really a kid. The time-traveling Troll opened his mouth to ask the question, and Mike stared back expressionlessly and dared him to ask it, and Karf closed his mouth and went back to his cards.

Mike's triceps began to ache from the strain of holding Conway vertical with his elbow, and he remembered a minor question that had been nagging at him. He knew Annie would have some brilliant answer for it, but he decided it was time to learn what it was. The room was filling fast, and soon it would be time to do whatever it was she had planned. He turned and muttered past Conway to her, too softly for the others to hear. "So what do we do about this guy?"

She shrugged. "Any suggestions?" she murmured back.

Mike was horror-struck. He realized at the last instant that he'd never be able to control his voice if he spoke aloud, so he only lip-synched the words *You haven't got a plan?*

She shook her head.

Unable to consult his wristband without dropping Conway, he looked wildly around the room, located a clock. In a few minutes this room was going to empty out, and it would be time for all of them to leave. Karf and Hormat and Durl and their friends out to the parking lot, and from there to wherever their next port of call might be; Mike and Annie back into Dreamworld. But it was going to be very difficult for them to walk away from a large muscular man who could not sit upright unassisted, without drawing attention to themselves.

Mike sat there and thought furiously, turning over possible scenarios in his mind. None of them worked, even in his fantasies. Seconds ticked away, then minutes. People around him perceptibly began to gather themselves to leave, and Mike began to panic. If Annie couldn't think of anything, what the hell was he supposed to do? He sneaked another look at her. She seemed utterly serene . . . but by now he knew her well enough to realize that she was badly worried herself. His heart sank.

He glanced away. Not wanting to meet the eyes of any of the time-travelers and spook them, he looked at the people nearest the table, employees standing around waiting for the hour to strike. Two of them caught his eye, and suddenly a ludicrous picture formed in his mind. His arm throbbed from the strain of supporting Conway.

He measured angles, made his decision, turned to Annie and said, "Follow my lead."

Her eyes widened slightly, and she nodded.

Just then there came the sound of a bell being gently struck three times.

The room came alive, and under cover of the commotion he said, "Everybody stand up," just loud enough for the table to hear, and, "Help me get him up," to Annie.

Between them they got Conway to his feet plausibly. All the Trolls likewise stood up, looking uncertain. Karf gathered in the cards, frowning ferociously.

"Good-bye," Mike said to them, and nodded toward the exit. They needed no further urging and left at once.

"Let me have him," Mike said, and when Annie let go of Conway, Mike gave him a twist and a shove that caused him to fall headlong in front of the two employees he'd picked out. He landed bonelessly and hard, blocking their path.

"His heart," Mike cried. "He stood up fast and then said something about his heart—"

The two employees bent over Conway, solicitous looks on their faces. Others were watching, but only with idle curiosity. Nothing really bad could happen to you in Dreamworld. Once they were sure Conway wasn't someone they knew, and the problem was being dealt with, most glanced away and continued heading for the door.

"Start CPR," Mike barked at one of them, and "You—help him," at the other. They nodded and obeyed.

Annie was staring at him. Past her he could see the time-travelers approaching the exit, not looking back. As he watched, the first of them passed out the doors.

"His brother just went on shift at Power House Three," Mike snapped at Annie. "Go tell him what happened. I'll get the Healers." He spun her, pushed her ahead of him, and together they ran back into Dreamworld.

Mike couldn't help grinning as he left the room. Properly done, cardiopulmonary resuscitation often broke ribs, and every Dreamworld employee had passed the course. The one Mike had chosen to administer it was a Frost Giant, muscled like a movie barbarian. If having his chest compressed by a monster brought Conway out of his drugged stupor, he would find himself being kissed by a Bearded Lady from The China That Never Was who, Mike happened to know, had remarkably bad breath.

His feet seemed to have wings. This was *fun*.

• • •

THEY USED MAXIMUM caution in returning to Annie's place, doubling back on their tracks four times, but saw no signs of pursuit or surveillance.

It was uniquely exhilarating for Mike to stride through Dreamworld victorious, and full of secrets so marvelous that Thomas Immega himself would gasp to hear them. This whole vast colorful kaleidoscope of compatible fantasies that he loved so well seemed to shimmer around him, more real than it had ever been, more real than Mike had ever dreamed anything but pain could be. He had entered it fully at last; he was a genuine sidekick. Whenever they were above ground, along the way everyone they passed seemed to smile at him. Whenever they were Under, other employees grinned at him. Yet he was absolutely certain that he was not smiling himself: he was doing his best to imitate a sober adult maintenance man just coming on shift. But people smiled. Since none of them challenged his right to be Under, he decided not to fret about it.

Once they were safely back home, with the door sealed, Mike allowed himself a muffled whoop and a victory dance. "We *did* it, Annie!" Out of sheer exuberance, he tried to bring her into the dance. It was like trying to dance with a tree; he gave up at once. "Sorry."

"We did *what*, exactly?" she asked sourly.

He blinked. "Why, we—"

"We know that time-travelers are passing through Dreamworld. They know we know. Apart from that, things stand exactly as they were yesterday. All we basically accomplished today was to get home alive."

"So . . . that's good, right? What's wrong with survival? I can live with surv—"

"I was surviving just fine before you came along," she snapped, and turned away and walked very quickly to the bathroom and slammed the door behind her.

Mike was too shocked to move or call after her. He stood there staring stupidly at the closed bathroom door. The sound of running water from the sink came through the door, then intensified as she turned the taps wide open.

It was not ignorance that held Mike frozen. He knew what it meant when they locked themselves in the bathroom and ran the water loud. It was the shifting gears, the instant change from triumph to concern, from thinking of Annie as his partner in crime, hero to his sidekick, to thinking of her as a woman crying in the bathroom. Mike had been doing a lot of instant emotional 180s lately, and it didn't seem to be getting any easier with experience. His thoughts came slow and hard, like footsteps in deep mud.

She's crying in there. Got to make her stop. Why is she crying? Doesn't matter, gotta make her stop. If they go in there and cry and you don't make them stop, sometimes they try and die in there. Hard to make them stop, though. Be even harder, not even knowing what she's crying about. What's she crying about?

The question was beyond him; his first instinct was to take it to some older, wiser head . . . like Annie. Briefly he fantasized himself knocking on the door and asking Annie to advise him. But then he heard a sob over the sound of the rushing water, and: *gotta make her stop!* so he thought about it some more.

What's happened that Annie might be sad about?

Well, let's see. Her whole life turned upside down without warning. Thirteen years of hermitage shot to hell. Her beloved home threatened by unknown forces of two different kinds, both terrifyingly powerful, both with unknown motives and agendas. The past twenty-four hours spent basically scrambling to stay alive and maintain her status Under, bluffing on a tightrope in a high wind. With a partner who thinks the whole thing is the neatest adventure ever. And all she can do now is try and get a night's sleep and wait to see who contacts her first tomorrow, Haines or the time-travelers, and hope she can keep outbluffing and out-thinking them.

Okay, maybe you know why she's crying now. Some of it, at least.

Maybe you anyway know enough to construct some sympathetic, soothing things to say. How do you get her to turn off the water and listen to you?

He went to the bathroom and knocked firmly. "Annie? No hurry, but I have to go."

The door opened almost at once. She had made no effort to disguise the fact that she'd been crying—but it was clear she had stopped. "I'm sorry, Mike."

"No problem," he said. "I could have waited."

"I'm sorry for what I said," she insisted. "None of this has been your fault."

"Oh, that," he said, shrugging it away. People when they cried said unforgettable, unforgivable things they didn't mean; everybody knew that. "No biggie. You were upset."

"That doesn't excuse it."

It doesn't? "Okay, then I excuse it."

She started to smile and stopped herself. "Thank you."

"Okay if I pee now?"

She did smile then, just a little, and stepped out of the doorway. "Sure."

"Too bad," he said. "I don't have to. I was bullshitting to get you to open the door."

Now she was grinning outright. "Then make us both some coffee, and soon you *will* have to pee. Meanwhile, we can discuss the events of the day together, and plan our strategy for tomorrow."

He grinned back. "Really?"

"Why, do you have to be up early for school in the morning or something?"

He hesitated. "Well, we have a big day tomorrow. Two important messages coming in. They could get posted two minutes after Opening. Actually, I'll be kind of surprised if they don't."

"I don't recall promising to pick up either message by any particular time. If they don't like the hours I keep, they can negotiate with somebody else. Let 'em stew—all of 'em! And let us brew . . ." She made a go-on gesture with her hands, and he went to make the coffee, and she went back into the bathroom and ran the taps again, this time to wash her face.

AN HOUR LATER Annie put down her empty second cup of coffee and frowned so ferociously that her eyes all but disappeared. "We're spinning our wheels," she said angrily. "Wasting good skull sweat."

Unused to coffee in the evening, Mike was still nursing his cold first cup. "We are kind of going in circles," he admitted.

"Everything depends on the answer to one question. The same one I asked Hormat. What in the name of God's golden gonads could they possibly be *doing* here, in our time? That's why I never believed in time-travel for longer than it took to read a good sci-fi novel—until I had my nose rubbed in it. Altering history is supposed to be utterly catastrophic—well beyond comparative trivia like nuclear winters or asteroid impacts. It seems axiomatic that stupid people don't develop time-travel. Having developed it, what purpose could induce a sensible person to risk *using* it?"

She got up and began the process of making herself a third cup of coffee. "I want to like these time-travelers," she said over her shoulder as she worked. "I've met them. They seem like decent enough people. Hormat impressed me, and none of them caused my Jerk Alarm to go off. Furthermore, anyone Haines sends a man like Conway after ought to be a friend of mine." She slid the filter basket into place, triggered the machine, and with her palms flat on the countertop, stood with her back to him long enough for the carafe to start filling. She lowered her head, and when she spoke again her voice was soft. "But after much thought, I have only one theory on what could have made them take the hair-raising risk of traveling back in time." She straightened and turned to face him.

"And?" Mike said.

"And, I really, really hate my theory."

She pushed away from the counter, came back, and resumed her seat. The only sound for a minute or so was the chuckle of the coffee dripping.

"Annie, Hormat and Durl are Good Guys," Mike began finally. "I'm sure of that."

"I know," she said angrily. "I said that. Good Guys can do bad things, Mike. For what seem to them good reasons."

He knew that was true.

She searched for words. "Try this: describe them in a single word. The way they act—all six of them. What is their predominant emotion?"

He thought about it, took a shot. "Scared?"

She nodded. "And what else?"

He thought harder. "I guess . . . well, sad."

She nodded again, more vigorously. "Yes! I'd have said 'resigned' myself. But 'sad' is just as close. With a subtle little flavor of something else I can't put my finger on."

He thought he knew what she meant. "Embarrassed," Mike suggested.

She nodded a third time and made a pointing gesture at him. "That's it. Embarrassed. Almost . . . almost ashamed."

"So?"

"Mike, they come across like refugees."

He blinked. "From what?"

The coffee had stopped dripping. She added cream and sugar, then opened a cabinet and took out a bottle of Irish whiskey, added a generous slug to the coffee. She took a deep experimental sip, sighed in approval, and brought the cup back to the table.

"I'm not sure," she said then. "But they're acting like people running for their lives, too terrified to count the risk. Either they're fleeing some unimaginable natural cataclysm, or . . ."

"Or what?" he asked, starting to get spooked. The fear in her voice, controlled though it was, was contagious.

She took a second long drink of her Irish coffee. "Or else maybe someone—or . . . something—is after them. I think they met up with something so horrible that they tore a hole in space and time and dove in to get away from it, and they're scared spitless it might come out of that hole after them at any moment."

"Like bad aliens. Real scary ones."

"That is the scenario that springs first to the mind."

Mike sat quite still and listened to his pulse roar. After what seemed a long time he said, "What are your views on kids drinking whiskey?"

She looked at him for almost as long. "I can't say," she said finally. "I've never seen one. Why don't you have some of this, and tomorrow I'll tell you what I thought." She handed him her cup, and he took a sip as large as the two she had taken.

It changed the flavor of the coffee in a way he was not sure he liked, tickling the roof of his mouth. But the warmth spread even faster than usual from his esophagus through the rest of his body. After a while his pulse slowed, and soon it was once again possible to fully inflate his lungs. As the symptoms of fear receded, so did the fear. Now he understood why grown-ups drank the stuff.

"If you stop right there," Annie said, "you'll stay calm, but you won't get stupid."

He nodded. "Why don't people always stop here, then?"

She grimaced. "Generally because they were stupid to begin with and don't notice any change."

He didn't want to think about that now. "Annie, what do we *do*?"

She sighed. "Silly as it sounds, I think we kill time until we start getting sleepy, and then fall asleep."

"*How?*"

"Reading is always good. Or you can Web-crawl, or play some game with the computer. And there's always laundry to be—" She saw his expression and stopped. "Okay. I know that's not how you meant the question. We get a good night's sleep because that's the only thing we can do. And it happens to be the smartest thing we can do as well, just now. We're not going to get any new information tonight, so we may as well maximize our ability to take advantage of the new information we're going to get tomorrow."

"Aren't you worried?"

She got up, went to the bed, and lay down. "Sure. Nothing wrong with fretting: it must be a good thing to do sometimes or the instinct wouldn't be so powerful. But I've *done* my fretting. I used it up. I fretted for over an hour and still didn't think of anything brilliant, so it's time to stop, before it becomes counterproductive." She gestured toward the coffee cup she'd abandoned. "Like booze: a little bit makes you smarter, a little bit more makes you stupider." She turned on the reading light over the bed, took a book from her bedside table, and settled herself more comfortably. "So the same rules apply: if you want to get drunk on it, it's all right with me. Just don't be noisy about it." She opened the book and began reading.

Mike opened his mouth, closed it again.

After a while he got up and put the cups in the sink. He decided to wash them, and when the sink was empty he decided to do the laundry and kept the water running. He was still fretting when he was done, but calm enough to consider reading. He decided he knew Cuppy too well; he needed novelty, so he picked up the Perry he'd been reading, found his place, and lay down beside Annie with it. At first he had to read each sentence two or three times to grasp its meaning, but within a page or two he was captured.

Presently he noticed that his eyelids were heavy and his focus blurry. He had read nearly sixty pages. He realized Annie had been asleep beside him for some time, not snoring but with a whistle in her breathing on the exhale that she would have suppressed if she'd been awake. She had fallen asleep with her clothes on. Okay, then he could, too. He glanced around, saw nothing within reach that would serve as a bookmark. He started to fold over the page corner—remembered it was Annie's book. Instead he tried to memorize the number of the page he was on. Page

83. An 83 is an 88 with a couple of pieces busted off the second digit. A busted 88 is a broken piano. What page am I on? Broken piano. The mnemonic was just goofy enough that he knew he would remember it. He closed the book, set it aside, flipped off the reading light, and was asleep before he had time to remember exactly what it was he wasn't fretting about.

BUT HE WAS not used to drinking coffee at night and woke after an hour or two of uneasy dreams. He could not remember their specifics, but the substance had been that he was in terrible danger. He seemed to recall a lot of fleeing from a Troll with Conway's face—nightmare fleeing, in which no amount of effort will widen the gap.

Mike emphatically did not believe that bad dreams were precursors of reality. He'd had many bad dreams that had failed to come true. But he knew he would not get back to sleep until he had exorcised the murky images somehow. Reading was always good in such cases, but if he turned the reading light back on he'd probably wake Annie. He considered playing Maelstrom on the computer, with the screen darkened and the sound turned low—but it seemed to him the computer had been shut down with its volume set all the way up: if he booted it now there would be a loud *bong* chime before he could turn the sound down.

He decided a short night walk might do the trick. Go up Johnny's Tree, watch the little blue microbots cleaning everything up, healing all the little accidental wounds inflicted on Dreamworld today by those who loved it a bit too hard—visible reminders that nothing in here could go wrong for very long. He slipped silently out of bed, located his shoes in the dark. He had to pee, badly, but there was no need to use Annie's sink—lots of places out there to pee; he'd made a study of them. Before leaving, he did his best to scribble a note—*Gone for a walk*—in the dark and left it on the table, just in case she woke while he was out.

He held his breath as he used his wristband to disable the door's security system—but the chirp sound, even though it sounded twice as loud as it did in daytime, did not wake Annie up. He stepped out into the alcove and decided against rearming the system until he'd come back from his walk. That way if it woke her the second time it chirped, he'd be there in person to reassure her. He checked his Command Band to make sure the corridor outside was empty, and stepped through the hologram wall and out into the corridor, squinting against the sudden comparative brightness. He felt very weary, but there was a mild exhilaration in being alone and footloose in Dreamworld, after hours.

Five minutes later he came to the service elevator that led up to the top of Johnny's Tree. He was so groggy he walked a few steps past it before snapping out of the fog. He turned and retraced those steps, and as he did so he heard a pair of odd sounds. A sort of *chuff!* in the distance, followed by a closer sound he vaguely recognized, just behind him. The sound of a dart sinking home in the dartboard. He glanced over his shoulder, saw a small dart sticking out of the corridor wall where none had been a moment ago. It made no sense to him, but even so his brain insisted on extrapolating its trajectory and forcing his eyes toward its probable point of origin, a branch corridor about ten meters distant. For a second he saw nothing there. Then he noticed a shoe tip.

He spun and raced down the corridor, took the first turn he could, banged through a door and sprinted up metal stairs, threw open another door at the top and exited at high speed. He was at ground level now, out in Dreamworld proper, customer country. Good news: dozens of directions to run. Bad news: the ground he was trying to run on was a seething carpet of blue cleaning microbots. They were programmed to recognize and avoid moving humans—but not running humans. Within five strides he was crunching them beneath his shoes. He knew they were only mindless machines, but he hated to destroy anything of Dreamworld's, and besides, their crushed remains would make it absurdly easy to track him.

He realized he was just passing the public elevator that led to the top of Johnny's Tree. Since he had just been spotted trying to take the service elevator to the same destination, it was probably the dumbest place he could make for now. That made it good misdirection. And at least he wouldn't be leaving an obvious trail anymore. He leaped for the elevator door, slapped at the button. The door hissed open at once and he thundered in, rebounded off the back wall, heard running footsteps outside, frantically slapped the button to close the door. It seemed to close in nightmare slow motion, while he fought not to pee in his pants. *Just* before it could close all the way, fingers appeared in it. At once it stopped closing and began opening again. Mike sank into a crouch. The doors parted to reveal a short broad man dressed entirely in black from head to foot, only his eyes showing. His right hand came up with some sort of sidearm in it, and Mike stopped breathing. Oddly, the man did not meet Mike's eyes. His weapon made a sound like a sewing machine and sprayed about a dozen more darts in a left-to-right pattern. Every one of them struck the back wall of the elevator—half a meter above Mike's head.

Of course—in this elevator, he was invisible! The magic was all turned off for the night, but there was no need to turn off the invisibility effect, since it only activated when it detected retinas.

He knew the shooter would realize his mistake in another moment. And once he stepped into the elevator, he would be invisible, too. Without hesitation Mike launched himself forward with all the power of his thighs and calves, ducking his head at the last instant. The top of his skull impacted the shooter's groin with great force; the shooter dropped his weapon and *flew* back out into the corridor, clutching at himself. Mike rebounded from him and collapsed on the floor. The doors slid shut again, unopposed this time. The elevator began to ascend.

Mike let his breath out in a great sigh of relief and got to his feet. He was safe now: he knew several ways down from Johnny's Tree, including a few unknown to the general public.

The elevator lurched to a halt.

The lights did not flicker, but somehow—instantly—there was someone there in the elevator with Mike. He leaped away, slammed against the wall, slid down into a defensive crouch again—and only then realized the new arrival was his own reflection in the elevator's mirrored wall. He was visible again! They'd shut down not just the motor but the invisibility effect as well.

Mike was wide awake now. Whoever was after him had the power to hack into Dreamworld engineering control systems, on short notice. Any minute somebody would be rappelling down the elevator cable from above, to catch him as he popped the emergency hatch and climbed out. If he tried to stay put, they could pop the hatch, train a gun on him, and *make* him climb up. He had read enough adventure stories to know what a "choke point" was, and realized now with shame that he had let himself be driven into one, herded like a sleepy cow into the chute, just like the clueless nimrod protagonist in any one of a hundred—

—wait a minute.

Mike had the power to hack into Dreamworld engineering control systems on short notice! His right index finger flew to his Command Band—paused centimeters away. Time came to a stop while he considered. His first instinct was to send the elevator hurtling skyward again, faster than normal, and try to get whoever was up there while they were on the way down. But . . . he might *kill* somebody that way. So far nobody had done anything worse than fire tranquilizer darts at him.

Who the hell was after him, anyway? Conway's men? Or the time-travelers? The man he'd just head-butted had been short, might have been either a short normal person or a tall dwarf. Mike hadn't noticed his face much, hypnotized by his weapon during the second or two he'd been visible. Mike was willing to risk killing one of Conway's men . . . but less willing to kill a time-traveler. And a third possibility occurred to him then: it was just barely possible that he himself had screwed up in some small way on the way here, dialed some lock code wrong or something out of fatigue—that could be Dreamworld Security out there hunting him! He *couldn't* risk killing or even injuring a Dreamworld employee, he just couldn't. Why, if it was them, they were just doing their job: he *was* an unauthorized intruder.

All this went through his head in a second or two. He would have dithered even longer, but heard faint noises overhead that he knew meant someone was coming down the cable. His finger stabbed at his Command Band. He left motor control carefully alone—but restored the elevator's special effects. His reflection on the walls went away.

Someone would lift the hatch and poke his head and the snout of a weapon down into the elevator, expecting to control Mike at once with it. In the second or two the guy would waste trying to figure out where the hell his quarry was, Mike would leap up and yank the weapon out of his hands, and then . . . well, then there'd probably be a standoff, but that would constitute an improvement in the situation.

Footsteps on the roof overhead. Mike crouched and got ready to spring.

The hatch opened.

But only a few centimeters. Nothing at all came through the crack.

Mike waited, heart pounding, gaze fixed intently on that slender gap. He wondered if he ought to leap up now, hit the hatch and smash it up into the face of whoever was up there. But the more he thought about it, the more it seemed that he had been so clever and brave and resourceful so far, nobody could possibly fault him if he took the opportunity to rest his eyes for just a second . . . well, just a minute or two . . . no need to open them until he heard the hatch move again, really . . . he was perfectly safe until then . . . in fact, now would be a good time to deal with that pesky pressure he'd been feeling in his bladder . . . yes, that felt good, no matter what Mommy said. . . .

Preoccupied with the good warm feeling, so long absent, he never felt his face hit the floor.

CHAPTER 14

BAD TIMES

"Broken piano," Mike said.

"What?"

"Broken piano," he repeated irritably.

"Hell is *that* supposed to mean?" the voice asked, but somehow Mike knew it was not asking him.

"He's just babbling," said another voice, just beyond the first one. "Takes them a while to come out of it."

Mike knew that voice. He tried to open his eyes, discovered they were already open. Apparently the universe had turned to beige nothingness, with a slight texture to it. Then focus came back, and with it peripheral vision. The textured nothingness was a painted beige ceiling. He was lying on his back looking up at it. He tried to get up, and failed. Then he tried to move his arms and legs, and failed again, for reasons he could not analyze.

"See?" said the second voice. "He'll be with us anytime now. Be patient."

Yes, it was Conway. This was bad. Very bad. Mike's head throbbed with the hammering of his pulse.

"I'm not a patient guy," the first voice said, coming closer as it spoke, and suddenly Mike was backhanded *hard* across the face. The blow snapped his head to the right, and when it rebounded to the left again he found himself facing the ugliest man he had ever seen in his life. Bald misshapen head, simian brows, ice green lizard eyes in wrinkled bags, greasy skin, fat jowls, tiny mouth with blubbery lips parted in a cruel smile. "Good morning, you little rat-bastard," he said happily.

Mike's eyes slid away. He saw his own outflung left arm and the leather wrist cuff that restrained it, inferred the other three cuffs, and immediately felt all four for the first time. They were quite snug, securely anchored. He was restrained spread-eagled on his back on some sort of X-shaped padded leather piece of furniture, at about waist height from the floor. Like most kids his age, Mike had seen such furniture a few times, on Usenet— enough to know at least vaguely what it was for. If it is possible for total terror to double, that is what happened to him then. If it had been possible to break his bonds, his titanic whole-body convulsion would have done so.

The ugly man laughed at him. Involuntarily Mike turned to look at him again, and again had to look away from that ghastly smile. This time he noticed Conway, standing just behind the ugly man. Conway was *not* smiling, had no expression on his face at all, and somehow that was even scarier.

Too much fear to be borne; in self-preservation Mike's brain converted it into rage, and he began screaming curses at the top of his lungs, the foulest words he knew followed by the direst threats he could concoct.

They simply let him exhaust himself. Then the ugly man— Mike realized he had to be Haines—leaned over him, smiling, and said, "Are you done now?"

Mike said nothing.

WHACK! A second slap, harder than the first. "I said, 'Are you done now?' "

Mike saw stars and tasted blood. Grudgingly, he nodded.

"Good. Before we start, here's how this discussion is going to go, from this point. I am going to ask you questions. You are going to give me immediate, responsive, accurate answers. Any-time you don't, and anytime I doubt one of your answers, something horrible is going to happen to you, and keep on happening until I like your answer better. You understand me?"

Mike hesitated and nodded again.

Haines smiled happily and shook his head. "I don't think you do," he said. "See, if you'd've understood me, you'd've said, 'Yes sir, Mr. Haines sir,' nice and loud, and right away. I don't think you're completely clear on what I mean by 'something horrible.' Conway, give him an idea of the kind of thing I'm talking about."

Conway stepped around Haines, lifted Mike's hand as far as the cuff would let him, and bent Mike's pinky backward until it popped out of the socket.

He fainted.

When his vision cleared, Haines's face was still hovering over his own. "We clear now, kid?" Haines asked cheerfully.

Mike nodded groggily. His pinky was a ball of agony; he tried to turn his head and look at it but his head would not obey him. This was worse than very bad. This was awful.

"He still didn't get the memo," Haines said. "Show him again."

"YESSIRMR.HAINESSIR!" Mike bellowed.

Haines giggled. "That's better. Never mind, Conway. Now we got the ground rules straight, we can have what they call substantive discussions. What's your name, kid?"

"Mike."

He realized belatedly he hadn't offered his last name, but Haines didn't press him for it, so he let it ride.

"And the midget bitch—what's *her* name?"

"Alice," Mike said without hesitation.

Haines sighed. "You just don't get it, do you, Mike? See, everybody's got a talent. Some guys can paint, some broads can sing, some guys can find oil in the middle of nowhere. Me, I always—always—can tell when somebody is lying to me."

Conway started forward.

"That's all right," Haines told him. "I'll get it."

Mike immediately balled his hands into fists, aware that the dislocated finger was still sticking out vulnerably . . . but instead Haines reached toward Mike's head, with something in his hand. Instinctively Mike turned away from it. Agony exploded in the top of his left ear and kept on getting worse.

"That's about number five in the Top Ten Worst Places to Use a Stapler," Haines said conversationally, "so you can see that you got maybe two more screwups max before things start getting *really* ugly. Ration them carefully. What's her name?"

"Annie," Mike cried, and felt a shame-bomb go off in his mind.

"Christ," Conway muttered. "Little chickenshit gave up his own mother."

They still thought he was Annie's son. Mike didn't correct the mistake; when you thought about it, Conway wasn't that far wrong. Annie was more to him than his mother had ever been. And he had just given her up.

"See how easy that was?" Haines said. "Now all you have to do is tell me where to find her and what the deal is with all the extra Trolls, and we're done here."

Like every young boy, Mike had wondered how he would behave under torture, if burdened with a secret more important than his life. This was turning out worse than even his most pessimistic fantasies. He had broken in less than a minute.

This was worse than awful. This was utter disaster. In about another half dozen questions, *everything* was going to be blown . . . and there was nothing Mike could do about it. In his childhood fantasies about a moment like this, there had always been an ultimate escape hatch, one he had read about in one of his favorite books and stored away. If you found you couldn't endure torture, you could always preserve honor by biting off your own tongue. Even if you didn't manage to drown in blood, you couldn't give away the Precious Secret to the Bad Guys if they couldn't understand what you were saying. He set his teeth tentatively on his tongue . . . and knew with a burst of sorrow that there was absolutely no chance he could make himself do it. Maybe later, when the pain got so bad his mind went, but certainly not until then.

For days now, off and on, Mike had been pretending to be an adult—confident, resourceful, and independent—and had succeeded so well in the impersonation that he had almost begun to fool himself. Even Annie had shown him respect due another adult. Now his new self-image imploded, and he knew he was a little kid and a coward. Probably the cowardly little kid who had doomed the universe, as if that made it any worse. He became aware of cool dampness at his crotch, remembered that he had pissed himself when they gassed him. He began to cry, and didn't even try to make himself stop. Why not add crybaby to the list?

They let him cry for some time, both seeming to enjoy it. Haines even chuckled aloud a few times. Mike had made them both very angry, over the last few days: this was the part they had been looking forward to most. The actual interrogation to come was merely business; no hurry. Mike's understanding of this fueled his sobs—and they knew that, too, and savored it—and he knew that, but still couldn't help himself. At least it delayed things.

As he bawled, it slowly came to him that this was all he could do: delay the interrogation. There was no point to it—there was no cavalry to come to the rescue. Even if by some miracle she knew he was missing, Annie *never* left Dreamworld—and even if she made a once-in-thirteen-years exception for him, Mike knew she could hardly have the means to track a creature like Conway to his lair. Stalling was utterly futile.

But it was a thing he could do . . . and absolutely the only other things he could do were betray his trust or be tortured.

So he didn't stop crying when he could have, dragged it out until he was afraid that Haines, with his eerie instinct for lies, was beginning to suspect. He tapered off at once, wiped his nose as best he could on the shoulder of his T-shirt, and spoke before either Haines or Conway could resume grilling him. "How did you guys ever catch me?"

As he'd suspected, they were delighted to pause and discuss their own cleverness; it was the digression most adults were a sucker for. Even cowardly little kids weren't completely helpless.

Haines giggled delightedly, and even stone-faced Conway snickered.

"I knew you'd be wondering about that," he said. "You and Annie think you're smart little bastards. That was a cute stunt you two pulled on me. But you see, the definition of a smart little bastard is one who never tries to take on a pro. Take a good look, sonny—" He came in close and suddenly thrust a finger so close to Mike's left eye that for a terrifying moment Mike thought Conway meant to put his eye out. But the fingertip stopped a few centimeters away and stayed there, rock steady. He blinked, stared, blinked, refocused . . . and saw it. A circular patch of flesh that was a slightly different color from the skin around it, like a tiny flesh-colored Band-Aid.

Mike understood at once, but the idea was to drag this out as long as possible, so he played dumb. "What's that?"

Conway snickered again. "Never saw one of those, did you? It's a locator flea. A traveling bug. Press it to anything with the temperature of a human body, and it jumps ship."

"Jesus," Mike said, and squirmed away from the fingertip.

"It starts transmitting right away, powered by your own body heat, tells us exactly where you are."

"Eww," Mike blurted, "is it still *on* me?" He writhed in his bonds, straining to see his right wrist.

Conway smirked. "What for? We *know* where you are now. It's not the kind of technology you leave lying around on some smart-ass kid."

"Got that right," Haines grunted. "Expensive shit."

"I had one on each fingertip of my left hand, back there in the Lounge today," Conway continued. "The idea was to tag five of the dwarfs, to identify them for the snatch teams out in the parking lot, and follow the sixth one out myself. You two clowns bitched that up . . . but you shouldn't have let me get my hand on you."

Mike remembered, now, the faint grasp of Conway's fingers at his wrist, the triumph he had felt as they loosened altogether and fell away.

"You made it easy for us by going for a midnight stroll up near the surface, giving us a stronger signal, but sooner or later we'd have nailed you even if you'd stayed down underground."

"I don't understand," Mike said. "How can you possibly get guys into Dreamworld at night? And get out again carrying . . . me?"

Conway smiled. It was the first time Mike had seen him smile, and he didn't like it. "There's an old expression: 'I could tell you . . . but if I do, I'll have to kill you.' You really want to know?"

Letting himself think that far ahead for the first time, Mike knew they were going to kill him. They had to. He had seen Haines's face, and Conway's. Conway was trying to give him a smidgen of false hope, out of sheer sadism. A wave of sorrow suffused his entire body, like a fever chill but warm.

"But it doesn't make sense," he blurted, still stalling for time for no reason he could think of. "Look, I know you hate Dreamworld, Mr. Haines—but if you can put mercenaries in there anytime you want, and you got stuff like that flea thing . . . I mean, Jesus, you could destroy the place anytime you wanted. You could have done it *years* ago."

"I thought you said this little bastard was smart," Haines said to Conway; then to Mike, "Hey, retard, I do that and the possible suspects are, like three governments, maybe five multinationals, Bill Gates, and me. I don't want people to see Dreamworld destroyed. I want them to see it self-destruct. It has a little quiet help, behind the scenes maybe; the public don't need to know all the details."

Mike was running out of questions. When he did, the interrogation would resume. And there would certainly be pain, because even Haines with his internal lie detector would not believe the truth the first time he heard it. Mike knew he ought to be feeling panic because of that, but for some reason he wasn't. He remembered one of his favorite authors saying something to the effect that a boy became a man on the day he understood, deep down, that he was going to die, and took that knowledge into account in making his plans. Mike knew he was going to die now, and roughly when, and there was a weird kind of comfort in it. "And what do you do then, after you wreck Dreamworld? Take on Disneyland?"

Haines snorted. "Disney? Forget Disney: the Rat is history. I'm already as big as the Rat; they blew it a long time ago. Once Avery goes down, and I get all his secrets, I'll pick up all his market share and the Rat can eat my garbage."

His voice changed subtly in the midst of the last sentence, and Mike knew the subject of secrets had reminded him what he was here for. The stalling time was almost over now. He closed his eyes tightly, and time came to a stop.

Okay, he had broken, minutes before. Awakened from drugged stupor to sudden bright pain, he had surrendered his will, failed the test of bravery. Okay, pain hurt more than he had ever imagined it could; his throbbing pinky and burning ear testified to that. Bogart had told Sydney Greenstreet that torture didn't work unless it had the threat of death behind it, and Bogey was wrong— Mike knew now that when the pain exceeded a certain level, the body took over and told the mind what to do.

That didn't mean he was beaten. He was still smarter than Haines.

"It won't help, Pigface," he said.

Haines had just started to speak, to end all this conversation and get back to finding out what he wanted to know, but this diverted him. "What did you say?"

"You can't win."

Haines sat up straight. "I can't? Hell I can't. What do you mean, I can't win?"

"Just what I said. You'll never be rich enough. You can't be."

Haines leaned back in, grabbed Mike by the top of his T-shirt, and yanked until their faces were centimeters apart. "What the hell are you talking about, you little punk?"

Mike smiled at him. "Say Conway's goons are good enough to keep staying one step ahead of Dreamworld Security. Say you're even smart enough to beat Annie, which is a joke. Say all your dreams come true: Dreamworld dies, and then you knock off all the other parks one by one, Disney, Six Flags, all of them. You still lose."

Haines's pudgy fingers took Mike by the hair. "What do you mean lose? Lose how?" he snarled.

Mike looked him square in the eye. "Because even if you can get Phillip Avery framed for embezzlement and child molesting, there'll be millions of people all over the world who still love him, and always will. And no matter how rich you get, you'll still be a fat ugly old Pigface with a raisin for a heart until the day you die." Haines's face went utterly slack. "Even Conway is a better man than you, and he knows it. He hurt me to get what he wants and because he's mad at me—you did it because it's fun for you. That's who you are, Pigface: somebody who likes hurting kids. Nothing can change that. There isn't enough money on the planet to get anyone to *like* you, and even your mother didn't love you."

Haines snapped. Roaring incoherently, he shifted his grip from Mike's hair to his ears, and began slamming his head up and down on the leather bench as hard as he could.

"Even if you win," Mike cried, "up in Heaven Thomas Immega will look down on you and laugh at how pathetic you are. Thirteen years it took you—and you *still* had to cheat."

Haines howled, released him, and produced a knife. Mike felt a brief thrill of triumph. It would end quickly, now.

And then Conway caught his employer's wrist.

Haines struggled ferociously, but even with his enormous mass he could not break free of Conway's grip. In useless rage he beat at Conway's forearm with his other hand . . . until he regained enough wit to realize who he was assaulting, and ceased struggling. The two men locked eyes.

"Not . . . until . . . he . . . talks," Conway said.

Finally Haines nodded, and Conway released his wrist, and Mike knew he had failed.

Okay. He had *tried*. It had *almost* worked.

Haines tore his eyes away from Conway's and turned back to Mike, shaking his knife hand to restore the circulation. "Fine," he said. "First he talks. No problem. I want to hear him talk in soprano." He slid the blade of the knife under the waistband of Mike's shorts, and lifted. The damp fabric parted almost without resistance. The knife was very sharp.

Mike's mind melted. *"Wait!"* he shrieked. *"WaitI'lltellyoueverythingI'lltellyouanythingyouwanttoknow—"*

Haines showed his teeth. "Yeah, I know." He leaned forward.

Mike looked away—as far away as he could, until he was staring over his head at the wall behind him—and to distract himself, thought how odd it was that utter horror could cause visual hallucinations. It looked as though the wall were starting to *glow* . . . as if a circular section of it about half a meter in diameter, a meter and a half up from the floor, had suddenly become a heating element . . . no, an *over*heating element, turning a cheery red, then white, then almost blue-white. The color transformation seemed to Mike to take place in dreamy slow motion, but it could not have, for that circle of wall had completely ceased to exist an instant before he felt the cold blade touch his bare flesh.

Through the new hole in the wall a face was now visible: Even upside-down, even stripped of the Troll makeup they'd worn the last time Mike had seen them, the features of Hormat were unmistakable.

MIKE SIMPLY COULDN'T help gasping Hormat's name, but that was all right: Haines and Conway naturally mistook it for a babble of terror. Hormat held a finger to his lips for silence, then inverted that hand, pinched his nose shut with it, and puffed out his cheeks. The effect was ludicrous in the extreme, but Mike got it, and held his breath, puffing out his own cheeks to show that he was doing so. He felt Haines's damp hand on him, felt the cold blade on his belly. Hormat nodded grimly and held something up to the hole. Haines let go of Mike, left the knife on his belly, and lay down with a wet sigh. Conway started to say "Goddamn it," got as far as the second *d,* and fell down, too, landing hard on his knees and pitching onto his face. Hormat signaled *wait,* mimed holding his breath again, and disappeared from view.

Mike held his breath. At the age of eight he had discovered that you could endure Social Studies without losing your sanity if you spent the time secretly practicing holding your breath. His record that year had been a full two minutes ten seconds, and to this day underwater distance swimming was one of his best things.

A rectangular portion of the wall began to glow now, as silently and rapidly as had the circular piece enclosed within it. The result was a Hormat-sized door. Hormat stepped through it, signing again for silence. Mike nodded. It was weird to see Hormat without his Troll costume, dressed in civilian clothes, but the dwarf's protruding lower lip, massive eyebrows, and I'm-too-tired-to-limp walk were still unmistakable.

Hormat consulted his fingertip watch, then he caught Mike's eye and mimed exhaling. The gas, or whatever it was, had dissipated by now. Mike nodded a second time and resumed breathing. There was no unusual smell in the air that he could detect. Apparently whatever had destroyed the wallboard did it so thoroughly that not even enough survived for a burning smell, and Hormat's knockout gas was as odorless as the grease he'd given Annie to use on Conway back in the Employees' Lounge.

That had to be the wall-destroying widget in Hormat's left hand: a small black thing that looked kind of like an electric razor. Mike's guess was confirmed when Hormat used it to release him. It sliced through the metal links that secured his cuffs to the table with no fuss at all, no squeals of metal or sprays of filings. It also took the wings off the staple in his ear without cutting flesh; the staple fell off at once. Then Hormat put the tool away and signed for silence again. He put his lumpy fingers on Mike's left hand, gave the boy time to see what he was going to do and get braced for it, and popped Mike's pinky back into the socket. Mike managed to keep the scream behind his teeth . . . and almost at once the pain began to abate to something that could be lived with.

He had the wit not to try to get up right away. He worked his arms and legs first, restoring circulation and relaxing cramped muscles. Then he tucked himself away in his ruined shorts, swiveled his legs around and over the side of the bench, and tried sitting up. Hormat helped him.

He decided he was ready to try standing. But he didn't want his shorts to fall down when he did, and he needed both hands free in case he fell. He got Hormat's attention, pointed down at the floor, gesticulated until he managed to get Hormat to roll Haines over. The man was a tub, but with considerable effort the dwarf managed to shift him. Beneath him lay the stapler he'd used on Mike's ear. Hormat handed it to Mike with a quizzical look. Mike used five staples to repair his shorts: three at the waistband and two down the length of the slice. It hurt his damaged pinky to use the stapler, but not intolerably. The result was ugly but serviceable. He set down the stapler and stood up carefully.

His knees felt a little weak at first, but the sensation passed quickly. He took a few experimental steps . . . then met Hormat's eyes and made a little bowing gesture toward the hole in the wall, as if to say *After you, Alphonse.* Hormat returned it with the complementary *No, after you, Gaston.* Mike nodded, took one last look around the room—his first real look at it; it was like something out of a porn video—and stepped through the hole in the wall.

HE FOUND HIMSELF in a luxurious basement room that appeared to be a kind of . . . well, den, or rec room, or grown-ups' playroom. Well-stocked bar along one wall, comfortable furniture everywhere, large flat-screen TV monitor hanging on a wall, excellent stereo system visible, plushly carpeted stairway leading upstairs. The effect was surreal. On the way through the wall he had noticed just how *thick* it was: soundproofed. There had been no access from here to the torture room behind him until Hormat had created one. Mike wondered if people had ever partied out here, unaware that a few meters away, someone else was screaming . . .

Hormat touched his shoulder, again signed for silence, and led the way upstairs.

Two large men slept at the top of the stairs, one of them snoring. Hormat stepped over them both and led Mike down a hallway, into a room that looked like an unused guest bedroom, and out its window into darkness.

When his eyes had adjusted, Mike found himself standing outside a large home in a wealthy neighborhood, almost as thick with trees as parts of Dreamworld. The night air was cool on his arms. He guessed that it was sometime between midnight and six in the morning. Hormat got his attention, pointed past manicured shrubbery toward where Mike could tell the front door must lie, briefly made his hand into the shape of a gun, and held up two fingers. Mike understood: two more guards at the front door, still active.

Hormat crept away from the house, moving from shadow to shadow, and Mike followed him, trying not to make any noise. There were enough trees, bushes, and other foliage on the grounds that shortly he could no longer see the house when he glanced behind him, and there was just enough moonlight and starlight for him to see where he was putting his feet. It did not make him slow his pace. He had no idea how long Hormat's knockout stuff lasted—all he knew was that he wanted as much distance between him and that house as possible.

Just as Mike was trying to frame his thanks, they reached the edge of the woods and came out onto a road, and what was waiting for them there seemed so incongruous that Mike couldn't help laughing out loud. He had been subconsciously expecting some sort of futuristic vehicle, something out of a Hollywood movie, bristling with phallic weaponry and ready to leap into orbit on command.

Hormat's ride was an ancient Honda with rust spots, bald tires, and a cracked windshield.

As Mike tried to suppress his laughter, Hormat looked first uncomprehending, and then annoyed. "We must work with local technology whenever possible," he said.

"I know, I know," Mike assured him. "It makes perfect sense. I just wasn't expecting it. Come on, let's get out of here."

Hormat unlocked the car and they both piled in. "This is actually good," Mike said as the seat belt fastened itself. "If they wake up and chase us, they'll blow right past. No way is Haines gonna believe he could've got taken by somebody who drives an old Honda."

Hormat started the car and drove away.

Mike watched him drive. He seemed to know how, and was smart enough not to speed away from a crime scene. The seat and controls had been modified to accommodate a dwarf, with an accelerator/brake lever that resembled an antique gearshift sticking out from the steering column, just behind the wheel. Mike tried to catch Hormat's eye, but Hormat would not take his own off the road, even though he could have afforded to at the speed they were traveling.

"Hormat?" Mike said finally.

"Yes?"

"I ought to wait to say this until I can look you in the eye . . . but I can't. Thank you. Very much."

"Welcome you are," Hormat replied. His syntax told Mike as clearly as his tone of voice that thanking him had, for some reason, been a mistake. He pointed to the glove box with a finger so gnarly it looked like a condom full of walnuts. Inside, Mike found a bottle of water. For the first time he became aware of the foul taste in his mouth; he uncapped the bottle and drank deep. The water was indescribably delicious.

At first they drove winding residential streets, through a neighborhood better than any Mike had ever expected to live in, but then they came to a main drag, took a right, and followed that a few kilometers. Everything was closed for the night, even the gas stations. Hormat tried to set the cruise control, but did not seem surprised when it didn't work. A genuine, authentic, piece-of-crap '08 Honda.

Mike had a million questions, but found he was in no real hurry to ask them. For the moment it was enough to be heading away from Haines and Conway. He wasn't at all sleepy, but he closed his eyes and let himself drift, conscious for a while only of the sensation of motion through space, and of the lingering dull aches in his pinky and ear.

CHAPTER 15

TO BEAT THE BAND

Eventually they came to an entrance ramp for a highway whose name Mike didn't recognize, and Hormat took that up onto a huge ten-laner. Even at this hour, there was a fair amount of traffic on it, but most of it whizzed by them in the controlled lanes to the left. The Honda had not been retrofitted, so they had to stay in the two autonomous lanes, restricted to a top speed of 110 kph.

At that Mike started thinking again, at least enough to become confused. As far as he knew, only a few states had computer-controlled roads in place so far. He hadn't noticed the plates on the Honda in the dark. "Hormat?"

"Yes?"

"Where *are* we?"

He realized as he asked it that his question was indeterminate, but as he was trying to rephrase it, Hormat answered, "About eighty kilometers from Dreamworld."

Mike was startled. From the moment he'd woken to find himself in Haines's torture chamber, he had been assuming that he was on the opposite coast, somewhere near Thrillworld: that Conway had flown him there unconscious on a private jet or something. He'd certainly felt as if he'd been out for long enough to have been hauled across a continent. But if not—

"Then . . . this is still the same night I . . . I got caught?"

Hormat nodded.

Jesus. Annie might not even know he was gone yet. "But Haines told us he couldn't fly out here until tomor . . ." He trailed off and slapped the dashboard in disgust at himself. "What a maroon! He was trying to fake us out. Shit, he did fake us out." He had a horrid thought. "Jeeze, they didn't get Annie, too, did they?"

"No," Hormat said.

Mike released his breath. With relief came the realization that there was something odd about Hormat's voice and manner. They were nearly as strained as they had been when Mike had insisted on thanking him. Mike glanced over his shoulder to study the sparse traffic behind them, saw nothing that looked or acted remotely like a pursuit vehicle—or a cop, for that matter. What was Hormat so uptight about? He studied the look on the dwarf's face until he realized where he had seen it before.

In a mirror . . .

"You're AWOL," he blurted suddenly.

Hormat frowned. "I do not know that word."

"Your people don't know you're doing this."

Hormat took his hand off the accelerator involuntarily, then resumed speed, stone-faced. He said nothing.

"They don't, do they?" Mike persisted. "You could get in trouble if they find out, right?"

A gnarly muscle swelled in Hormat's jaw. He nodded.

"Jesus." It took an almost physical effort not to say, "Thank you," again.

Perhaps Hormat realized he wasn't going to, after a few seconds, and appreciated it. Something made him unclench his jaw and unbend far enough to say, "Much worse than that could happen." For the first time he took his eyes from the road and looked Mike square in the eye.

Mike met his gaze. "They won't hear it from me."

Hormat returned his eyes to the road.

Mike did the same. Time and white lines went by. Slowly he realized the landscape was beginning to look vaguely familiar. If he had it right, Dreamworld was over *that* way, just beyond that rise. With any luck, he might actually get back home to Annie's place before she woke up! He saw himself preparing their breakfast, and nearly doubled over with a savage spasm of previously unsuspected hunger.

"Ill you are?" Hormat asked sharply.

"Starving," Mike said, and took another long drink from the bottle of water. "God, I could eat the ass end out of a whale with a plastic spoon."

It just slipped out, an expression Uncle Walter had used to annoy Mom, and for a moment Mike was afraid he had offended Hormat, too—

—and then the dwarf brayed with sudden laughter.

Mike was so relieved, and Hormat's laugh was so intrinsically funny, that he couldn't help breaking up himself. The contrast of his tenor laugh with Hormat's baritone honk was even funnier, to both of them. Soon they were roaring together, laughing so hard that Hormat had to pull into the slow lane and steer with the elbow of his accelerator arm so he could have a hand free to wipe the tears away. It took them several tries to stop; one of them would almost manage it, and then the other would set him off again. It was Mike's aching stomach muscles that finally forced him to quit, but he didn't mind a bit; he felt *great*.

Still chuckling, Hormat wiped tears from his eyes and said, "I have nothing you can eat, Mike."

Mike nodded. "No sweat. I'll be home soon." He glanced out the window. "Hey, what time is it?"

Hormat checked his finger. "A little after five o'clock."

That was good. With luck, Mike would be able to sneak back into Dreamworld before morning shift change without being spotted. He knew at least three good ways to do so. Now, which would be best?—

He caught himself. If he was over the shock now and ready to start thinking again, he might as well do so intelligently. Getting back home would take care of itself—more important questions remained unanswered, and his window to ask them was closing fast. And as he tried to formulate them, several things that had been puzzling him below the conscious level suddenly started to make sense—or so it seemed.

He felt he'd formed a bond of sorts with Hormat; time to see how far it would stretch. Start slow. "Hormat?"

"Yes, Mike?"

"How did you rescue me? I mean, how did you manage to tail a pro like Conway all the way to Haines's place? For that matter, how did you even know I was in trouble?"

The dwarf blushed, enough to see even in the poor light inside the car, but didn't duck the question. "I, also, placed a tracer on you," he admitted. "Just after we met, when you were taking us to meet Annie."

Mike nodded. "Sure. I should have guessed. If Conway has the technology, so do you. Is yours still on me?"

Hormat shook his head. "We have left it behind us."

Something in his voice told Mike the answer was true but incomplete. "But you put one on Annie, too, when you shook hands with her. Right?"

Hormat's silence was a tacit admission.

Okay so far. Go for one of the big ones. "Hormat?"

"Yes, Mike."

"*Why* did you rescue me?"

This silence conveyed no information Mike could read.

"I mean, I see why you had to go AWOL to do it. As far as your people know, me and Annie are as big a threat as Haines and Conway. They want to know why you're here so they can use you to destroy Dreamworld somehow; we want to know why you're here so we can be sure you won't; and you guys don't want to tell either side anything. I understand that, kind of. So it seems like as far as you guys are concerned, if we all kill each other off, that's good news. What made you stick your neck out?" No answer. "In fact, why were you even monitoring me at one A.M., or whenever it was they snatched me?"

Hormat not only did not reply, he actually stuck his tongue a little way out and bit down on it as if to prevent himself from doing so. That was okay; Mike suspected he already knew the answer. He checked their surroundings and saw that they were getting close to Dreamworld. The window was nearly shut. Time to roll the dice and go for broke.

"You want to tell me, don't you?"

Hormat sucked his tongue back in and frowned so thunderously that for a moment Mike thought he was about to burst into tears.

"Your friends don't want us to know . . . but you want to tell me why you're here. Or 'now,' or whatever. You'll be in big trouble if anybody ever finds out, but you want to tell me anyway. You came to do that, and you saw me get grabbed."

The dwarf spoke through clenched teeth. "Read minds, do you?"

Annie had asked him something like that, once. She was not the first, either, but her comment had caused him to give it a little thought. "No," he said. "It's just . . . well, I see people do funny things, and I just think, well, why would I do that if I was them? Really, I think anybody could do it if they tried."

Hormat made a *hrrrmph* sound.

Mike had no time for the subject. "Look, Hormat, you saved my life. You tell me, you don't tell me, either way you're my bud, okay? But if you're *gonna* tell me, you better get to it. We're gonna be back at Dreamworld in ten or fifteen minutes, and I want to get back Under before the sun comes up and makes everything harder."

Hormat's hands tightened on the wheel and accelerator until the knuckles whitened and ropy muscles stood out on his arms, but he said nothing.

At first Mike held his breath, but soon he had to quit that and just waited and hoped. After a while he got tired of both waiting and hoping and just watched the road, and some indeterminate time after that, they both knew that so much time had passed that Hormat would not be able to answer Mike's question before they arrived. The window had closed.

Hormat spoke then, startling them both. "You are right."

Mike waited, and thought about hoping again.

"I do want to tell you."

He resumed hoping. Maybe the secret could be told in a few sentences.

"But I cannot. My decision to make, it is not."

Mike went back to watching the road.

"The right I have not. Can you understand?"

If something bad's after you guys, maybe Annie and me can help! Mike wanted to say, but the pain in his new friend's voice made him bite his tongue. "Chill, Hormy. Like I said, you saved my life. You can't tell me, you can't."

"Thank you," Hormat said, and his arms and hands relaxed. But he kept frowning just as ferociously.

"But we're gonna find out, you know. Me and Annie."

Hormat turned his head, and Mike looked him in the eye. Hormat returned his own eyes to the road and nodded slowly. "Yes. I expect you will," he said wearily.

They rode on in silence. Mike kept wanting to make conversation, but every neutral subject he thought of sounded idiotic in this context. It was hard enough to chat with any grown-up, much less a time-traveling dwarf. Eventually he quit trying and instead passed the kilometers trying to guess, or deduce, or intuit, just what the *hell* Hormat and his friends were *doing* here/now. He had no success at all.

A while later the turnoff for Dreamworld came into view in the distance, and Mike decided it was time to start planning his break-in. A faint rosy glow was apparent behind the hills to the east, but there was still plenty of darkness to work with, and Security would be at its most sleepy. The first thing to do was—

—Oh, SHIT—

"Oh, SHIT," Mike said aloud.

"What is it?" Hormat cried, alarmed.

"My Command Band!" Mike blurted, pawing uselessly at his bare left wrist. "Oh shit, this is terrible. This is freakin' awful! Hormy, those two assholes cut off my Command Band—it's probably still back there—oh God, we gotta go back for it—"

"No," Hormat said forcefully. "There is no time."

"You don't understand—*I can't get back inside without that Band.*"
This was the last straw for Mike. Too much had happened to him,
and his nerves were shot; he began to blubber. "Hormat, what
the hell am I gonna *do*? I'm screwed, I'm totally screwed—"

Hormat could not put a hand on Mike's shoulder because he
needed both hands to drive. Instead he touched his foot to Mike's
calf and rubbed it. "Can you not merely wait until the park opens,
and—"

"I got no money," Mike said, feeling his voice take on a singsong whining quality and helpless to stop it, "I got no ID, I got
no place to hide until Opening, if I *did* get in they'd lock a regular
Dreamband on me and the only way I know to beat that takes
props I haven't got—Jesus, Haines and *Conway* can get in and
Under faster than I can: I gave them the key! They're probably
on their way after us right now, or sending guys, they'll nail me
right in the parking lot waiting for the doors to open—" He
buried his face in his hands and wept.

Hormat removed his foot from Mike's leg and sighed. "Sit
back," he said.

Mike ignored him, giving way to hysteria.

"I said, sit *back*," the dwarf repeated sharply.

Grudgingly, Mike straightened up, but kept sobbing.

Hormat braced his left arm against the steering wheel, rechecked his rearview mirror, and yanked back *hard* on the accel-
erator/brake lever.

Things happened too fast for Mike to register then. When he
caught up with events again he was sitting with an air bag in his
face, listening to the dopplering horns of cars and trucks whizzing
past on the left, so shocked he had stopped crying and too shocked
to speak.

They were on the shoulder—*just* on the shoulder, with their
left front fender almost over the line into traffic. The Dreamworld
turnoff was only a hundred meters or so ahead. Mike was unhurt,

save that his hips and chest were sore where the belt had grabbed them, and his face stung where it had impacted the air bag. He tasted blood, realized he'd bitten his tongue. Some was trickling down his chin, but he couldn't get his hands high enough to wipe it away.

Hormat retracted both air bags, switched off the SOS system, and turned to face him. He reached out and took Mike by the shoulders, and even in his daze Mike noticed how gently he did it. "Do I have your attention?" he asked.

Mike nodded dumbly.

Hormat held his eyes and spoke slowly, and with unmistakable sincerity. "You have a right to be hysterical. You have the right to despair." He shook his ugly head from side to side. "You do not have the time right now."

Mike took a deep, shuddery breath, wiped at his nose with his forearm, and nodded.

Hormat released his eyes and his shoulders, got him a tissue from a box between their seats, and restarted the stalled engine. "A right to be hysterical *I* have," the dwarf muttered to himself, "and I also the time have not."

"Hormy, what am I gonna *do*? I got about half an hour to get in there, and I don't know *how*."

Hormat shrugged. "Then it's simple. I must get you in."

"You? How?"

"If we could wait until Opening, I could simply pay our admissions, and then cut off our Dreambands once we were inside, with the device you saw me use earlier—"

Mike shook his head. "I can't wait that long, Annie'll be—"

"It doesn't matter," Hormat said. "Even if you could wait, I cannot. By coincidence, half an hour is almost all the time *I* have, too. It is important that I get back before I am missed."

"So then, how—"

"I've already started," Hormat said, and put the car back in gear. He stayed on the shoulder for the hundred-odd meters it took to reach the Dreamworld turnoff, and exited there. The familiar skyline approached. Safety, tantalizingly near.

"What are we gonna do?" Mike said urgently. "What's the plan? What's my move, Hormat?"

"Say as little as possible and act stunned," Hormat said, concentrating on his driving.

Mike gave up trying to figure it out—gave up trying to figure anything out, ever. "I can do that," he agreed.

"Good," Hormat said, the irony lost on him.

He drove them to the extreme north end of the parking lot, took the road marked Do Not Enter, hung a right at the end of the wall. He drove past the fake VIP entrance, and pulled up just before the real one. Even though it was well out of sight of the parking area, it was most inconspicuous, a plain door with no knob. The fake entrance a hundred meters behind looked much more plausible, with canopy, spotlights and red carpet . . . but it led only to a holding area. Not many noncelebrities knew about the real one—but Mike was not particularly surprised to learn that Hormat did.

"You're Joey Wilson; I'm your Uncle Ed," Hormat murmured as he shut the engine. There was enough spill of light from the fake entrance to see by, here.

Mike nodded. The door was already opening. A Security man came out, apparently unarmed; his partner remained in the doorway, one arm out of sight, in case he needed cover. He circled the car, stood by Hormat's window, and rotated his finger, clearly intending to ask Hormat, politely but very firmly, who he thought he was and what he was doing here.

Out of his view, Hormat hit the *window down* button—but when it was open a decimeter or two, he also hit the *window up* button. The window stopped closing, but kept whining. He shrugged and released both buttons. "It's jammed," he told the guard through the crack, and gestured at the two deflated air bags. "Must have happened when we had the accident."

The guard's eyes widened when he saw the air bags, and again when he took in the blood on Mike's chin. At once he postponed the question of who Mike and Hormat were and made an *it's okay; come here* gesture over the top of the car to his partner as he said, "Can you unlock the door?"

"I think so," Hormat said, and did so, unsteadily.

At once the guard had the car door open and started checking him over. "Are you all right, sir?"

"Yes, I think so," Hormat said. "Just a little shaken up. Nothing hurts."

Mike's own door was opened, and he found himself being examined by the second guard. Past her, he could see that the VIP door had shut behind her. Her hands were gentle, knowing, and thorough. By the time her eyes got back up as far as his face, he'd had time to reopen the cuts on his lip and ear, and cross his eyes. "I'm fine," he said.

"Does your neck hurt?" she asked. "Or that left hand?"

"Nah."

"Okay, let's try getting out. Lean on me."

"I'm okay," he said.

"Lean on me," she insisted, and helped him from the car. On the other side, the first guard was doing the same with Hormat. Once she was sure Mike could stand unassisted, she said, "Okay, let's see you walk a straight line for me."

Mike wobbled a little, careful not to overdo it, taking his cue from Hormat.

"All right," Hormat's guard said, "let's get them inside and call it in."

Mike's guard nodded and steered him toward the door. "What's your name, son?" she asked.

"Joey Wilson," Mike said, dragging his feet to let Hormat catch up with them. "He's my Uncle Ed."

"What happened to you guys?" she asked.

"I'm not sure," he temporized. "Uncle Ed, what exactly did happen?"

"And why did you come *here*, instead of the main gate?" she added.

Hormat held up a horny hand, and winced as if it hurt his ribs. "Let's get in out of the chill and sit down for a moment and I'll tell you the whole story," he said.

Mike's guard nodded, glanced down at her Command Band to punch the unlock sequence. Hormat caught Mike's eye, and just as he had back in Haines's torture room, pantomimed holding his breath. Mike did so. The door opened and he followed his guard in. As soon as all four of them were inside, both guards dropped bonelessly and silently.

Mike waited until he saw Hormat was breathing again, and said, "Once they come to, they're gonna report this, and then—"

Hormat was shaking his head, looking around. "They cannot report what they do not remember—and they will remember nothing that happened to them within the last half hour or so." Mike blinked at that, but said nothing, and hastily put on his poker face. Hormat had spoken without thinking.

They were in a short wide corridor, and the two chairs by the door were obviously where the guards were in the habit of sitting. Each chair had a paperback on the floor beside it; one was an adventure novel and the other a romance. "Help me," Hormat said, and with Mike's assistance soon had his own guard propped up on the former chair, and Mike's on the latter. "With any luck," Hormat said, "each will assume he dropped off to sleep, and be too embarrassed to mention it to the other."

"Did it work the same way with Haines and Conway, too?" Mike asked as casually as he could.

Hormat nodded impatiently. "Save that they will *know* something happened, yes. They had you for much longer than half an hour. And they have more evidence from which to form deductions. You can find your way from here safely?"

"Huh? But aren't you—"

"Good-bye, Mike."

"Hormy, *wait*," Mike said urgently.

The dwarf shook his head. "I cannot," he said, and turned to go.

"Hormat, this isn't far enough! I *can't* get back home from here without help—not without my Command Band!"

Hormat froze in his tracks, turned, and regarded Mike closely. Hormat's craggy pouting face *always* looked suspicious, but this stare was his masterpiece. For a moment his eyes almost slid away to the wrists of the two sleeping guards, but even as the thought occurred to him he must have realized they could not afford to have either of the guards wake up Bandless. His eyes reacquired Mike's, locked on, and began firing bullshit-piercing beams.

Mike met them squarely. Most people's poker faces fade under pressure because they think too much about the bluff they're running, and the force of the other's will. Mike was busy, trying to think of a route back Under that would plausibly require assistance.

Hormat continued to apply eye pressure, his brows curling down over them in clearly increasing skepticism.

Mike didn't flinch. He'd thought of a route now, and the tiny added bit of confidence in his eyes came across as sincerity. "Your help I *need*," he said earnestly.

Perhaps phrasing it verb-last helped touch an emotional chord in the time-traveler, as Mike hoped, or perhaps the artistic flourish was unnecessary. Either way, Hormat bought it. He sighed hugely, released Mike's eyes, and consulted his watchfinger. "Twenty minutes from now, I *must* walk out that door and drive away," he said flatly. "Even that will leave me no margin at all. I *cannot* risk a speeding ticket."

Mike let most of his relief show. "Five minutes going in, tops," he assured the dwarf, "and once I get another Band I can have you back here again in less than that. Thanks, Hormat. I just don't know what I would've done if you—"

"Wait here a moment," Hormat growled, and went back outside. Mike watched from the doorway: a group of seemingly decorative architectural structures not far from the door provided a place to discreetly conceal as many as half a dozen limos, and

Hormat moved his car there. He was back inside nearly at once, his bandy legs moving quickly.

"Lead the way," he said.

Mike turned at once and did so, wondering for the first time—now that he had the luxury—whether he had just done a smart thing or a stupid one.

Well, at least it was the first thing he had *done*, all night, except let himself be tossed around by events. He couldn't report back to Annie with nothing to show for the evening but a long dismal tale of disgrace, humiliation, and incredible luck; a boy had to have some pride.

THE WAY MIKE took them did indeed require someone to stand chickee at three different points, the last just before the corridor off which Annie's place lay. And they got there in well under five minutes, as he'd promised. Along the way Mike had assessed Hormat's familiarity with Dreamworld procedures and routines, and found it almost as good as his own: the time-travelers had obviously studied their drop zone carefully.

So when Mike stepped through the wall, he did *not* immediately turn right. As he'd hoped, when Hormat followed him, the dwarf did turn right, automatically. Mike gave him a two-handed shove between both shoulder blades that flung him forward; he flung up his hands with a startled cry and cannoned into Annie's door. As he did, Mike hit the switch that Annie had showed him on his first day Under, and the holodoor they'd just come through turned solid, locking them in together.

Hormat spun around, put his back against Annie's door, and raised his hands defensively. "Insane you are?" he cried.

Mike raised his own hands in a quite different way, signifying peaceful intent and apology. "Sorry, Hormy," he said, "but once you knew we were home you would've turned on your heel and split. I want you to come in first. Just for a minute, honest."

"Why?"

"You've been up all night, and you've got another drive ahead of you—on manual. You gotta have some coffee or you'll wipe out."

"There . . . is . . . no . . . *time*," Hormat said through clenched teeth.

"Take it with you in a hot-cup," Mike said. "Come on, there's more than fifteen minutes left of the twenty you said you had. You can't afford to get pulled over for erratic driving." He was noticing for the first time how truly awful Hormat's teeth were.

Hormat closed his eyes. His shoulders slumped, his arms lowered, and he shifted his weight from his heels to the balls of his feet.

The instant his back was no longer touching the door, it opened. Hormat whirled around and recoiled as if straight-armed again, but from the front this time—nearly backing into Mike, who barely had time to sidestep.

"You should have phoned ahead first," Annie said coldly to Hormat.

Mike's heart leaped at the sight of her. She looked *regal*, somehow wore her bathrobe and slippers as if they were the formal vestments of some elaborate ceremony of state. Whose protocol Hormat had oafishly screwed up.

"I—" the dwarf began.

She cut him off, raising her scepter. No, Mike was getting a little giddy with fatigue and relief—it wasn't a scepter, she just brandished it like one. It was a remote control. The one for the computer.

She gave Hormat time to recognize that, then pointed behind her with it, toward the computer. "If I do not like your explanation for why you took that boy away in the middle of the night," she said coldly, "I will use this to send a summary of everything I know about you people to Phillip Avery, the National Security Agency, and the *New York Times*. It's on a deadman switch: if my thumb should relax for some reason, you'll never find the right code to stop things before the message finishes uploading. Start talking whenever you're ready."

CHAPTER 16

UNDER: THE CIRCUMSTANCES

"It's okay, Annie," Mike said quickly. "Hormat didn't grab me—Haines and Conway did. Hormy *rescued* me. If it wasn't for him, I'd . . . well, skip that . . . but I owe him *big*. I told him he could have some coffee to take with him: he's gotta make a long drive right away, on no sleep."

As he spoke he was communicating with her on a second level with his eyes and body language. "There is no telephone in your car?" she asked Hormat.

"No," he said stiffly.

She nodded. "Very well. Come in."

As he crossed the threshold she said, "Wipe your feet," sternly. Hormat backed up and did so, winning another imperious nod. Mike came in on his heels, and found himself caught in a hug that crushed the breath from his chest. He locked his knees and returned it with what strength he had left, his head swimming with too many powerful emotions to even try to sort out.

Finally she released him. She held him at arm's length, and this time her eyes demanded information of a different kind.

"I'm fine," he said. "I'm sorry I scared you. I was just going out for a walk, to think . . . only Conway put a tracer on me yesterday."

Her hands tightened on his shoulders like clamps. The one on his left shoulder really hurt; she had the remote in that hand.

"I'm fine," he insisted. "It's gone now. Hormat tailed them and

sprung me. Then he helped me get back in, 'cause—oh shit—"
He hesitated. "Annie, I'm sorry, but they got my Command
Band. I couldn't help it, I was—"

She shook her head. "Don't worry about it, boy."

"But they've still *got* it—"

"Don't worry, I said." She released his shoulders, disarmed the
deadman switch on her remote, punched in a new combination,
aimed it at the computer, and fired. "Your Band is just a bunch
of plastic and silicon now," she said. "It can't do anything, and it
can't be traced to us. Come on inside; we have coffee to pour."

Mike relaxed and let her lead him in. Hormat was looking a
little pale; Mike suddenly understood that the brief interval between Annie's firing the remote and her explaining why must
have been a bad time for him. Annie realized it at the same instant.
"Pardon me, Hormat," she said. "I should have told you what I
was doing first."

"You needed to deactivate that Band quickly," Hormat said.

She shook her head. "Not that quickly. It was thoughtless. Do
you take cream or sugar in your coffee?"

He bowed slightly. "Both, please. But I fear I must drink it
quickly."

"He's AWOL," Mike put in. "He's gotta get back before they
miss him or he's in deep shit." He lifted Annie's wrist, checked
her watch. "He's got to be out of here in fifteen minutes. Less,
if one of us doesn't go with him." He went straight to his side of
the bed and swapped his ruined shorts for a coverall; one of the
staples had already torn loose and he was tired of worrying that
his pants would fall down.

One of Annie's eyebrows lifted slightly. "Indeed? Then it's fortunate the coffee is already made. Please take a seat there, Hormat.
Mike, you there when you're ready."

She soon had them sorted out, with mugs of coffee before them
and pastries laid out, and took her clothes and shoes into the
bathroom. Mike fell on a cherry Danish, inhaled it in a couple of

gulps, and poured coffee on it to dissolve it on the way down. Hormat stuck to the coffee.

Annie came out fully dressed and with her hair brushed, seated herself at the head of the table, and raised her own mug. "Thank you, Hormat, for rescuing Mike," she said formally. "Our home is yours, now and forevermore."

Hormat blinked. "I—" He broke off, tried again . . . failed again. On the third try he managed, "I do not think I . . . can convey what that means to . . . to one like me." He looked down at his coffee, looked back up at Annie. "No one has ever said such a thing to me. When I am from, no one would say that to a stranger." He dropped his eyes again and sipped coffee.

"Then you understand how seriously I meant it," she said. "The only other person I've ever said that to is Mike."

Mike felt a warm glow.

"If there is trouble with your friends over this," Annie went on, "you are always welcome here."

"Thank you," Hormat said gruffly. He tried to glance around the room without being obvious about it, from under lowered brows, but Mike caught him at it. So he looked around himself, to try to see the room as Hormat must be seeing it.

Probably the same way Mike had seen it, his own first time. There wasn't actually much here. Bare-bones household utensils scrounged from Dreamworld inventory, a computer, a couple of bookshelves. Nothing permanent; as baldly functional as a hotel room. Annie could move everything here to another location in a single afternoon if she wanted to. Or abandon the lot, just cut and run, and reproduce most of it out of available stock in a few days . . . all except the books, anyway. For all he knew, this was the fifth, or the twenty-fifth, address Annie'd had since she'd gone Under. If it wasn't, it looked like it was. Annie's real home was not here, but all of Dreamworld itself.

So was his now, came the thought.

Hormat was trying not to look confused now. "I do not wish

to pry, but may I ask you both your job titles here? I confess I am not familiar with the operations of your section."

Mike and Annie exchanged a glance. The time-travelers still didn't get it. They clung to the idea that he and Annie held some sort of official capacity in the Dreamworld organization, something undercover (since Mike had needed Hormat's help to get back inside) but legitimate. They must think he and Annie were some sort of Internal Affairs–type spooks, used to keep a quiet check on Security perhaps. The misconception might give the pair enhanced negotiational clout. Mike sensed that she was asking his opinion, and moved his head a few millimeters from side to side.

She turned to Hormat and smiled faintly. "Our titles," she told him, "are Annie and Mike. We have no job except enjoying ourselves. Dreamworld does not know we are on their property. We're Under—underground, out of sight, unofficial—just like you and your friends."

Hormat sat stock-still. Mike could almost hear the wheels turning inside his head, the sprockets clicking into place. "I see," he said. He hesitated over the next question, then risked it. "May I ask . . . how long . . . ?"

"Thirteen years," Annie said.

His eyes went round.

"About a week," Mike said.

Hormat's eyes opened even wider. He kept looking back and forth between Annie and Mike, and the longer he looked the more surprised he looked. Finally he made himself stop, looked down at his coffee, and took a long drink of it. He set the cup down on the table, folded his big wrinkled hands around it, and said to it—Mike knew he was addressing both of them—"Thank you. For sharing your secret with me."

He and Annie both said, "You're welcome," at the same time.

Hormat hesitated, turning his coffee mug around and around in his hands.

"Go ahead, ask," Annie said. "Whatever it is. You rescued Mike and placed yourself at risk to do so. If anyone ever had a right to ask nosy questions, you do. I don't promise to answer, but get it off your chest."

The dwarf nodded his thanks and asked his question. "Why? Why are you each . . . 'Under'?"

NOW IT WAS Mike and Annie's turn to hesitate. This was a turning point, and both knew it. For Mike, at least, time came to a stop while he writhed on the point of the dilemma.

Mike had dragged Hormat here in the half-conscious hope that together, he and Annie might be able to befriend him—or more accurately, to cement the tentative friendship he had already offered by saving Mike's life—and using that new intimacy, pump him for all he was worth. Mike knew Hormat *wanted* to tell them why he and his friends were all here/now; the dwarf had come right up to the very edge of explaining things on the drive here— and then changed his mind and pulled back. Mike and Annie had about fifteen minutes, tops, to change his mind and push him over the edge: their one and only window. In a few hours it would be time to start meeting and trying to negotiate with both Haines and the time-travelers, and they dared not do so in ignorance.

But charm alone wasn't going to cut it. If they wanted Hormat to trust them enough to answer their intimate questions, they were going to have to answer his. Fast.

But—*this* question? Of all the things he could possibly have wanted to know?

It was the one question they had both solemnly sworn never ever to ask *each other*: that single promise constituted their sole contract with each other. Whatever Annie's reasons for coming Under, she was not prepared to discuss them even with someone she was willing to share a bathroom with, and there was only one of those on Earth. As for Mike, up until a few seconds ago he had planned to make it through his entire life without ever telling anyone why he'd come Under. He didn't even know if he could make himself tell *Annie* . . . and Hormat was just—

—the total stranger who'd just saved his life, at no benefit to himself.

Mike opened his mouth to speak—

—and Annie cut him off.

He was so shocked he failed to grasp the meaning of her first half dozen words or so, so startled they were being spoken that he could not comprehend them. After that he paid close attention.

"I came here," she said, her voice hoarse but firm, "because I had to. It was this or die. I moved into Dreamworld full-time because I could find no place for me in the *real* world."

Hormat nodded slightly at once, as if he understood. Mike did not have a clue what she was talking about, and without looking directly at her, let his face say so.

"When last measured," she went on, "my IQ was over one-seventy. This world is not a comfortable place for the highly intelligent. I have never been physically attractive. My personality is abrasive. And I am a midget. I have had, I think, an unusually lonely life. Children of my own were never a realistic hope. I kept hoping anyway . . ." She stopped speaking for a moment, cleared her throat noisily, and continued. "At forty, I stopped. By then I'd long since found a reasonable form of sublimation. I was a social worker, in child services. I will not tell you where. I had *dozens* of children, and they all needed me. I had a place in the world, a purpose. I worked very hard. But—" She paused again, and rubbed the bridge of her nose. "But the social services system was badly flawed, and kept getting worse. Overextended, under-funded, understaffed, overmanaged. Overwhelmed. One day there was bad trouble. Ugliness . . . even beyond what we had come, God forgive us, to accept as normal." She glanced at Mike, took a slow deep breath, and went on. "I will not describe it, but when it was done a child was dead, another badly injured, and two others severely traumatized. And I had put two foster parents and my boss in the hospital. They pulled the plug on the foster father a few days later. The judge who arraigned me for that said he wished he could give me a medal instead."

Mike wanted to go to her, might have done so if he'd had a clue what to do once he got there.

"I was out of work, for good, and I needed a lot of money for attorneys. Bail had cleaned me out. Dreamworld was just about to open, then, hiring all the little people it could find. I came here for an interview, looked around . . . and went Under that very day.

"I could no longer be part of a system that *can't* protect kids at risk or in terror, can't supply decent care. It no longer helped, enough, to know that for all its abominable failures it's by far the best system the world has ever seen. I just couldn't choke down one more restaurant meal knowing that somewhere in the same city mothers were scavenging for their babies. I had to leave the world . . . and I preferred to do it without dying."

She broke off for a moment, got her voice back under control. Mike sat with his jaw open, listening.

"Here in Dreamworld, no child suffers, no adult is exploited, all are made joyful. The place charges a lot—but the customers get their full money's worth. This is a pocket universe, a little island of Right and Good and Fair. A writer I like named Hiaasen once argued that the very attempt to build such a perfect pocket world is intrinsically evil—he was talking about Disney, Dreamworld wasn't around then—but he never did say why. I discovered that I utterly disagree."

Hormat kept nodding; Annie's words seemed to resonate with him.

"So I decided to stay forever," she went on, "because I found that here I can stand the pain of being alive . . . and . . ." She paused, admitting something to herself. ". . . and because *here*, I can be of real help, actually accomplish something. I didn't realize that at first: I thought I was just hogging a free spot in the lifeboat, and did it only because I *had* to . . . but after a few months, I came to see that I might, if I stayed alert and kept busy, perhaps *earn* the right to stay here." She put her hands flat on the table. "So I did."

Hormat let several breaths go by before saying, softly, "I see." Then he and Annie both turned and looked at Mike.

HE HAD BEEN so absorbed in Annie's speech that it took him that long to comprehend that it was his turn now. He began to hastily reassemble for inspection the entire structure of Why I Should versus Why I Mustn't and What If I Do versus What If I Don't—

Annie saw his face and tried to let him off the hook. "I don't see any need to press Mike for specifics of his own situation, Hormat. I said earlier that this world is not a comfortable place for the highly intelligent—and he is, I assure you, considerably smarter than I am. That alone should satisfactorily—"

Mike found that he was talking, and listened to hear what he would say.

"Mom was all the family I ever had. My father died before I was born. She was a schoolteacher, high school physics. We were happy a long time. Then when I was nine, it got hip for a while for middle-class people to do crack—I don't know if you heard about that in here, Annie. Mom had this asshole boyfriend, and he turned her on. You know what crack cocaine is, Hormy?"

Hormat nodded. "I know what it is."

"I don't really understand why she started. It doesn't matter: she did. After a while she wasn't a teacher anymore. There was no family to help us. Everything we had went into Mom's pipe. Up in smoke. Mom's money, my college money, then the house . . . it took a long time. Years.

"I really busted my ass. I really did. I read everything I could find, I talked to counselors and doctors and priests and ex-crackheads and social workers and cops, I found out everything they knew, I tried all the theories they had and invented stuff of my own. None of it worked.

"I stopped going to school and tried to take care of both of us, but it was hard. The only time she ever showed any gratitude was if I stole money and gave it to her. So I did. Or if I went out and scored for her, when she was too sick. So finally I did that too, sometimes. I mean, I couldn't stop her doing it, I could at least make it easier for her—I felt like I *had* to do *something* for her."

He discovered that Annie had hold of his right hand; he didn't remember her taking it.

"Then a couple of weeks ago I scored her some and screwed up the purity test and it was a bad batch and she died right in front of me."

Annie *squeezed.* Good thing it wasn't the other hand. He didn't squeeze back. He wanted to cry, but seemed to lack the necessary tears. Might as well finish the story.

"So now I had a no-brainer choice. Drop out of the world, or go into the system Annie was just talking about. I know kids who went through that system. I know a lot about it. So I figured wherever I was gonna run to, I was probably gonna have to stay there like forever. So I asked myself where I wanted to be forever, and then I studied the place and made my move and Annie helped me and here I am."

Annie topped off his coffee. It was the first he'd realized she was not still holding his hand. He took the cup and drank. It stayed down. There were no more words inside to come up. He was done.

He waited for their reactions. He expected Annie's first, so it was a surprise when Hormat spoke, and the words he chose Mike found baffling.

"Well done," the dwarf said.

Mike grappled with that a little and gave up, set it aside for later and looked up at Annie.

She had nothing to say. She simply stood there, holding the coffee pot and looking at him. Her face was calm, serene, quite composed. But tears were *pouring* down her cheeks. The effect was striking. He had never seen anybody cry with their eyes without also crying with their face.

"I screwed up, you see?" he said to her. God, now he was doing the same thing! He knew he wasn't crying, but his eyes were leaking. He wiped away the water impatiently. "It was important and I screwed up big-time. So I came here, because nothing ever gets that screwed up here."

She nodded.

He found a tissue and blew his nose.

She put a gentle hand on his shoulder. "I believe my role at this point is to produce soothing clichés," she said softly, "but I do hate sounding like an idiot. I can't say 'I know how you feel,' because I don't. I can't say 'It wasn't your fault,' because you obviously know that and it doesn't help, enough. I can't say 'You did your best,' because you just told *me* that, and it obviously doesn't help enough, either. Hell, you've never once done less than your best for *me*, and you've only known me a week."

He tried to smile. "It's okay, Annie."

"Perhaps it will be," she said, "if you'll listen to just one cliché. One you may *not* already know."

"Sure."

"It's okay to be glad it's over."

The idea was astonishing. "It *is*?"

"Relieved I would be," Hormat agreed quietly.

"So would I," Annie said. "It is permissible to feel relief on the way out of Hell."

"It is?"

She squeezed his shoulder. "You say you screwed up. The fact that you had no choice at all doesn't help: you screwed up, and nothing hurts like that. Your mother screwed up, too. Twice as bad—no, more than that—because she was responsible for you, and still committed slow suicide. It was only a matter of time. She was smart, you say, so she must have known that . . . and that must have hurt her, too."

"Yeah."

"And now neither of you is screwing up anymore. How can that not be a relief? To both of you?"

"Uh . . ." Something began to unknot inside him. He knew it would take a long time . . . but now that the process was begun, time was all it would take.

"Don't grunt. Good God, boy, look at it this way: no matter how long you live, you'll never screw up that badly again—and you're twelve years old."

In spite of himself, he grinned. "That is something to be proud of, isn't it?" he said.

She smiled and let go of his shoulder. "I wish I could say the same. Now excuse me, all right? There are pressing matters on the table. Hormat?"

"Yes?" the dwarf said, seeming to come out of a fog.

"Your time is nearly up, is it not?"

He started and hastily checked his finger. "Yes," he said. "Another few minutes."

Shit! They'd taken too long—spilled their guts for nothing—Hormy *had* to go . . .

Annie nodded. "Tell me, Hormat: why have you and your friends come back to this era?"

Mike dropped his jaw.

Hormat's face turned to stone. He and Annie locked eyes for at least ten seconds, and then he closed his eyes for at least another ten. Oddly, he was for once not frowning. Then he opened his eyes and looked at Mike. Something happened to his face that Mike couldn't pin down. There were no discernible muscle movements, but somehow it lost ten years in the space of a few seconds.

Hormat smiled. It was the first smile Mike had ever seen on his face, and it was wondrously ugly.

"We came to bring you a free lunch," he said.

CHAPTER 17

COMPLIMENTARY COMESTIBLES

Mike's determination not to interrupt was strongly tested. Everybody knew there was no such thing as a free lunch; it was a Heinlein proverb, one he himself had always found to be true. He was positive there was no such thing as a free rock of crack cocaine. But he kept his mouth shut. Everybody knew there was no such thing as time-travel, too.

"Why, Hormat?" Annie asked.

Hormat shifted his eyes to her. "For the same reason you came Under, Annie," he said, still smiling. "We could no longer bear not to." He turned back to Mike. "For the same reason you came Under, Mike. Because all our other choices were worse."

This was all a little too philosophical for Mike; he was aware that Hormat was getting himself in deeper shit with every minute. "We figured something was after you guys," he prompted. "Aliens or something."

Hormat shook his head. "No. We're running from history. Nothing more. Human history."

"What do you mean?" Annie asked.

Hormat's smile slowly faded. "I've thought about this," he said. "How to tell you . . . whether to tell you . . . how much to tell you—I wish I could think about it another month. . . ."

Annie reached across the table and took his hand. "Just tell us," she said.

He closed his eyes. "The future is horror," he said.

"Of what kind?"

"Of all kinds." He opened his eyes and saw that they did not understand. "In my time," he said, "there are fewer than a quarter of a billion humans."

Mike was aghast. His own world held over seven billion.

Annie looked startled. "On Earth, you mean?"

"Alive," he corrected. "Anywhere. Less than a quarter of a million live off Earth. Our birthrate is below replacement." He winced. "*Well* below."

"My God," Annie breathed.

"Wait," he said. "You have seen my friends and me?" He looked down at himself and then back up. "*We are the best of us.*"

Mike stared. "You're—"

"We are the biggest and strongest and healthiest volunteers that could be found," Hormat said. "I know to you we seem small and weak. But when I come from, I am considered a giant, of abnormal strength and endurance. There may be a hundred people in all my time who could take me in a fair fight—and most of them are on this mission."

"Dear God," Annie breathed. "What went wrong?"

Hormat sighed. "*Everything*. All at once. No man can say with certainty which happened first or caused the other—but the global economy collapsed utterly, and the Ice Age came, and technological civilization all but died, and the planetary ecosystem was ruined, almost beyond our ability to repair. And the 'almost' does not matter, for in the process, the gene pool was hopelessly corrupted. Civilization had lasted just long enough and been just reckless enough to fill the biosphere with more toxins, carcinogens, and other mutagens than it could handle . . . and they all interacted.

"There was a Dark Age that was nearly the last . . . and science was rediscovered too late. My generation has, by the skin of our teeth as you say, and by enormous good fortune, just barely staved off an ecocatastrophe so total that nothing vertebrate could have survived—and we have even made some remarkable scientific breakthroughs. We have limited use of nanotechnology, which your time only dreams about so far, and two other powerful technologies you have no names for because you have not even dreamed of them yet—" He broke off and smiled a bitter smile. "It is the best joke of all time, when you think about it. We could easily feed and clothe and house and amuse a population larger than yours, if we were lucky enough to need to. But we ourselves are doomed. Our DNA is irreparable. We have made our time a comparative paradise for those who remain alive in it . . . but the end is in sight. And we can no longer bear to look at it."

"What year do you come from?" Mike asked.

Hormat seemed not to hear the question. "So we looked away. We looked at the past, because there was nowhere else to look. We traced the roots of our doom, with bitter hindsight. We identified a point in history when—if only they had known what we knew now—everything might have been made right, and disaster averted."

"The early twenty-first century," Annie whispered.

"And then one of the scientific breakthroughs that had come too late to help us produced a spin-off: time-travel."

Mike followed a thought train until it crashed. "But," he blurted, "but if you *succeed*—if you guys manage to change history—even if you pull it off—"

Hormat nodded calmly. "Our time—our world—ceases to exist. Yes."

"But—don't you disappear with it, too? You and all your friends back here?"

"How can we know that?"

"Why . . . by . . . by—"

"How would you design an experiment to answer that question?"

Mike thought about it and felt his head spin. "Jesus, Hormat—"

"Probably we will disappear, yes. Never have been. We will know we have succeeded if we notice ourselves fading out of existence. If it is given to us to know that. If we succeed."

"But how can you just—"

"As with you and your mother," Hormat said, "it will be very sad—but a relief for all concerned."

Mike told himself to shut up. "But aren't there—I mean, don't you have—?" He got control of his mouth back and closed it.

"Loved ones in the future?" Hormat finished for him. "Whom I will miss as badly as you miss your mother? Yes, Mike." He closed his eyes briefly. "We all do. But like you, we *must do something*. Even if it turns out to be wrong. We hope the future we bring about will be better. And if it is not, at least we will not know it."

Annie shivered slightly; sat up straighter, and squared her shoulders. "I have always prided myself on being able to handle three impossible things before breakfast," she said. "Two to go. What exactly do you and your friends plan to do?"

"I told you," Hormat said.

"You're going to give us a free lunch."

"Exactly. We plan to make you all rich—without letting you catch us at it."

"Huh?" Mike said in spite of himself. "Isn't that exactly how we screwed up everything for you guys? All of us trying to get rich?"

Hormat almost smiled. "Most of you do not want to be rich," he said, "although you think you do. Except for a few freaks, most of you do not really want anything so unreasonable. You want only a privilege you have been told belongs to the rich: freedom from fear. You want to be free of want, free of burden, free of worry, so that you may sit by your own vine under your own fig tree long enough to either grow bored or find someone to play with. You want enough to take care of your loved ones and indulge their reasonable whims."

"I guess," Mike said.

"Mike, history is a complex subject, and economic history is the worst. But most of the problems the human race has ever had—the real problems—trace back to the same cause. Insufficient wealth."

"Don't you mean inadequate, inequitable *distribution* of wealth?" Annie asked.

"In a sense, yes," Hormat agreed. "But while you cannot control individual greed, you can overwhelm it—with enough wealth."

"Can you?" she asked, looking dubious.

Mike started to see it. "Annie," he said, "every society has parasites, right? They suck as much money out of it as they can, so they can play Who's Got the Most Toys with their parasite friends. If there's enough of them, and they're greedy and short-sighted enough . . . well, the society dies, one way or another, and their wealth doesn't mean shit anymore. But suppose there was so much money that even after they hauled off all they could carry, there was still enough to go around, enough to keep everybody fed and working."

She was grimacing. "That does sound like what America's been trying to do for the last century or two—get rich faster than the parasites could steal it."

"And it has done so more successfully than most cultures in history," Hormat agreed. "Even so, the racing has been . . . what is the expression about throats?"

It was Mike who got the reference. "Neck and neck."

"Yes. So my friends and I are going to cheat."

"I repeat," Annie said. *"How?"*

He smiled. "By injecting wealth into the system—by stealth."

"Like pickpockets in reverse," Mike breathed.

"Yes," Hormat said.

Annie shook her head. "I don't understand."

Things were falling into place in Mike's head, like a mental game of Tetris. "I think I do," he said. "Annie, listen: a truck leaves a warehouse with a load of five hundred widgets, okay?

Any truck, anywhere on earth. When it gets where it's going and they unload it, how many widgets are sitting there on the loading dock?"

"Four hundred and eighty," she said.

"Tops," he agreed. "Suppose that stopped happening?"

Her jaw dropped. Hormat smiled.

"Suppose five hundred and twenty widgets came off the truck. Who'd complain?" Mike went on. "Somebody will probably pocket the unexpected bonus—but who cares?"

"It's in the system now," Hormat said, "part of the economy . . . and without being documented because it falls into a gray zone."

Annie was staring into space. "It's a truism that you never *quite* get what you pay for, anywhere except Dreamworld—my God, we're all so cynical that if it ever stopped being true, or reversed, it *might* be quite a while before anyone even noticed . . ."

"Suppose a little more oil—of slightly better quality—started coming out of the Alaska pipeline than was pumped in?" Hormat said. "Just possibly it might be noticed . . . but would it be remarked? Who profits by investigating the phenomenon?

"Suppose the generators feeding the national power grid started to perform just a little better than their design specs said they should—almost as if power were being fed into the system from some outside source? Who would complain?

"Let's say you were a geologist who could *prove* a massive new oil dome or iron deposit or copper vein or coal seam was in fact *not there* until ten minutes before the first exploratory drill discovered it—who would believe you?

"Suppose sitologists suddenly made unexpected breakthroughs in genetically enhanced food crops—how many would deny that their own genius was responsible? How many would even mention, much less credit, their grad-student slave—that funny little dwarf?

"If your computer never ever crashed again . . . well, you would notice, eventually—but would you actually call the newspapers? If you did, could anyone possibly track down the specific individual whose virus had rewritten and improved your operating system software?"

"You and your friends can do all those things?" Annie asked.

"And much more," Hormat said. "We hope."

A thought occurred to Mike. "Aren't you guys doing it the hard way? I mean, why can't you just . . . I don't know, like, hack into the world banking system and diddle all the computers into *thinking* there's more wealth? Increase everybody's bank balance by a few bucks a month—Mom never used to even look at her bank statements, and anyway, nobody's gonna say anything if they do find a discrepancy in their *favor*."

Hormat and Annie were both shaking their heads. The dwarf let her take it. "That just creates more *money*, Mike—not more wealth. Money with nothing to back it up is one of the principal reasons the world economy is in the fix it's in."

"What you need is more of what one *buys* with money," Hormat amplified. "Raw materials. Power. Calories. Drinking water. Things nanotechnology can produce 'out of thin air,' very cheaply, by using invisibly tiny machines to build new molecules an atom at a time out of available parts. You will have the same amount of money in your bank account—but soon you will be able to buy more with it."

Mike nodded dubiously. "If you say so."

"I've listed only some of just the first-aid measures. We will do many other things. But those convey the overall idea. Your dying descendants have come back to hang an IV drip for your ailing civilization—to build its strength and make it healthy enough to survive the coming crisis. Our immense wealth is useless to us, for it cannot be left to our own descendants. So we must give it to our ancestors."

WHAT KIND OF other things?" Mike asked.

Annie shot him a look, moved her head from side to side, and unobtrusively moved her wrist so that the watch on her Band showed. *We've got the general idea, Hormat's late already, and there are more important things to—*

"Give me a couple of examples," Mike said. Annie frowned, but he ignored her. Hormat was a big boy; he could take care of himself.

Hormat apparently failed to notice the byplay. "Well, some of it will consist of persuading you to use more intelligently the resources you already have. Some of the most important things we want to bring you are not material goods, but *ideas*."

"Like what?"

Hormat pursed his lips, consulted an imaginary list below him and to his right, and picked one. "Microwave roasting."

"You can't roast with a microwave," Mike said.

"Not by itself, no," Hormat said. "How much do you know about coffee, Mike?"

He thought about it. "Use good beans and a pinch of salt and clean the gear immediately, without soap, every time."

"All anyone needs to know," Annie murmured.

Hormat sighed and nodded. "This will require a brief lecture, then."

Annie again shot Mike a dirty look, which he again ignored.

"There are three basic strains of coffee plant," Hormat began. "Arabica is the most expensive—not just because it is the best-tasting, but because it is the most delicate. It can only survive in very specific and narrow conditions, in ecological niches that occur only a few places on earth—and with luck. Each year, a whole nation's crop may fail without warning. Slightly less feeble is Robusta coffee—it requires slightly less strict conditions and is a little less vulnerable to disease. But it is usually blended with at least a little Arabica, because its own brew does not taste as good."

"The cherries are too big," Annie said before she could stop herself.

Hormat nodded vigorously. "Exactly. They yield a much larger bean."

"Isn't that good?" Mike asked.

She shook her head. "When you roast them, by the time the inside is done—" She broke off suddenly and knitted her brow.

"—the outside is burnt," Hormat finished for her.

"*Cushlamachree,*" Annie said softly. "I see where you're going now."

Mike shook his head. "I don't."

She turned to face him, an odd expression on her face. "The third kind of coffee, Liberica, grows *anywhere*. Almost like kudzu, you couldn't kill it with an ax. It laughs at parasites and disease, doesn't care what the weather is. And it's perfectly worthless—because it produces cherries the size of golf balls. The coffee tastes like hell."

It hit Mike all at once. "Microwave and roasting, together." He and Annie chorused the next sentence. "The inside and the outside get done *at the same time*—"

Annie still had that funny look on her face. "The coffee industry is one of the biggest, most profitable industries on the planet," she said, seeming to be talking to herself even though she was looking right at him. "Billions a year. Lots of billions."

"We can increase its productivity at least fivefold within a decade," Hormat told her, "simply by whispering the idea in the right ears. They'll be able to do their own arithmetic."

Her eyes were getting wider. She turned back to Hormat. "Liberica will grow anywhere," she said, a singsong tone entering her voice, "but most of the places it happens to be growing already . . ."

"Are some of the poorest countries on earth," he said.

"*Now,*" she said, and they both smiled broadly.

"A lot of our work will be like that," Hormat said. "Spreading ideas. Encouraging your people to think in new ways about resources they already possess—and to reexamine things they take for granted."

"Like what?" Mike asked. "Tell me another." Annie glared at him reprovingly, but he failed to notice.

"Software," Hormat said at once, and then hesitated.

"What do you mean?"

Hormat chose his words. "Mike, for several reasons I want to tell you just as little as I can about exactly what went so horribly wrong to produce the world I come from. But . . . are you familiar with the basic notion of nanotechnology?"

"Tiny robots," Mike said, "way too tiny to see, small enough to take molecules apart into atoms and then reassemble them into different molecules."

Hormat nodded. "The key to infinite wealth. And each tiny robot must be run by an even tinier computer, yes?"

Mike and Annie nodded agreement.

Hormat pointed to Annie's computer. "How reliable is yours?"

Annie's face began to change as she took his meaning. "Oh my God," she breathed.

"What is it, Annie?"

"That thing crashes at least once every other day. They *all* do. I mean, it's not like back in the twentieth, when they crashed twice an hour and nobody thought anything of it . . . but even today . . . God, Hormat's absolutely right, and I can't believe I never realized it before. Don't you see, Mike? Nanobots could theoretically multiply faster than a plague. One teeny nanobot, running software as reliable as, say, the best-selling word processor on the market, might well be able to turn the entire planet into gray goo by this time next Thursday."

Mike thought about it and started to shudder. "We're nowhere near *ready* for nanotechnology . . ."

"You need a new computer language, an operating system and applications that are one hundred percent bug-free and crash-proof," Hormat said. "Nothing less will do. Ninety-nine point nine nine repeated out to the thousandth decimal place is not good enough."

"And you'll give us those?" Mike said. "But *how?* How are you gonna persuade all the nano guys in the world to give up all their own software and use yours?"

"We probably couldn't," Hormat said. "Instead we hope to release a worm, which will eventually infect every piece of software already in existence. Think of it as a bug-eating worm. When it is through conquering the noosphere, computers will not crash anymore."

"But—"

Reluctantly, but firmly, Annie interrupted. "Mike, that's enough. Hormat's out of time. He's going to get home late as it is."

The dwarf shook his head. "Let him ask his questions, Annie. It does not matter. I am no longer in any hurry."

She looked dubious. "But surely the later you get back, the worse it—"

"Thank you," he said with great kindness, "but there is no later than late. The moment I missed my deadline, I became a dead man."

MIKE AND ANNIE both cried out at the same time, and cried the same word, but each meant separate things. *"Why?"*

Hormat answered Mike first. "Because what we are doing can have *no* slipups. It is simply too dangerous. If we are to succeed, we must have not only great determination and exhaustive training . . . but *perfect* discipline. The moment my absence is noted, they will know what I've done. And why. I've committed the ultimate crime: anachrognosticism. I have given knowledge of future events and of our present plans to . . . we call you 'locals,' among ourselves. In effect, I've given you two the same power *we* all fearfully bear: the power to end the universe at any moment, simply by revealing our existence. If you had carried out the threat you made to me a while ago on your doorstep, Annie, and told even what you knew *then* to any medium of historical record . . . the End of Everything might have come."

She repeated her own question, more anguish in her voice than

Mike had ever heard. "*Why,* Hormat? Why did you stay and answer our questions? Why sacrifice yourself?"

To Mike's astonishment, Hormat smiled broadly and actually emitted a rumbling gurgle that might have been his version of a chuckle. "I doubt I can explain it to you. I'm not sure I understand it myself." His expression sobered, and he looked as sad and skeptical as ever again. "Here is the best answer I can give you. I told you because I decided I owe it to you both."

Mike was appalled. He'd known he was pushing Hormat by dragging him home—Hormat had *said* that he *mustn't* be late. When the appointed hour came and went, and the dwarf just kept on talking, Mike had suspected he was probably getting his new friend in a jam—but Annie needed all the information she could get to make her decision. So Mike had kept pumping him, on the assumption that Hormat would know when he really *really* had to go. Mike himself had once taken a beating rather than leave a friend in need just to get home on time.

But, *death*? Some of his horror and guilt tried to transmute into indignation. "You *owe* it to us?" he cried. "What the hell does *that* mean?"

"It means he's a jerk," Conway said.

CONWAY STOOD IN the open doorway, aiming a shotgun at them.

Mike froze like a rabbit. His face tingled, felt hot. His scalp crawled. He could hear his pulse thundering in his neck. Maybe this was okay. As long as Hormat still had some sleepy-gas left . . .

Behind him he heard some very odd sounds, which suddenly converted themselves into a mental picture. Hormat had just leaned across the table, put his broad palm over Annie's mouth, and pinched her nostrils shut. Mike was already holding his own breath. He began to flood with relief, at the same time trying to keep it from his face—

Conway grinned broadly. "Nice try, Sneezy," he said to Hormat.

Mike kept holding his breath, but all the relief seemed to sigh out of him. Scrubbing Conway's memory hadn't kept him from deducing what must have happened to him and Haines back in the dungeon.

"I'm man enough to admit you clowns made me look stupid twice in one day," Conway said. "But I learn from my mistakes." He took his left hand from the shotgun barrel just long enough to point to his own nose. "Filters," he said. "Should have had them in when I was working on you, kid, I know. I didn't realize you had pals with magic powers, then." Despite his words, he was still looking directly at Hormat, speaking to him. "I do, now."

"How much did you hear?" Hormat asked.

"Enough," Conway told him. Since Hormat was speaking, Mike relaxed his diaphragm and took in a tentative breath. Nothing happened; the gas was dissipated. He heard Annie breathe, too, behind him.

"*Really?*" Hormat pressed. "Do you truly understand the *danger,* now? How close you came to destroying everything—even yourself?"

"I think so," Conway said. "Don't worry, Shorty, I have no intention of blowing your cover. I'm not even going to tell Haines. I like the universe just fine the way it is: I won't risk changing history." His insolent smile faded. "But I won't let *you* clowns change it, either."

"What do you intend to do?" Annie asked. Her voice was so tightly controlled Mike wanted to turn around in his chair and look at her, but he could not tear his eyes from the mouth of Conway's shotgun. He had seen a gun like it before, during a drug raid: small, compact, with a thirty-round magazine. They were called "alley sweepers."

"After I kill you clowns, you mean? Nothing that'll make the papers, don't worry. Just as quietly and unobtrusively as all those little runts from the future are infiltrating the world, I'm going to hunt them down and kill them to the last man. I've got the manpower and I've got the skill and I've got the motivation."

"What motivation?" Annie asked. "Why do it? Haines doesn't give a damn about the world or its woes, all he wants is Dreamworld shut—"

"Forget Haines. I have."

"Then who's your client?"

"All of them," he told her.

"I don't understand."

"I think I do," Hormat said sadly.

"Think about it," Conway said. "I don't get hired by rich people much. I get hired by *powerful* people. People that are into power only care about money when they can use it as a club. *And you can only do that when it's scarce.* Powerful people don't want the world to be rich—just them. And I have to agree. The kind of world Shorty there wants to build, pretty soon they won't have as much use for guys like me. When I think about it, I *like* the world with a whole lot of losers in it . . . and a handful of winners to milk. Makes it easier, you see?" He grinned again. "If I ever wanted to retire, I could probably do it just on what the coffee industry is going to pay me for making sure that anybody who ever says the words 'microwave roasting' out loud winds up dead. I'm going to be bigger than Pinkerton. I'm going to be *planetary*."

As Conway boasted, Mike's mind was running around the inside of his skull like a rat trying to escape from a trap. What were they going to *do*? It was like watching a movie where you knew the Good Guy was going to win in the end, because he was too big a star not to, but for the life of you, you couldn't figure out how. First you tried plausible ways, and if that failed, you tried Hollywood ways. Did he and Annie have anything here that could be turned into a plausible weapon? Wait a minute: the computer remote! No, he remembered where Annie had set it down—out of reach: she'd be cut down as she dove for it. So he entertained fantasies: Durl would show up to cover his pal's back; Phillip

Avery would pick right *now* to become aware of Annie's presence and send a squad to arrest her; Hormat would have some other secret weapon besides his sleep gas, that he was only holding back to build up suspense; Conway's gun would explode—

He stopped all at once and faced the truth. This was real life. He wasn't a star. He didn't have to win. For the second time since midnight, Mike accepted the certainty of death. He began trying to think of *ways* to die that might improve his friends' chances, however slightly. Such as charging the gun—

Annie spoke. "I know a guy who can stop you. And he's right here."

CHAPTER 18

FIXING THE RACE

For a moment Conway bristled like a cat and seemed to grow eyes in the back of his head. He carefully backed up a few steps and stopped just outside the doorway in the atrium, where he could still cover the entire small room, but could also keep track of the holowall entrance on his right with his peripheral vision. Then he let a corner of his mouth curl. "Oh yeah? Who?"

"A Mr. John Nurk," Annie said clearly.

Conway frowned. "Hell is he?"

Mike was almost as puzzled. He got the reference at once—any Dreamworld regular would: John Nurk, half of the Nurk Twins, aka John Lennon—but he didn't understand what Annie was driving at.

"Hormat knows," Annie said. "You remember, Hormat: you met Mr. Nurk only minutes after you met Mike—although you never did see him."

Mike was even more confused. The next person Hormat and Durl had met after Mike had been Annie, as far as he knew.

"Who *is* he, I said?" Conway snarled. "And how's he going to stop me?" He was trying not to show it, but he was just the least little bit rattled now, more by Annie's obvious confidence than by anything she'd said.

"It's perfectly self-evident," she replied elliptically. "I mean, it must be high or low."

Mike got it at last.

He understood now not only what she was driving at, but why she was talking about it in code. She had a plan—she had a weapon after all—and it was crucially important that he and Hormat both take right action the instant she employed it. Which would be sometime in the next few seconds.

"Last chance," Conway said, pointing the shotgun in Annie's direction.

"Okay," she said. "I'll tell you: it's high. Not low."

Conway frowned slightly, sighed in exasperation, and took a bead on Annie's face. At that range, the blast would get all three of them, clustered as they were at the table. "Fine," he said. "The hell with it. So long—"

Annie laughed aloud. "The funny part is, you're not an ignorant man. You've probably read it yourself a dozen times, in adventure stories. What's the one way to ambush someone that *always* works, Conway?"

His frown deepened as he thought about her question in spite of himself. Mike didn't have to look behind him to know where Annie's right hand was. It was near her left wrist . . .

She chuckled again. "Silly, considering our species used to live in trees once—but for some reason, even the most alert, cautious man never looks *up* . . ."

And everything seemed to happen at once, then.

CONWAY'S EYES WIDENED as he took her meaning. Even if he'd had more time to think, he'd probably have reached the same decision. All it would cost him to find out if Annie was bluffing was a split-second glance upward. A lesser man might have decided not to risk it, but a part of the combat computer that lived in Conway's skull had long since inventoried this tactical situation and was quite certain all three targets were at least a full second away from anything in the room that could pose a serious threat to him. So taking his eyes from them momentarily was the lesser risk, and he chose it. And sure enough, it took him well under half a second to be absolutely certain there was nothing dangerous overhead, that just as he'd thought the bitch *had* been bluffing, stupid enough to think she could dodge a scattergun in a small room. Conway was almost smiling as he flicked his eyes back down and began to bring the barrel back down, too, but he stopped smiling and moving almost at once because the room was empty now.

Even then he did not stop thinking clearly. He never did figure out that all Annie's baffling remarks had been veiled references to Johnny's Tree in Strawberry Fields, did not waste any time at all wondering exactly how the three little bastards had managed to make themselves invisible. He didn't care how; how was a good trick he could steal later; the point now was to counter it, and the counter was perfectly obvious and perfectly simple: just let off two rounds into that little room, three tops, and wherever they were hiding they'd probably be hamburger. Again, a lesser man might have done so without even thinking about it—but Conway, the master survivor, never lost sight of one important factor. Dreamworld Security was, in his professional opinion, almost as good as he was. The moment he pulled the trigger, he was going to have to turn on his heel and run like hell, *instantly,* if he was to have any hope of slipping through the cordon that would begin closing in at once. He was very reluctant to do that until he was *certain* all three of his targets were dead. So he delayed half a second, hoping to catch movement somewhere or hear footsteps or furniture banging, *something* to aim by.

But then he decided the hell with it, lowered the barrel and began to take up slack on the trigger, and again his own competence betrayed him. Force of habit wanted him to aim his shotgun blasts at the traditional correct height, at waist level—but he was professional enough to remember that his targets were a midget, a dwarf, and a short kid. He adjusted his aim accordingly, laid the muzzle at what would ordinarily have been a little under crotch height, and as he squeezed off the first round almost forty kilograms of absolutely nothing hit him square in the face.

That started his head and upper torso moving backward, and he might have been able to backpedal quickly enough to keep his feet under him, but the shotgun went off again. It blew a large ugly hole in the ceiling and gave him additional momentum both backward and down: the first thing to hit the atrium wall behind him was the top of his skull, with a sound almost as authoritative as the gunfire. Remarkably, he did not lose consciousness then, or even a moment later, when the forty kilos—now visible: the goddamn kid—rebounded more gracefully from the wall, fell on Conway, bore him down to the plasteel floor, and whacked the *back* of his skull against *that*. But he did lose the shotgun.

No matter. It was worse than useless now anyway: they would be looking for a man with a shotgun. Time to break off the engagement and get clear. Shouting inarticulately in rage and pain, he flung the boy from his chest, got his feet under him, and without even stopping to snap the brat's neck, hurled himself through the holowall and out into the corridor, taking what consolation he could from having nailed two out of three.

MIKE SHOOK OFF Annie's help and got to his feet, glaring at her. "You never told me you had the place tricked up to do that," he accused.

"You never asked. Security here is *good*; I had to be prepared for a raid." She tapped at her Command Band and canceled the effect; behind her, Hormat became visible again, standing on the tabletop.

And visibly upset. He leaped to the floor, crying, "Catch him we *must*," and tried to muscle his way between and past them.

"Whoa," Annie cried, and Mike helped her restrain him. "Are you trying to get us busted? Let Conway look out for hims—"

"He either gets away or Security gets him," Hormat grated,

struggling feebly with them. "Either way . . . *what happens next?*"

Mike looked at Annie and Annie looked at Mike, and then they both shoved Hormat away from the door—but only accidentally, in the process of using him as a starting block.

In those first couple of running steps, while he was still planning how to make his right turn as he passed through the holowall, Mike assumed it was hopeless. Conway had a lead of several seconds on them and did not care if he attracted notice as long as nobody stopped him. Mike and Annie had to *live* here. And even if they threw caution to the winds and raced flat-out . . . Conway was over two meters tall, with long legs, and he looked to be in the peak of physical condition and training. Mike was a short twelve-year-old, and Annie was an aged midget. They were both unarmed except for Annie's Command Band, and she couldn't very well have *all* of Dreamworld tricked out with booby traps. Mike was prepared to give it his best shot—he understood the fate of everything was at stake—but he didn't give much for his chances.

Until he passed through the holowall and into the corridor, where he saw two things, one happy-sad and the other just happy, which between them explained some of the odd half-heard noises out here that had been nagging at his subconscious.

The happy-sad thing he saw was a pair of semiconscious midgets lying in the corridor in his path, both moaning feebly. A heavy pipe wrench lay near the larger one. With no idea how he could possibly know it, Mike knew who they were and why they were there, though he had never seen either face before. They were Max and Amparo—the tunnel rats who had almost caught him in the air shaft. The only explanation for their presence here, far from their station, was that they had noticed a stranger skulking through Dreamworld, carrying what looked like it might be a weapon, and tailed him. Why hadn't they just reported it and let Security handle it? Because Max either knew or guessed that *the guy was heading straight for the Mother Elf's place!* Annie wasn't quite as Under as she thought she was. Max and Amparo had waited outside in the corridor, unable to hear anything, debating their move . . . then they *had* heard the shotgun blasts, and that gave them time to get into position before Conway came out. It hadn't helped them enough, of course; they were civilians and Conway had taken them both easily.

But even he hadn't been able to do it without breaking stride: the *happy* thing Mike saw at the same moment he saw Max and Amparo was Conway's right foot, only just now disappearing around a corner down the hall. There was now at least a hope in hell of catching him.

Mike leaped over the prone pair and poured on the steam—and soon he saw a really *startling* thing. Annie was at least thirty years older than him, he was sure of that, with legs just as short as his, and he had seen little in the few days he'd been here to suggest that she lived anything but a sedentary life, and furthermore she was a girl—

—and she was smoking him.

Trashing him; by the time he got it through his head that she had a lead and was going to keep on widening it, it was up to thirty meters. He almost grinned, until he realized it made her more likely than him to get killed by Conway first, and then he stopped thinking altogether and concentrated on running.

She was better on straightaways, he was better on stairs. By the time they burst out into the open above ground, they were neck and neck again. People who had just been staring after Conway turned and stared at them. Many were Guests, both adults and kids; Dreamworld had opened for the day while he and Annie were playing out their real-life drama underground. Mike blinked at the bright sunlight and reacquired Conway. He was racing straight into Heinlein's Worlds, the most direct route to the nearest exterior wall of Dreamworld. The parking and entrance area was over at the other end of the park; there was nothing beyond the wall Conway was heading for but forest. He glanced over his shoulder and saw Mike and Annie coming, increased his pace. Mike frowned—

Then he caught sight of one of the omnipresent clocks and began to hope. Once Conway was into Heinlein territory, he would almost certainly race right past Podkayne's Mars and straight into Westville. It was, again, the most direct route to the outer wall. But Mike knew it was not necessarily the *fastest*—not at this time of day. Just now it was smarter to deke left through Kip Russell's place—what was it, Centerville?—to avoid Westville. Where Lummox the huge Star Beast was just about to reenact his awe-inspiring March to the Bon Marché for the first time that day, eating Buicks as he went . . . and blocking the whole street.

Maybe they could pass Conway, beat him to that wall, be waiting to surprise him when he got there.

There was no time or breath to explain his logic to Annie; all he could do as the turnoff approached was yell, *"Follow me,"* and hope she would trust him. The shout caused her to turn her head and miss a stride, just as a bullet passed through the space her head would have been occupying. *Bang!* At once she was down and rolling. Mike started to do the same, but saw that Conway was running again now, so he stayed in motion. He could see the little holdout gun Conway had in his right hand; he must have had it all along, for Mike had never seen him pull it. This was really not good. Conway could turn and fire again at any moment . . .

And then inspiration came to Mike.

He sucked in all the air he could and let it out in a desperate bellow, using his "adult" voice. *"Stop him: he tried to shoot the Mother Elf!"*

The world went silent. He had not noticed until then that it was making sounds. Everyone stared at him. Annie stared up at him, openmouthed, from the position of cover she'd rolled to. Then she sprang to her feet, tilted her head back, and brayed at the top of her lungs.

"Hey, Rube—"

If there was any place on earth where the carny's ancient emergency call to arms was still remembered, it was Dreamworld. Many if not most of its older employees were ex-carny, and the rest had heard the legends. As one, every employee in sight, and one or two of the Guests, stopped staring at Mike and Annie—

—and turned to look at Conway.

All heaven broke loose then. Those still in a position to stop him began moving, while those behind him started yelling variations of the things Mike and Annie had just said to bystanders farther ahead who hadn't heard it. The words "Mother Elf" were heard more than once. Conway began running broken-field, trying to avoid being boxed into a gauntlet, but at first he kept assuming kids would be harmless, and that was wrong. Two of them almost succeeded in tripping him by rolling a trash can into his path while he was looking in another direction.

Never for an instant did Mike hope any of them would actually stop Conway. But he was pretty sure they'd slow him down— and so would eight-legged Lummox, taking up most of the road in his path. And Mike felt that Conway, already at risk of being caught or identified by Security cameras, was not stupid enough to make things even worse by shooting any Guests or legitimate Staff who got in his way if he could possibly avoid it. Mike had caught up with Annie now; he stopped watching the traveling chaos, helped her up, and hissed again, "Follow me!"

They took the left into Centerville, and luck was with them: Conway was too distracted to notice until they were out of sight. Within a block Annie must have figured out Mike's plan; she again moved out in front of him and began building a lead, just as the Russell Family came boiling out of Kip's House, wondering why the spaceship had come early today. In no time Annie and Mike were thundering past the spaceship itself; he could see Peewee and the Mother Thing gaping from its airlock.

Less than a minute later they had reached the far end of Centerville. They paused a moment to get their breath back, saw no pursuit behind them. Before them stood the outer wall. To their right was the inner wall that separated Centerville from Westville. Both appeared unscalable, but as Mike had prayed, Annie had another trick up her sleeve—*just* up her sleeve. She tapped her Command Band, and a doorway appeared in the inner wall.

Then she cursed as he pulled her backward by the collar and beat her through the door into Westville.

She tried to follow on his heels, but he stayed in the doorway, blocking her. *"Wait,"* he said, and looked over the situation. He could feel her impatience, but she said nothing and waited, still trying to get control of her breath back.

Conway was not yet in sight, but this was where he was going to end up, sooner or later; not far from where Mike stood, a section of outer wall had been breached by a new hole large enough for an adult. You could only tell that from Mike's position, too: a strategically placed Dumpster obscured the opening from people in Westville. Mike measured angles, rechecked them, and turned to face Annie. Just as he did so, he heard the first sounds of approaching commotion in the far distance and knew he had no time to explain. "Stay there," he hissed urgently, and closed the door in her outraged face.

He made it to a crouch behind the Dumpster in plenty of time, at the cost of a badly scraped knee, and spent his remaining seconds in the careful positioning of his right foot. If his calculations were right, the first few centimeters of its tip were now visible to anyone approaching the Dumpster. Happily, his shoe was a dark color that would stand out well against the default soft blue of Dreamworld plasteel. He glanced over and saw that the door he'd come through wasn't there anymore: Annie had figured out his plan and improved it with her Command Band.

He heard a shout, a thud, a grunt, and then Conway's approaching running footsteps. He began planning what he would do after Annie popped out behind Conway and slugged him. Go for the ankles, that was it: chop the big son of a bitch down to where they could work on him conveniently.

The footsteps slowed and stopped, two or three meters away. Conway chuckled. "Nice try. Come out of there, both of you. You're the only people in this park I can afford to kill right now."

Mike stepped into view, his empty hands prominently displayed. "There's just me," he said.

Conway's eyes narrowed suspiciously. Instantly he dropped to the ground, lay prone with his handgun extended, sighting underneath the Dumpster in search of another pair of feet. He failed to find any, and he could see that the three visible sides of the Dumpster offered no ledge or handgrip or other means of holding one's feet off the ground. A quick glance to either side showed no other potential hiding place nearby. He stood back up and sneered at Mike. "What happened? Mom have a heart attack?"

Splendid idea. "Yes, you creep," Mike blurted, and started to cry. To his surprise, real tears flowed. "You crummy rat-bastard! Somebody oughta . . . oughta do to *you* what you were gonna do to me back at Haines's place."

Conway grinned. "They don't make a blade that sharp. Good-bye, you little shit." He raised the gun, and just behind him the door reappeared and opened silently, and Mike waited for Annie to charge straight through and whack Conway on the back of the head with some utensil. And instead she came charging through at an angle, at the *wrong* angle and empty-handed; instead of passing behind Conway she passed in *front* of him—

—so quickly that Conway's peripheral vision failed to warn him until she was already going by at high speed, snatching the gun from his hand with an overhand sweep, then spinning and twisting and skidding to a halt and bringing up the gun before he could gather himself.

Conway blinked at her, too astonished to curse. "That was *nice*," he said.

"Thank you," she said, and shot him through the heart. As he fell she stepped closer and put a make-sure shot through his brain. Then she spun on her heel, flung the gun into the Dumpster, and burst into tears.

Mike, who had stopped his own fake tears in shock when the gun went off, resumed crying too, this time for real.

•   •   •

STILL SOBBING, ANNIE came and yanked him away from the Dumpster, spun him, pushed him toward the door, muscled him through it, and closed it behind them. She tapped her wrist, and it went away. Then she rummaged in her pockets until she found a wad of Kleenex, peeled off two tissues, and handed one to Mike. "Blow your nose," she said, for all the world like a maiden auntie. "And wipe your eyes."

Numbly Mike obeyed. "We shoulda gone out that hole behind the Dumpster," he said.

"First place they'll look. Hurry, we've got to go!"

"Where?" Mike asked. "Why?"

"Right now we've got to get Under and hole up somewhere nobody's looking for us."

"What's the point? We're *blown*. Security's probably in your house right now."

She took him by the front of his coverall and shook him twice. "I trusted you twice in the last five minutes, when you had no time to explain. Your turn. *Come on!*" She let him go, turned, and ran away.

He followed automatically.

He did almost no thinking at all in the next few minutes, didn't even note the route Annie took, didn't try to guess where they were going or what she had in mind so he could be ready. He had been thinking too hard and too fast for too long, the past day or two, had been filing away so much trauma to deal with later that the hopper was full. In his immediate past was violent death, in his immediate future was—at the very least—the end of his life in Dreamworld. His mind went on strike; most of what little consciousness he retained was fully occupied in forcing his exhausted body to keep moving. His calves ached, his chest burned, his feet hurt, his lacerated knee stung; his damaged pinky throbbed; that was more than enough to deal with for now.

An eternity later—perhaps three minutes—Annie found a spot remote enough to suit her, a supply depot in a seldom-used corridor, hustled them inside it, and sealed the door. Mike collapsed gratefully onto some piece of gear he didn't recognize, and concentrated on not throwing up. He quickly found that keeping his eyes open helped a lot.

She waited until she had enough breath back for speech, then panted, "We'll be safe for a few minutes here."

Mike nodded dully. So what?

She raised her Command Band to her mouth. "Annie calling Hormat. Can you hear me? Annie calling H—"

"Are you all right, Annie?" Hormat's voice said. He sounded extremely worried.

"Out of breath," she said, "but triumphant."

There was a pause. "You got him?" Hormat said excitedly then. "Where is he now?"

"Hell. No question in my mind."

A longer pause. "I see. I'm sorry I—"

"Shut up, please, I'm in a hurry. Just outside the entrance to the Administration Area there's a maintenance closet, marked: meet us there as quickly as you can without being seen."

The longest pause yet, and Annie had no time for it. "Damn it, Hormat—"

"Annie," he said, "I thank you for what you are trying to—"

"Shut up again, I'm trying to save your life—"

"That is not poss—"

"*Yes, it is*—I'm telling you it is."

"But how—"

"No time. Trust me and live. Mistrust me and die. Out." She switched off. "Come on," she said to Mike. She opened the door, peered cautiously out in both directions, and then ran from the room.

Mike stared after her for a moment with his mouth open. Then it sank in. *Hormy might not have to die.* He lurched to his feet and raced after her.

• • •

HORMAT WAS WAITING for them in the closet when they arrived. "Annie, my leaders will not change their minds," was his greeting.

"They won't have to. Now please be quiet: we were interrupted in the middle of this conversation when Conway dropped in, and there's no time for any more delays. Now: *do not* tell me where you're supposed to be right now. Don't even tell me how far away it is. But tell me this: is it in this state?"

Hormat nodded. "Yes. It is—"

"Shhh. I don't need to know. I can get you home in time. Probably plenty of time."

He looked dubious. "How? To meet my deadline now I would need—"

"I can get you a brand-new car," she said. "Not only that: one with unquestioned maximum privilege."

Mike's eyes went round. A new car would let Hormat use the automated lanes—up to 50 percent faster than the maximum speed manual drivers were permitted—and maximum privilege would let him use the 175-kph lane reserved for emergency vehicles, cops, and VIPs. Annie was right: Hormat could still make it home before roll call!

"You have the codes?" Hormat asked.

"Memorized long ago," she said. "You'll have to dump it as far from your destination as you dare and hoof it in the rest of the way, then tell your people your own car must have been stolen in the night."

He nodded. "That could work. But . . . what about you?"

"What about me?"

"What will you do? You and Mike?"

She shook her head. "I haven't the foggiest. I haven't had time to think about it yet. And I don't now—come along. Mike, take rearguard."

He and Hormat did as they were told, lining up behind her. She slipped the closet door open, peered out, then flung it wide and stepped boldly out into the hallway. They followed, trying to look as if whatever they were doing, they were supposed to be doing it. She led them *away* from the door to the Administration Area and nearly at once ducked through an unmarked door into a stairwell. One flight down they left it and emerged into a long wide corridor. Halfway along its length she held up a hand to warn them and stopped. She fiddled with her wrist, and a door appeared in the wall. An elevator door. She frowned in concentration, tapped the Band again, and there was a distant hum. The elevator arrived, the door opened, they all piled in.

Mike looked for a control panel as the door slid closed, saw none, wondered briefly if they'd walked into a trap. But Annie tapped another code and the car descended. "Once this stops, we have to be very quiet," she said.

The car stopped, the door opened, and they stepped out into a garage. It was large enough to accommodate perhaps twenty vehicles and currently held only five. The one Annie led them to was clearly the finest of the lot, and they were all luxury machines.

As she neared it, she tapped her Band and held it out toward the car. Mike was too groggy to catch the significance of the fact that it failed to chirp in response; when Annie and Hormat stopped short, he cannoned into them from behind.

Annie reentered the code with great care, tried again. No result. "Shit," she said forcefully. "He must have changed the code, and for some reason not told his diary. Now why in the *hell* would he—"

"No, he didn't," said a voice behind them.

Mike whirled and looked. Fifty meters away, a tall gray-haired man stepped out from behind a pillar. Mike knew him at once.

"He just overrode you," Phillip Avery explained.

MIKE SAW THAT he was right. Avery was holding up his own left wrist. His Command Band outranked Annie's. "I have sealed off the room," he went on, "and Security will be here in minutes. If any of you do anything that I interpret as threatening I will—"

"Phillip Avery, do you know me?" Annie said loudly, interrupting him. Her voice echoed harshly in the enclosed garage.

He looked closer, squinting. Slowly his face changed, smoothed. "Why yes," he said in a softer voice than before, "I believe I do." Unconsciously he straightened his collar. "You are the Mother Elf. Aren't you?"

"That's right," she said.

He frowned and smiled at the same time. "You're real. My God." He shook his head, and both the smile and frown intensified. "That does put a different complexion on things."

"Listen to me," she said, with the kind of emphasis used to convey life-and-death information. "It's important."

He nodded. "I will."

She pointed to Hormat. "I don't have time to explain now, but this man saved Dreamworld today. At immense risk, and without committing any crime. You can do as you will with me and Mike. But *this man has to walk*. Now. And he has to have your car."

Avery was clearly startled. "Do I get to find out who he is and what he did?"

Annie didn't duck. "No. You never get anything but my word that he deserved to walk."

Avery was expressionless for a long moment, and then he burst out laughing. "Do I get my car back, at least?"

"Undamaged, within a day," she said, without smiling back.

He finished chuckling, and sobered. The decision took him less than five seconds. "All right: for the sake of what I owe you I'll go this far. I will let him go if you will tell me why a man died here today."

She spoke rapidly. "His name was Conway; Haines sent him here today to destroy Dreamworld; I killed him for it; this man was a kilometer away at the time."

With each clause, Avery's eyes had widened a little further. "And the boy?"

Same machine-gun delivery. "My son Michael; he helped me stop Conway; the bastard was about to shoot Mike when I took his gun away and used it on him."

Avery's eyes must have started to hurt; he closed them for a moment. An electric shock had gone through Mike when she called him her son; he turned and stared at her, but she ignored him.

"Mr. Avery, Mike and I will tell you the whole story in detail, but this man needs to go *now*," she said urgently.

He opened his eyes again and slowly shook his head from side to side.

"I'm telling you the truth!" she insisted.

He held up a hand as if to interrupt her. "I believe every word you say," he told her. He tapped at his wrist, and behind them the car chirped and opened its doors and started up. Beyond it, the garage door begin to hum upward. "He can leave. But I think you and your son had better go with him."

Now it was Annie's turn to stare with wide eyes. All the urgency drained out of her slowly; her shoulders slumped and her mouth went slack. "Oh my God," she murmured.

"Mother, you know you can't stay here anymore," Avery said gently. "I don't know where else you belong . . . but I'm sure it isn't in jail, or on the *Six O'Clock News*. Thank you with all my heart for everything you've done these last thirteen years. I wish Tom could have lived to meet you. I love you, and he did, too. Now get the hell out of here and don't ever come back—without a good disguise. I'll take care of Haines." He turned on his heel and left the room.

Mike was halfway into the car when he realized Annie was still standing there, looking at the spot where Avery had stood. He went back and took her by the hand and led her to the car. When they were seated together in back he had to adjust her seat belt and opaque her window for her, too. Then he had to lean forward and help Hormat program the unfamiliar autopilot. By the time he sat back and turned to opaque his own window, they had already emerged from the garage into sunlight.

He had already left Dreamworld. His life there was over.

· · ·

HORMAT STAYED AS alert as if it were necessary—as if he could have reached the pedals—until the car stabilized in the privilege lane. Then he stopped craning his neck to see over the dashboard and turned in his seat to face Mike and Annie.

"He was right," he said to Annie, his gruff voice as soft as he could make it. "You could not have stayed there."

She blew up. "Of course he was right! *I killed in Dreamworld.*"

He shook his head. "That is not why. Even if you had not killed Conway, you could not have stayed."

"Oh yeah?"

Hormat nodded. "As you said, he interrupted our conversation. You were about to tell me you could get me a fast car. I was about to tell you what my friends have decided to do."

Her eyes narrowed. *"Oh."*

Mike sat up straighter. Wasn't this ever going to end? "About us, you mean."

Hormat nodded. "And Haines and Conway, too. As of last night, all of you knew things you should not know. You two now know everything, but even then you all knew too much. Enough to let any of you figure out all the rest, if you kept thinking about it. There was a council." He hesitated and looked embarrassed. "And it was decided—"

Mike's weary brain made one more intuitive connection. "—that later today sometime you guys would hunt us all down and scrub our memories."

Hormat flinched and stared at him.

Mike shrugged. "You slipped up on our way in this morning," he said. "You let me know you guys can erase memories. If you can do it to a guard for half an hour, I guess you could do it to me for a week. Take away a week from each of us, rewind us back to just before we all spotted you, and . . . well, we'd all be confused as hell, I guess, but I don't see how we could ever have figured out just what had happened to us. Not enough clues."

Annie was looking back and forth from one to the other like a spectator at a tennis match. She settled on Hormat and studied him closely. "That's why you told us everything, isn't it?" she said. "So at least we'd get to know the whole story before we were made to forget it."

Hormat sighed. "I knew you would not be permitted to keep the information," he said, "but it seemed to me you deserved to have it. However temporarily. I suppose it makes no sense, but—"

"No," she said, "it makes sense to me. Thank you, Hormat."

Mike was also grateful—but paranoid, too. Memory erasure was one of his favorite sci-fi nightmares. "So what now?" he said. "What happens now?"

Hormat turned to him and shrugged. "Conway is gone. Haines knows no more than he did last night; my friends will deal with him and he will forget even that. You and Annie . . . are gone, they know not where."

Mike didn't want to ask, he knew he was disrespecting Hormat by asking, but he couldn't help it. "Are you gonna tell them?"

Hormat forgave him his need to be certain. "No, Mike."

"Can they, like, probe your brain and find out?"

The dwarf shook his head. "In theory they could. But I am going to be home before I'm missed, now. There will be no reason to suspect me of complicity with you, and I cannot be made to undergo a probe without grounds."

"Will they be able to track us down?" Annie asked.

"I don't think so. Not if you are careful. We are . . . not like Conway. Not hunters. And we dare not hire such a one, lest he notice our existence. If you stay out of sight long enough, my people will decide their safest course is to stop looking for you and pray that you are dead."

The totality of his predicament slowly washed over Mike, as if his mind had just decided he was ready to deal with it now—and he did not agree. "Annie," he said, hearing the growing panic in his voice, but unable to suppress it, "where *are* we gonna go? What the hell are we gonna *do*?"

She blinked at him. "We'll think of something," she said calmly.

"What the hell do you mean we'll think of something?"

"Hormat, once we're over eighty klicks from Dreamworld, you can drop us wherever you like."

Mike could not believe she was shrugging the whole matter away. "Annie, don't you get it? We haven't got any money. We have no ID. We're gonna have to live off the books—do you have any idea how *hard* that is?" He could hear his voice rising. "I did that for almost three weeks while I was figuring out how to get Under, and I broke my butt just to get a safe place to crash and admission money. Nobody's hiring kids or midgets out there, Annie! I mean, Jesus Christ, you've been . . . you've been living in a dreamworld!"

She laughed in his face at that line, and Hormat chuckled, too, and after a moment's pause, Mike had to join in; he was too tired to fight it.

"Good lad," she said when she could. "As long as you can still laugh at yourself, you'll be okay. I'm going to be laughing at myself a lot in the near future, too, and I hope you'll join me."

The laughter had taken the edge off his panic, but Mike was still upset, and his face must have showed it.

"Mike," she went on, "you're exactly right. I've been living in a dreamworld . . . a small one. I've *been* living off the books for thirteen years there, in plain sight, with warrants out for me. The outside world is going to be a *lot* easier to fool, I suspect. Don't worry about it: we'll get by."

He didn't believe her. But the "we" reminded him suddenly that she had claimed him as her son before Phillip Avery, and he became so confused he shut up. Hormat went back to pretending to drive. Annie cleared her window and watched less privileged drivers fall behind on their right. Mike sat in silence and tried to sort out his emotions.

After a while he decided he was mad as hell.

He was mad at *everything*. At Annie, and himself, and God if there was one or Fate if there wasn't, and Hormat and all his friends, and Conway, and . . . and especially . . .

An idea dropped into his head. He prodded at it, held it before his mind's eye for inspection, shook it to see if it rattled. Slowly he began to grin.

"Annie?"

"Yes, Mike?"

"What's Haines gonna do?"

She turned and regarded him curiously. "I don't understand your question."

"Hormat's friends get him and delete a week from his memory. Right, Hormat? About a week?"

"Perhaps more. Back to before whenever it was he first thought of hiring Conway."

"So now he forgets he ever knew us, or the Free Lunchers, or Conway. But what does he still want to do, more than anything?"

Her eyebrows rose as she took his meaning. "Destroy Dreamworld! Make his disgusting Thrillworld the number one theme park in the world."

"Right!"

She glowered for a moment, then brightened. "Well, at least Avery is warned now; he said he'd take care of it, remember?"

Mike found he was still grinning. "Maybe he can. Maybe. You want to bet Dreamworld he's right? He has to stay within the law, remember."

"What are you driving at?" she asked suspiciously.

He could *not* stop grinning. "Now, Ms. Elf, for the dining-room set *and* the orbital vacation package, answer this next question within twenty seconds. Listen carefully: what is the one place on Earth where *not only* could people of our size and skills probably get themselves hired . . . but neither Haines nor the Free Lunchers would think of looking for us in a million years?"

Her jaw fell. "Oh, *no*. Oh, you rotten, rotten child, you're not seriously proposing that we both go Under in—oh my God, in *Thrillworld*?"

"You got a better idea?"

Annie blinked at him in horror—then put her face in her hands and groaned.

In the front seat, Hormat began to laugh and laugh.

ABOUT THE AUTHOR

Spider Robinson is the winner of many major SF awards, including three Hugos, one Nebula, and the John W. Campbell Award for Best New Writer. He is best known for his Callahan books: insightful, lighthearted science fiction stories centered around the most bizarre blend of barflies you're likely to meet in this or any other galaxy. Other well-known works include three novels in the Stardance sequence, *Stardance, Starseed*, and *Starmind*, written in collaboration with his wife, writer/choreographer Jeanne Robinson. They currently reside outside of Vancouver, British Columbia.

For further information, contact www.spiderrobinson.com